RINGPULL

JAMES ROBERT BAKER

Ringpull

Published by Ringpull Press Ltd, 1995

Ringpull Press Limited
Queensway House
London Road South
Poynton
Greater Manchester
SK12 1NJ

A CIP catalogue record for this book is available from the British Library

ISBN 1-898051-22-4

Cover Illustration by Richard Jeffers
Printed in England by Clays Limited, St Ives plc.

For Kenny,
Wes and David

ONE

I WAS having a dream about Pete. We were at his old place in Venice Beach, in the bright, messy living room. We were arguing, the way we had toward the end in real life. But this time I was living there with Pete, I'd moved into his bungalow, and even though we were both angry, I could tell we still loved each other. And suddenly we stopped arguing, and there were tears in Pete's eyes, and the next thing I knew we were making out in this horrendous, cathartic way—kissing deeply, which we'd never done in real life. But this was a dream so we didn't have to think about saliva.

Then we were naked in the bedroom, the sun streaming in through the palm bushes outside the high, dirty windows. We were rolling around on the mattress on the floor, on the white sheets. My orange cat was sleeping at the foot of the bed. I saw the line of black hair on Pete's white stomach. Felt his smooth, warm back, his hard cock against mine. When we kissed now, it sent a surge of bliss back through my brain like an amphetamine rush and I thought I was going to come. I groaned, *Oh, Pete,* and he groaned, *Oh, Tim,* and—

I opened my eyes and saw a little pink sphincter where Pete's mouth should've been.

"Goddamn it, Jefty. Will you please get your fucking butthole out of my face?"

7

I pushed the wiry tomcat off my pillow. He yowled as he hit the hardwood floor. Yowled again.

"Shut up."

I looked at the digital clock: 8:59. I had a few more minutes. I rolled over, watched the blades of sunlight expand across the white walls, across the colorful 1950s travel poster ("Fly to Mexico by Clipper"), as the breeze puffed the white window shades. Listened to the waves crack against the shore three blocks below. Wished I could go back into the dream. Back to the rush of making out with Pete.

Except I shouldn't still be having dreams like this, thoughts like this, a year after Pete and I had broken up. I should be past all this by now. A year, I'd wasted an entire fucking year. I thought about Pete's bungalow on Cabrillo as it was in real life. A family of rednecks was living there now. The last time I'd driven by I'd seen the fat white-trash mama sunning her legs on the porch.

Jefty climbed back up on the bed, started clawing the pillow. "Knock it off," I told him. "You rip up my Ralph Lauren sheets, I'm shipping your ass to the research lab." I stroked the cat and thought about the mornings when he used to wake up Pete. When Pete and I would sit up in bed and drink coffee and talk, wired and loose, talking about all sorts of things, making up stories.

"On the Road," Pete said once. "You know who's who. We're driving cross-country."

"Across the Mojave," I said. "It's hot in the '46 Ford—"

"So we peel off our T-shirts."

"Right. Your sweaty torso knocks my breath out," I said. "I idolize you. I want you so bad I can taste it. But I get incredibly flustered."

"Suddenly we see the Flying Wing," Pete said.

"What?"

"The Flying Wing. Swooping down over the purple mountains. Swooping down right *at us!* It scrapes the top of the Ford. I screech to halt! We're so shaken—"

"—that we start kissing," I said.

"And sucking each other's cocks and fucking and everything."

8

"Families in other cars flash past, *screaming* when they see us, moms *keening* in horror."

"But we don't care, we don't stop!"

"We come laughing, exploding, jiz flying everywhere!"

Another time we were surfers, like the two clean-cut buddies in *Endless Summer*.

"We drive down to Baja in 1965," Pete said.

"We ride a bunch of waves at a deserted beach. But as we come up out of the water, there's a gang of raunchy Mexican outlaws waiting."

"With their uncut dicks hanging out," Pete said.

"Right. And they strip us and tie us up back-to-back."

"And in spite of ourselves we both get hard-ons," Pete said.

"Right. But the leader, who's really pretty cool and extra-appealing, like Pablo, deliberately leaves the ropes loose—"

"So just at the point where they're about to whip our gringo faces with their raunchy uncut dicks," Pete said, "we escape."

"And run along the beach—"

"Still naked—"

"For miles and miles, till we come to a village—"

I couldn't remember what happened then. What difference did it make? Why was I even thinking about this? I got out of bed to stop it.

I went into the bathroom, aimed my hard-on into the shower, took a leak against the white tiles. Went on to the kitchen, fed Jefty, grabbed the coffeepot and a mug, and came back to the bedroom. Watched MTV for a while, drinking coffee. Eric Clapton, Soundgarden, the Jesus and Mary Chain's "Reverence"—until it reminded me of one of Pete's songs. Chris Isaaks briefly on VH-1, "Don't Make Me Dream About You"—too close to home. CNN: a windswept George Bush addressing a crowd, an azure sea behind him. Thought of "the giggle factor," Bush's admission in '87 that there was still a "giggle factor" in the administration concerning AIDS. Imagined cutting off Barbara Bush's head with a chain saw, setting it on a stake. I'd giggle at *that*. On American Movie Classics: *Ramona*. Loretta Young, gorgeous, ruby-lipped, right-wing. An insipid Don Ameche. The color looked grimy.

I snapped up the window shade. It was already warm, the sky a clear blue over the Pacific, except for the brown band of smog just above the horizon. What Todd would call Gidget weather, and I should be getting into a Gidget mood. I sang a few bars of the Sandra Dee movie theme song, but instead of amusing me, it sickened me. The past was all used up. I imagined Gidget in a hospital bed, covered with KS lesions. "Moondoggie, why? I didn't do anything wrong. . . ."

In the shower I thought about the times Pete and I had stood there under the water, how he'd looked in the hard morning light, his blue eyes, his beard shadow, his amazing pale skin. How even at his worst, even at his grungiest, long after I'd realized he wasn't physically perfect, he'd never failed to completely put me away.

Once I'd mentioned something to Todd about Pete and me taking a shower together, and he'd said, "How sweet. I'll bet you hold hands at movies, too."

"Only at Arnold Schwarzenegger films," I'd said. "You're just jealous, Todd—because you and Phil are like a couple of grizzled old desert dykes who haven't bumped pussies since 1953." He'd laughed.

I wished Todd were in town this weekend. We might have gone to dinner and a movie tonight. But he'd gone back to New York for an ACT UP conference. In the last year he'd become increasingly involved in the L.A. chapter of the group. His own health was fine, although, like me, he was a hard-core refusenik when it came to taking the test. He'd lost a number of friends though, more than I had. But then Todd had always had more friends to lose. I'd given money to ACT UP, but resisted direct involvement, put off by all the bickering and in-fighting I'd seen at the meetings I'd gone to.

Todd and I had been friends for twelve years, since UCLA, where he'd been an art student while I was working on my graduate degree at the film school. He'd helped me a lot after the breakup with Pete. If it hadn't been for Todd, I might have done something truly extreme. Sometimes it was tempting to think of Todd as a role model in terms of relationships. He and Phil had been together ten years. They weren't monogamous though. Both had "safe adventures" on the side. I didn't have a moral problem with that—it wasn't any of my business anyway—but I knew that kind of arrangement would make me crazy. Pete and I had been monogamous, for as long as it had lasted. Neither one of us had wanted to be with anyone else for the entire six months.

I might have done something with Gregory this afternoon, but he was going mountain-biking with a guy he had a hopeless crush on. "Why do I keep doing this?" he'd say. "Falling for these guys who just want to be friends." "I don't know, Gregory," I'd tell him. "You must be getting something out of it." "I suppose," he'd say abjectly. Gregory took the test every six months. He was always negative, which was not a big surprise. He'd been celibate for more than four years.

Drying off, I talked to Jefty. "What am I doing? Why did I ever agree to go out with this guy? I feel like Blanche Du Bois going out with Mitch."

I got out my knapsack and packed a beach towel, sunblock, and *City of Quartz*, Mike Davis's refreshingly leftist view of L.A., parts of which I'd been rereading since the riots. "If I'm not back by seven," I told Jefty, "you'll know Dirk Bogarde's been transformed into Jason Patric."

That's a bit harsh, I suppose, and unfair to Dirk Bogarde, who despite his better-known creepy portrayals began his screen life as a juicy pretty boy. And I don't really want to trash Victor, in spite of what happened. He's not an evil person really, just an odd-duck British queen who'd slipped off the screen of a 1960s Joseph Losey film and ended up with Mum in southern California. Not bad-looking, I guess, by many people's standards, but he just didn't do it for me. His tan was far too deep, burnt-in and leathery. He wore rings, a gold bracelet on his bronzed wrist, and cologne. I

11

have a serious aversion to cologne, at least on guys I'm going out with. His smile wasn't all that pleasant either, a bit carnivorous, like a Hollywood agent's. And his teeth were yellow even though he didn't smoke. And sometimes he did have bad breath.

I had no trouble relating to Victor casually, as I had for several years. He was a writer of coffee-table movie books, and he'd come into the film archives every so often on a research matter, and if I wasn't busy, we'd talk. I enjoyed discussing films and Hollywood history with Victor, despite our radically different enthusiasms, and although I'd sensed early on that he might be attracted to me, I felt that issue had been subtly resolved years ago, the perimeters of our acquaintanceship by now well established. That's probably why he took me by surprise when he stopped in on Wednesday to check some facts in our Lubitsch file.

"So what are *your* plans for this Memorial Day weekend?" he said casually on his way to the door.

"Nothing special," I said. "Just going to take it easy. Catch up on my reading."

"And go to the beach, I'll bet." He had a voice like Robert Morley's. "You live near the beach, don't you?"

"Yes. I enjoy the ocean aesthetically. But I'm not really into spending a lot of time sitting on the—"

"You're pale though." He interrupted a lot. "Haven't been getting much sun, have you? Cooped up in here, watching *Kiss the Blood Off My Hands* all day."

"Well, I know you don't care for film noir, but—"

"Say, *I've* got an idea. I've got to go down to Laguna on Saturday. Told a friend I'd look after his condo. Just a few blocks from the beach. What do you say?"

"Well, I don't know. Saturday—"

"Oh, come on. It'll be fun. The gay beach, I mean. Do you know it?"

"No, I've never actually gone to the gay beach at Laguna—"

"Well, then, that settles it. You've got to come. These Orange County boys! Surfers for days! Let me give you my address. Why haven't we ever socialized?"

"I don't know."

I could have backed out later, of course, but I would have felt a little crummy if I had. I thought of Victor as an essentially lonely asexual forty-year-old mother's boy starved for friendship and conversation, and I didn't see what harm it could do to go to the beach with him once, on a date, if that's what it was. And of course it was. A *date*. A word I hated because it reminded me of tense, grim heterosexual high school ordeals. Corsages, sweaty palms, the waxy taste of lipstick on a church-sponsored hayride. A good-night kiss for Cindi under the bug light, then a pit stop at the Lido, where Ray, the married projectionist, would suck me off between reel changes. Home by midnight; how was your date, dear? Fine, Mom.

My recent grim dating experiences made me nostalgic for the old days of living a lie, the word, the concept, having made a depressing comeback in AIDS-era gay life. I could usually avoid it until New Year's Eve, but to be alone then was too pathetic, right? Not really. What's worse is to have to kiss Sidney at midnight; that spoiled 1989. I'd spent the next New Year's Eve fending off Roland: "But you *can't* say no. It's New Year's." Think again, Ro. I'd brought in 1991 with Pete. We'd stayed in, watched cassettes, and fucked our brains out. This New Year's Eve I'd gone to a party with Todd and Phil, where some guy in a SILENCIO = MUERTE T-shirt looked so much like Pete that I felt as if I were stuck in a queer remake of *Vertigo*.

Pete never used the word *date* except ironically, as in his song "Date Night at Dachau." Easy to imagine how Victor would react to that song title, without even caring to hear the song. "Oh, dear. If that's a *joke*, it's in dreadfully poor taste." There'd be no way of explaining that it *was* a joke and therefore also completely serious.

When Pete and I broke up, it was very bad for a while. Initially I got the flu, which I was certain at first was AIDS, and after I got over that I was emotionally twisted, alternately despairing and enraged, for the next two months. That passed. Life continued and I thought I was over him. Then, at about six months, it got bad again—this is my pattern. I started thinking about Pete again all the time for no apparent reason except that I still missed him so much I'd lie in bed at night and groan. One night, watching *Trouble in Mind* on cassette, I lost it. At the end of the film, where Kris Kristofferson drives off alone with nothing but his tenderest fantasies, while Marianne Faithfull sings an ineffably wrenching song of lost love, I started sobbing. I wanted to pick up the phone so bad. But I knew that was crazy, wildly inappropriate, and way too late, and I called Todd instead, and he told me to "let go of Pete, stop wallowing, turn the page." I was certain to meet someone else, Todd said, someone who'd make me look back to Pete and wonder how I'd been so upset about something so trivial and obviously "sex-based." In the meantime, Todd suggested, I might feel better if I went out and got laid.

"Fuck him out of my system, you mean?"

"Well—"

That's your solution to everything, I'd thought. I'd said, "No, I'll wait."

The period of retro-longing at six months passed, too. I started going out again, though not with anyone who didn't bore the shit out of me. But that was okay. I had my work, which I could get into as deeply as I wanted, and I had my friends, like Todd and Gregory. I knew I'd meet someone again eventually. I was "smart, witty, boyishly appealing," Todd reminded me. I was thirty-eight, though I could pass easily for thirty-five, which was good since that's how old I said I was. I wasn't discouraged. My life was not at all bad. I was healthy for one thing, and these days that's a lot. I'd learned some "important lessons" from what had happened with Pete that I could apply to my next relationship, whenever that was "supposed to happen," as Gregory put it. "The truth is, you just don't meet meaningful people every day," he'd say. No, but I didn't think I could wait four years. I'd waited much longer than that before I met Pete. If something didn't happen soon, I was afraid there might be a major explosion of inevitably soul-destroying "safe sleaze" (Todd's term).

*　　*　　*

I went out to my car, a restored metallic blue 1968 Camaro convertible. No point in putting the top down. Victor would want to drive. I waved to the crazy straight guy who lived alone in the house across the street. At night I sometimes saw him pacing in his living room, talking to himself. He ignored me this morning as he clipped his ivy. I drove off down the eucalyptus-lined street, making a left at Channel Road in Santa Monica Canyon. I remembered Pete once telling someone that I lived at the corner of "Isherwood Court and Don Bachardy Lane." (In fact, the Isherwood/Bachardy house was on the far side of the canyon.) At the top of the hill, I took a left on San Vicente.

I understood why I was thinking about Pete again now. We'd spent the previous Memorial Day weekend together, which I still thought of as our last good time, before everything turned to shit, though I knew Pete wouldn't agree. For him, things started turning to shit much sooner than they did for me. He'd seemed irritable and preoccupied that weekend. But then he'd quit smoking only two weeks before, right after we'd come back from France, so I'd tried not to take his mood personally. (In retrospect, it was obvious that he'd quit smoking as a passive-aggressive distancing device, since he'd known I wasn't ready to quit myself. Of course, he'd insisted that he didn't mind that I continued to smoke. He'd only asked that I not do it when we were together.)

Driving into Brentwood, the Lightning Seed's "Pure" came on the radio, a catchy techno-pop song I'd listened to obsessively on my Walkman in France before Pete joined me, a two-week period filled with quietly elated anticipation. I recalled the hyperromantic exhilaration I'd felt watching Pete walk in across the windswept tarmac at the Nice airport. That image still set off a buzz in my stomach, but I wasn't alarmed. These were only stray memories, last year's snapshots evoked by last year's pop song, not a true return of longing. And the dream—that was painfuly obvious. I always dreamed about things that were never going to happen. Like kissing Pete again, making love with him until we were both punchy, living with him. But it was

15

therapeutic to have that sort of dream, to have a final working out of the subconscious residue of desire. A psychic housecleaning.

More than anything it was a kind of wistful feeling I had toward Pete now, a sense that in spite of how badly it had ended, and no matter who I met in the near future, Pete would always be one of the half dozen or so great loves of my life.

I was aware that he'd moved to Laguna Beach. At least that's what I'd heard several months before. Todd followed the local music scene much more closely than I did. "Yeah, Drunken Boat broke up," he'd said last winter. "Pete's supposedly moved down to Laguna, fed up with L.A."

But Laguna Beach is a sizable community. The chances of a fluke encounter were remote. And one place I knew I wouldn't see Pete was at the gay beach. He hated sitting on the beach even more than I did. And I certainly wasn't going to look him up. I wasn't that much of a masochist.

I met Victor at his mother's prim white colonial house in Brentwood. We got into his new silver Jaguar convertible with its V-12 engine and I could tell it was going to be a long day.

"Do you mind if I smoke?" I said as we got on the freeway.

"As a matter of fact . . ."

He pointed like a fussy teacher to the no-smoking decal above the ashtray. I stuck the cigarette back in the pack.

"I didn't know you smoked."

"I don't that much really. Just at certain times."

"Oh? What are those?"

While I masturbate. No, edit that. He might think I'm being flirtatious. "Oh, you know. While waterskiing. At funerals."

"Oh, dear. I thought perhaps you meant after a good bout of sex."

"No, no, not at all."

The top was down. It was hot now, hot and dry, a mild Santa Ana wind, what Pete would call a Raymond Chandler condition. Victor shoved in a cassette. Barry Manilow, his greatest hits, volume one. "Mandy." I looked around for the barf bag.

"Did you see him at the Greek?" Victor said.

"No, I missed that."

"Oh, did you ever! He was absolutely incredible!"

"Yeah, I guess he's quite a showman."

"Say, know who's coming up in August? Liza Minnelli. Just got the tickets. Interested?"

I'd rather eat smegma. "Well, that's a ways off. Why don't we see."

"Sure. No pressure. I'll remind you."

It took over an hour to get there, while Barry sang the songs that made the whole world car sick. Laguna Beach was jammed because of the holiday and the heat, so parking could have been a problem. But Victor used his friend's card to enter the subterranean garage of the Villa Marbella condo building, and from there we walked down to the beach.

We spread out our towels and I took off my T-shirt and khakis while Victor took off his white tennis shirt and shorts. He was wearing skimpy navy blue Speedo's while I wore a pair of baggy 1940s swim trunks with a kitsch tropical design.

"Say, those are great," he said. "I like a little mystery."

He leaned back in his beach chair and adjusted his cock in his Speedo's. "But I say, if you've got it, flaunt it." He smiled. "Not that I'm all that obsessed with size. Cuteness definitely gets points, too." He winked.

I wanted to go home.

But I smeared on some sunblock lotion.

"Say, you *are* pale."

"Yeah, I burn easily."

"I like your skin though. And your physique in general. Do you work out?"

"Not really. I go out on my bike occasionally."

"*I* should do something, I suppose. What I'd give for a nice set of pecs."

Victor's dark, hairless body was as thin as a pharaoh's.

For the most part the beach was packed with what I'll call mainstream homosexuals. Smooth, tanned, muscle boys in pastel bikinis, with virtually no body hair and mean Reagan-era faces: West Hollywood south. There were a few silver-haired disco survivors—a guy who looked like Jeff Chandler off to the right. Groups of super-young queer clones here and there. I like goatees actually. My first boyfriend, Robbie, had one twenty years ago. The Bronski Beat remake of "Don't Leave Me This Way" was wafting from somebody's boom box, a song I can't hear without thinking of Diane Keaton under the strobe light in *Looking for Mr. Goodbar*, being repeatedly stabbed.

"So, taken the test?" Victor said.

"What?"

"The HIV test. Taken it?"

I squinted at Victor, his eyes closed, his shiny face to the sun.

"No, actually, I haven't. I've thought about it. I've come close a few times. But—"

"I was petrified," he said. "I didn't sleep for three nights. To be very candid, I feared the worst, considering some of the things I used to do. I was quite the party girl in my day, believe it or not. At one time, I absolutely *lived* at the baths."

"But you're negative?"

"Praise the Lord and pass the penis."

I cringed. "You're lucky."

"I'm something. God, when I think of the things I used to *do*. With absolute strangers, without a second thought. I don't want to burn your ears though. I can tell you're the conservative type."

This has sometimes been a problem for me. I *look* fairly conventional, I guess: prepped-out, short, parted hair, glasses. I feel more comfortable when I'm inconspicuous. I don't trust fashion trends. Part of this may be a WASP legacy, a fear of looking ridiculous: "Here comes Tim, with last spring's buzz cut. What a dork!" But I'm not conservative.

"What I mean is," Victor said, "I'm sure you're all right.

18

You haven't been sleeping around. I'm sure in your case the test would be just a formality."

I nearly laughed. He didn't know anything about me, not a thing. And he wasn't going to find out anything now.

"I've been careful," I said. Like all but celibate for six years before Pete.

"Well, that's all you *can* be."

"I'll bet *you've* been more cautious," I said, "since you found out you were negative."

He shrugged. "Same as before. I have certain rules. No come in the mouth and always wear a Rubber Johnny. That's the British term for condom, you know."

"Yeah, I think I've heard that."

"So that's where *I* stand. What about you?"

What if I tell him I've got a symptom? Diarrhea? Swollen glands? No, that's too sick. "I'm all for safe sex," I said. As long as it's not between me and you.

Eventually, I steered the conversation to Victor's favorite subject, musicals, and he burned up some energy gushing about Barbra and Judy and Vera-Ellen, until around three, when I said, "You know, I'm getting a little worried. I think I missed a few spots with this sunblock."

"Well—we certainly don't want you to look back on this day with any regret. Let's head back to the condo."

This place depressed me. Twenty years ago it would have been flocked wallpaper and chandeliers. Now it was designer Santa Fe—which was of course already shockingly passé. On the coffee table, *Architectural Digest*, *Vanity Fair* (which Pete called *Vanity Queer*), and—*National Review*? Like a Jew with *Mein Kampf* on display.

"If you'd like to wash off that goo," Victor said, "do be my guest."

"Thanks, I think I will."

I took a quick shower. As I reached for the towel, I saw that water had splashed out, soaking my khakis and shirt on the floor. So I pulled on my trunks again.

"Tim?" Victor rattled the knob.

I opened the door.

"Why did you lock the door? You're not afraid of me, are you?" Carnivorous grin, yellow teeth.

"No, it wasn't intentional. I must've just pressed the button."

"Thought I'd see if you'd care for a caftan."

He was wearing one, purple with gold threads. A lime green one over his arm.

"No, I'm fine."

I stepped out, drying my hair. By then Victor was in the living room, adjusting the stereo: an excruciating, wallowing rendition of "Send in the Clowns."

"Is that Shirley Bassey?" (*Gold-fing-ah!*)

"Yes. Still fabulous, isn't she?" Victor crossed to the bar and picked up a frosty pitcher. "Bloody Mary?"

"No. No, thanks. I don't drink."

"You don't? Oh, don't tell me you're one of those AA people."

I thought of Pete. "No. It just doesn't agree with me, it never has."

He opened the bar refrigerator. "Well, then, let's see? 7-Up? Tab?"

"Tab's fine." I needed the caffeine. I was getting a headache.

"You're not hungry yet, are you?"

Uh-oh. "No."

"There's a lovely little place down by the pier," he enthused. "Wonderfully intimate, excellent pianist, fabulous steaks. I should make reservations—"

"Victor, I thought we were going back this afternoon."

"Oh." He set down his Bloody Mary. "Oh, my." Looked wounded. "I thought . . . Well, to be frank, I thought you were going to stay over."

"No, no. I really should get back."

"Oh. Oh, my. I guess we got *our* signals crossed." He lowered the stereo volume, kept his back to me. I felt almost as bad as he wanted me to feel.

"I'm sorry," I said. "It's just that on the first date, I mean—"

"Say no more." His royal purple back. "I know when I'm being rejected."

"I'm not rejecting you—"

Softly but forcefully: "Why don't you just leave."

I laughed incredulously, which he took the wrong way. "Victor, I'm thirty miles from home."

He whirled around dramatically. "Who the *hell* do you think you are! Goddamn little tease! Parading around here bare-chested, drying your hair! You can't do this to me! I don't know who you think you're dealing with! Go! Leave! Right now, this instant! Do you hear!"

It was so extreme I nearly laughed again, as if that might somehow dissipate his anger. But this time I knew better. This obviously had less to do with me than with other, much crueler rebuffs in his past. Without saying anything else, I stuffed my wet clothes into my knapsack and went out the door.

I'd just reached the bottom of the stairs when Victor stepped out and called down to me plaintively, "Tim, wait! You must forgive me. Please! Hold on while I change. I'll drive you."

While I waited for him to come down, I reached in my T-shirt pocket. Almost five hours—I needed a cigarette bad. The pack was wet and mushy.

Victor came down in his shorts and we got into the Jaguar. He was stiff and silent as we swung onto Pacific Coast Highway. "The canyon's clogged now. Are you sure you wouldn't like to wait till later, grab some dinner?"

"No. I really do have some plans for tonight." To wit: jack off, feed Jefty, eat a Healthy Choice, get in bed with Jefty and *City of Quartz*, wipe today from my mind.

"You must forgive my fit of pique," Victor said as we inched along in the heavy traffic. "If I've been in any way too pushy . . ."

"No, no, I'm just in a funny place, that's all." Why was I making excuses?

"Well, I can certainly empathize with that. These aren't the easiest of times."

The top was down and the sun was bludgeoning. I began

to sweat and worried that I was going to burn since I wasn't wearing a shirt. I became aware that Victor was taking sneaky looks at my body. I needed a smoke bad.

"What's wrong?" he said. "Did someone hurt you, is that it?"

"I don't really want to go into it, Victor."

And it was then, right then, that I saw Pete, standing by a car back in the garage of a Chevron station. For a second I thought it was just my imagination. It wouldn't have been the first time I'd been startled by a man who resembled Pete at a distance. But it was Pete. It was definitely Pete. His straight, black, parted hair, his pale skin and beard shadow. The hair on his pale forearms. The light blue Chevron shirt, no doubt with PETE stitched above the pocket in red, like the shirt he'd been wearing at the Chevron station in Santa Monica the day I'd met him, the day he'd changed my oil and we'd talked much longer than we'd needed to, never taking our eyes off each other, though I'd still thought he was straight (but lonely), until he'd called me that evening, having gotten my number from the receipt, and asked me if I was gay, and if so, would I like to go out sometime.

"I'm right then," Victor said. "Someone did break your heart."

I looked back as we passed the station, vaguely aware that Victor was squeezing his crotch. My heart was flooded with adrenaline.

"See something you like?"

"No. But I really need some cigarettes. Would you mind stopping at this liquor store up here?"

I don't know what I was thinking.

"I thought we discussed this," Victor said, tapping the no-smoking decal again.

"Victor, I'm having a nicotine fit. I just need a few puffs. I'll smoke in front of the store. Be a mensch, how 'bout it?"

He swung into the liquor store parking lot. But instead of pulling into the open slot by the door he drove around to the side of the building. "I'll bet I know what you'd really

22

like in your mouth," he said. "And I can assure you, it won't give you cancer."

He threw the Jaguar into park and dug his semierect cock out of his shorts leg. "*This* will make you forget him."

I opened the car door. "You don't have anything I want, Victor." I looked at his big cock, at his scared, excited eyes. "Anything at all."

I got out and went into the liquor store, which was crowded with beachgoers. I waited in line and when my turn came, asked for a pack of cigarettes. That was when I realized that my wallet was in my khakis, which were in my knapsack, which was in Victor's car.

I didn't expect him to be waiting when I came out and he wasn't. But I'd been so shaken I'd forgotten about my stuff. He could have at least tossed my knapsack out on the pavement before he'd driven off. "You fuckhole," I said, and some teenage girls looked at me. But except for losing my wallet I was relieved.

In fact, I might as well admit I knew it was perfect. I looked at the red and blue Chevron sign several blocks back down the highway. I could tell Pete the simple truth, that I was stranded in Laguna Beach with nothing, no money, just my sunglasses, my baggy tropical trunks, my huarache sandals, the same ones he'd splattered the day we had mock-anonymous sex on the beach at Point Dume. He'd have to help me, have to give me a ride back. He might give me the key to his place so I could wait till he got off work. Then when he came in, we'd talk for a while and . . . realize how much we'd missed each other and . . . fall onto the bed, kissing, kissing deeply, groaning, *Oh, Pete. Oh, Tim* . . .

I still loved him so much.

TWO

THIS WAS crazy. This was fucked up. It was *over*. Over for a year. This was deranged. Hadn't I done something like this before? What a self-defeating pattern.

But what choice did I have? I started walking. This was clearly a mistake. But what else could I do? It had ended very badly. He might still be mad. He might still hate my guts. But it had been a year. People get over things. And wasn't that part of his AA program, to forgive people and let go of anger and resentment? He'd at least be cordial. He might even make an amend. God knew, he owed me one. The cold little fuck.

But when I got to the station, I didn't see him anywhere. I asked the manager, "Is Pete around?"

"Pete?"

For a second I thought maybe I *had* been mistaken.

"Pete Schindler. I think he's a mechanic here—"

"Oh, *Pete*. You just missed him. Got off at four." He yelled to another guy, "Hey, Charlie! Watch that Buick! Watch it, watch it!"

"Does he live around here, by any chance?"

"Who?"

"Pete Schindler."

"Hey, Charlie! Where's Pete living now?"

Charlie called back, "Down there on Cliff Drive! White place with a tower. 'Bout five blocks down."

I wished it had been closer. I had too much time to think. The worst possibility: that Pete was living with a new boyfriend. Cliff Drive curved along the beachfront bluffs, a pleasant, desirable area. A *rich* boyfriend. Rich and young and blond. *Scott.* Pete would have told Scott about the *awful guy* he'd been seeing for a while last year. "Scott, this is Tim. I think I told you . . ." Scott's initial smile giving way to hard blond attitude: I know what *you're* about, *Tim.* The body of a man but the brain of Sean Young.

This was a mistake. This didn't feel right. Pete's line about us: "This doesn't feel right anymore." I should have hit him when he said that.

Nice homes along Cliff Drive, but some a bit run-down with peeling paint, overgrown lawns. Scott might not be rich. Might be a student, at UC Irvine. Young, smart, and blond. "Pete doesn't want to talk to you. If you don't leave now, we'll call the police."

I passed an area where a few men were cruising on the bluffs. So this was where *that* went on down here. A bearded man kept watching me as I passed.

Finally, I saw the white house with the tower—really a turret. An old Victorian house with peeling white paint and an overgrown lawn. Pete's gray '65 Citroën was parked in front. Where there'd once been dents, it was primered.

The front door was open, music pounding from the house. Van Halen, which I knew Pete hated. As I came up the steps and saw the people inside, I thought I must have the wrong place. Big, shirtless, stupid-looking heavy-metal guys and trashy blond babes in thong bikinis. "Oh, Brack!" one of the women was saying, playfully slapping Brack's biceps, as if she'd just been teased.

"Fuckin' chicks, man!" Brack responded. He had tattoos up and down both of his arms and a mean baby face like Lars in Metallica.

"Excuse me," I said at the door. "Does Pete live here?"

Dope in the air. A ripple of apprehension as they all checked me out. "Yeah! Go on up!" Brack yelled.

"He's cute," one of the women said in a kittenish voice as I climbed the battered stairs.

Pete's door was ajar. He was on the bed with his back to me, in his gray Jockey shorts, wearing a Walkman, writing in his notebook, a poem or a song. I couldn't help looking at him a moment, his pale, smooth back, the black hair on his legs, remembering how he'd looked when I woke up beside him, put my arms around him from behind, my hard morning cock against his hairy butt. How I'd kiss his shoulder and he'd turn his head and kiss me on the mouth, burning my face with his beard growth, which I liked. How we'd make love in the morning, at night, all the time, for hours on end.

How I wanted to do that again right now. How impossible. How abject. I should go. This was not good. I should dematerialize now.

I knocked. Because of the Walkman he didn't hear me. My heart was pounding like you wouldn't believe. "Pete?" I said loudly.

He jumped when he saw me. He sat up, pulling off the headphones. "What the fuck are you doing here?"

His pink, glossy, eloquent mouth. His blue eyes, his jacked-up crazy blue eyes. Oh, Jesus. Why did he still have to look so good? I shouldn't be doing this to myself.

"Look, I'm sorry to bother you. But I came down to Laguna today with a friend, and we had a fight, and I'm stranded. He has my wallet in his car. And I happened to see you at the station, but when I got back there, you'd just taken off. Charlie told me you lived down here."

"Charlie?" He took off his glasses.

"Some guy at the station."

"Oh. *Charlie.*"

"I think that was his name."

He was as shaken as I was. He got up and pulled on his faded black jeans. "So what's the story? You're *stranded?*"

"Looks like it. No money, nothing."

Suspicious scowl as he buttoned his pants. "I still don't know why you had to come here."

That's right, we might as well be strangers now, you heartless fuck. "I just explained to you what happened. I don't know anyone else in Laguna. I didn't even know *you* were here, until I just happened to, you know . . ."

"So what can I do for you, Tim?"

Nothing, dick face. Fuck you. "I don't know. Let me use your phone, I guess."

"It's right there."

I picked up the phone and sat down on the edge of his bed. He snatched up his notebook before I could glance at it. I held the phone, hesitating. I didn't even know who I wanted to call. I didn't want to call anyone. Why did he still have to look so good? This was a bad mistake. I'd just bought myself weeks of turmoil and pain. He picked up his cigarettes.

"You started smoking again."

"Yeah, a few months ago."

"That's too bad," I said. "I know what you went through when you quit last year. Mind if I bum one? I'm about to go crazy." He held out the pack; I took one. "This guy I was with was completely unbelievable. Talk about dates from hell. Not that anything happened, but—" Pete lit my cigarette. "Thanks. In a way, it was funny. I mean, first there was Manilow, then back at the condo, Shirley Bassey doing a truly execrable 'Send in the Clowns.' And get this, he offers me a *caftan*—"

"Tim, are you going to use the phone?" Censorious, dadlike.

"Yeah, in a minute. Can I just take a few puffs first? Got an ashtray?"

He handed me an abalone shell.

"Oh, I remember this from Venice. You had this then, right? So how are you anyway?"

"I'm fine. I'm doing okay."

"How's your music?"

"That's fine, too. We've reformed the band."

"No kidding. That's great. You been playing many gigs?"

"Yeah. We've got one tonight. I'm going to have to start getting ready pretty quick." He looked out the window.

"Where you playing?"

27

"In L.A."

"Oh, yeah? Where?"

He sighed and looked at me. "Tim, I'm not really happy to see you."

"I got that."

"I think you should just use the phone."

I punched Gregory's number, thinking he wouldn't be home yet. As soon as he said hello, I hung up.

"Damn it. His fucking machine."

Pete was pulling on a T-shirt. I wished he'd sit down next to me on the bed, put his arm around me, so we could start kissing. Why couldn't that happen?

"Well?" he said.

"I'm thinking. Know what time it is?"

He looked at the alarm clock. "Four-thirty."

"Shit. Todd's out of town. Will's at work until ten . . ."

"Well, you can't wait here, Tim. I've got to go out."

"You been here long?"

"A few months."

"Nice crowd downstairs."

"Brack's okay."

"But he doesn't know you're gay."

"He does now."

"What's that supposed to mean?"

"Nothing. Forget it."

"I don't seem gay."

"If you say so."

"Look, I know I don't. That's one thing I'm sure of. I got a compliment from one of the bimbos."

"Tim, use the phone."

"What are you doing here, Pete? This seems hellish. A nightmare of repression."

"I needed the quiet."

"Right, with Sammy Hagar downstairs—"

"It's quiet most of the time."

"Bet you can't bring anyone home though."

"Maybe I like being with real people for a change—"

"Morons, you mean."

28

"—instead of a bunch of pretentious West Hollywood fags."

"But I see there's a cruising area right down the street," I said. "Some hot tearoom action, too, I'll bet. Probably lots going on down there at night. 'Think I'll get some air, *dude.*' "

"Why don't you fuck yourself?"

"I'd rather fuck you."

"I know. But it's not going to happen."

It was the *I know* that made me want to kill him. His fucking ego. He was so sure that everybody wanted him, it made me sick. I should hit him. Or say something really shitty, cut him bad.

I couldn't look at him. I stared at the phone. "I don't know who else to call."

He got his wallet. "Here's some money."

"For what?"

"Bus fare." He tossed a twenty on the bed.

"Bus fare? *Bus fare?* I don't want to take a fucking bus. Do you have any idea how long that will take? *Hours.*"

"I don't know what else to suggest."

"Well, where'bouts are you going in L.A.?"

He sighed. "The Wilshire District. But I'm not going straight there."

"Well, can't I tag along? It would really save me some time and it could save my life. I would not want to have to make a transfer at Florence and Normandie. Wait, I've got it. *Wilshire Boulevard.* There must be a bus that runs straight out to Santa Monica. You'd really be sparing me a tremendous ordeal."

"Tim, why did you come here?" Angry and jumpy.

"What do you mean? I told you."

"You're still obsessed with me, aren't you?"

"I was never *obsessed* with you, Pete."

He looked out the window. "Okay. If you say so. It doesn't matter now anyway." Heavy sigh. "Okay, look. I'll tell you what. I'll take you up to L.A. On one condition."

"What's that?"

29

"No discussions. I don't want to do a big autopsy on what happened. It's dead and buried and I don't want to dig it up."

"No problem."

"I mean it." He glared at me. "If you upset me, I'll put you out of the car."

"Jesus, Pete. I wish you'd lighten up just a tad. Come *on*."

"Look—I'm already very tense. This is a very important gig tonight, and I don't want to squander my energy."

"I won't make any demands, I promise."

"That would be unique." He walked across the hall into the bathroom and closed the door.

THREE

WHILE PETE was gone, I looked around his room. Not a bad place to be really. A bit cramped but bohemian. A fresh breeze, ocean view. If the slime-rock weren't screeching downstairs—Guns 'n' Roses now—you could probably hear the waves crash. A low shelf of paperbacks, but only a fraction of the books he'd had in Venice—this felt like a temporary retreat. *Querelle, A Single Man, The Atrocity Exhibition*, the AA Big Book, an oral history of the Velvet Underground, *Rimbaud: Complete Works, Selected Letters*. The Sam Peckinpah biography I'd given him. We both had ambivalent feelings about Sam. We'd laughed over one section Pete had read out loud: Warren Oates's grisly description of Sam directing *The Wild Bunch* with severe bleeding hemorrhoids. Yelling, "One more time! Reset those squibs!" despite the blood and shit "streaming" down his legs.

Gregory wouldn't see what was funny about that. He'd just make a sickened face. There was a time when Todd would have laughed, but not anymore. Something had happened to Todd's sense of humor. I was still always thinking of jokes and remarks that no one would get except Pete.

Next to his Rickenbacker guitar, I noticed his blue spiral notebook. I considered snooping, to see what he'd written about me. I imagined sarcastic, accusatory poems—"You, in your existential despair at Gelson's"—using things I'd

31

told him to trash me. But I decided there could be something genuinely scarring, so I didn't look.

His wallet was open on the bureau. I was looking at his driver's license when he came back.

"You were born in 1959. That makes you thirty-three. You told me you were twenty-nine."

He took his wallet from me. "So what?"

"I'm going to tell *Teen Beat* you're over the hill."

"You lied, too."

"What makes you think that?"

"I looked at your passport in France. You're thirty-eight."

"Who cares? I look like Alec Baldwin."

"Old, old, old," he said in my face. A reference to a grisly photo of Judy Garland with that caption in *Hollywood Babylon*, which we'd once laughed about.

"I am every man's fondest hope of what he'll be like at my age," I said. "I exude eroticism. I whip heads around everywhere I go. I find notes on my windshield all the time."

He didn't say anything, just picked up his guitar, put it in its battered black case.

I said, "You're not exactly chicken, you know."

"Let's go. And be cool, okay?"

"I'll try not to mince."

"I'd appreciate it."

As we stepped out the door, I said queenily, "Oh, Miss Pete. Girlfriend. I feel . . . *so gay.*"

"Tim—I mean it."

"Okay, I'll talk about snatch." I imitated Brack's stupid voice: "It's Saturday fuckin' night, man. Let's snag some gash. Fuckin' A."

"You're really pushing it."

"Don't worry. I'll just be my natural butch self."

We'd just started down the stairs when Pete's phone rang and he went back to get it.

"Oh, hi. How you doin'? . . . Oh, jeez."

His tone was so intimate I was certain at first it was a boyfriend. But eventually he said, "Look, the important

32

thing is you're still sober," so I knew it was someone in AA.

"Are you gonna be all right till then?" he said gently. "Look, it's normal to still think about it at this point, Joey. Sixty days is not a long time. Look, I gotta go right now. But I'll see you there and we can talk, okay?"

After he'd hung up, I said, "A newcomer?"

"Yeah. A guy I'm sponsoring. He's having some problems."

His concern for new men in AA had always impressed me. And I was relieved because I knew he didn't believe in "thirteenth-stepping" newcomers—that is, having sex with them.

Brack shouted, "Later, *dudes!*" as we went out the door. Pete waved. Cretin-rock still blasting, breathy laughs.

In Pete's Citroën I said as a joke, "You haven't gone straight, have you?"

"I thought about it," he said matter-of-factly. "After what happened with you."

The first stop was going to be Pete's mother's house in Anaheim. He wanted to pick up some old R&B albums he had stored in the garage. On the freeway I said, "So how's Pablo?" The group's bass player.

"He's fine. He's got a new boyfriend."

"That's good. I like Pablo. How's Soren?" The guitar player. He had a subterranean crush on Pete and had hated me on sight.

"He's fine."

"And Doug?" The drummer.

"Doug died last winter."

"Oh, Jesus. I didn't know."

"That's why we disbanded," Pete said. "It kind of knocked the wind out of our sails."

"It was AIDS?"

"Yeah. It was real sudden. I mean, he was fine until he got this shortness of breath. Which turned into the pneumonia. He died on the third day in the hospital."

"Jesus."

"Yeah, the suddenness was a shock. But in a way I think it's what he wanted. As opposed to going through a long ordeal. I mean, we'd talked about it in theory. That we both believed in suicide, you know."

"That's awful though," I said. "That's so scary. He had no idea at all that he had it?"

"No, I don't think so. He was fine. He hadn't taken the test, but, you know, he'd been careful for a long time."

I thought of several others guys I'd known or had heard of who'd gone almost that quickly. Bob, a friend from film school, who, as someone had said, "was diagnosed on a Tuesday, dead on Friday." To me that was much more terrifying than the usual case where people had lots of warning and time to prepare. I could also see why it might be preferable though.

Once in bed after sex Pete and I had discussed the idea of suicide at a certain point if either of us ever got it. He'd said, "I think I'd really do it. They say a lot of guys consider it at first, then get talked out of it, or decide to fight to the end. Which I understand. But I can't see it for myself. Going through all that. Blindness, dementia, all kinds of agonies, just to die in the end anyway. *Why?* I haven't done anything I feel I have to suffer for."

I'd agreed, but I'd been less certain that if I really had to face it, I wouldn't try to last as long as I could. But that was before I saw what my friend Roy went through for the last three months of his life. The chemotherapy, the way they fried him with radiation till his skin peeled off, just to keep him alive while this thing that looked like a piece of cauliflower grew out of his brain. Someone brought him a copy of *Final Exit*, but his sister from Iowa found it and flipped. I guess she felt he hadn't paid the full price yet for his "lifestyle choice."

I'd been thinking seriously about finally taking the test until I saw Roy like that. It's still the worst thing I've ever seen. When I'd tried to tell Gregory about the cauliflower, he'd held up his hand and said, "*Stop!*"

"How old was Doug?" I said.

34

"Twenty-six."

"Jesus. I'm sorry."

"I am, too. I miss him."

We got off the freeway near Disneyland, the Matterhorn and the spires of Space Mountain visible above the treetops. We turned into a residential area. I hadn't seen Pete's boyhood home before, and it wasn't really what I expected. He'd talked about his "middle-class background," but the neighborhood was more lower-middle class or blue collar. His mom's place was a scuzzy salmon-pink tract house with barren flower beds and a yellow front lawn. As we pulled up to it, a white-haired man in the driveway across the street stopped messing with his camper and stared at us. Pete noticed him, too, and apparently there was some history between them. "That's right, it's me, fuckhead," he said under his breath.

Before I could ask him what that was about, Pete was flooring it, tearing off down the street.

"What's going on?" I said.

"Nothing. Her car's not here. She must still be at work. I'm going to swing by. It's not far."

I'd never met Pete's mother. All I knew was that she was a secretary. He'd always been rather tight-lipped about her. He still saw her occasionally, he'd said, "but we don't agree on a lot of things." He'd told me more about his father, a truck driver who'd died in a crash when Pete was twenty. His father had been an alcoholic with a bad temper. Once I'd made a joke about "The Brady Bunch," and Pete had said, "I can't stand that show. I always think of trying to watch it while my parents were fighting in the next room."

Pete didn't say anything as we drove on through the ratty neighborhood. I could tell he was embarrassed about my seeing where he'd grown up, that he'd exaggerated so that we'd seem more equal.

One day after we'd known each other about a month, Pete and I had driven down to La Jolla to look at what was left of my boyhood home. A landslide in the late sixties had pitched several of the neighboring bluff-top homes into the ocean, and our once-sleek Richard Neutra dreamhouse was now a gutted shell at the end of Narcissus (or, circa 1968, Narcosis) Drive. Pete and I stepped through the space where the plate glass had been and looked around while I talked about my family history. You could see that kids had been coming there to fuck. There were beer cans and panties and an old mattress on the speckled linoleum floor. Homeless people had been there, too. A grungy sleeping bag, a rusty Von's shopping cart in the rumpus room. In the yellow breakfast nook where my mother had served Aunt Jemima pancakes on bright sunny mornings in 1959, someone had taken a dump.

We'd walked back to my old bedroom. It was late afternoon, yellow sunlight flickering in through the eucalyptus trees, reminding me of an afternoon when I was ten, when I'd sat on the floor in the same yellow light, sobbing after a fight with my father.

Pete looked through the dirty sliding glass door that led to the patio. "Jeez, you could step right out to the pool. You were spoiled rotten, weren't you?"

"Maybe I was," I said with an arrogant attitude that was facetious on one level, but also turned Pete on. "*So what?*"

He stepped over to me and began undoing my belt.

"So this is where you used to beat your meat?"

"Yeah, a lot. It felt great, too."

"I'll bet it did." Pete unbuttoned my pants. "You ever have anyone over?"

"Are you kidding? With Joe McCarthy in the next room?"

"I'll bet you wanted to though. I'll bet you would've given anything for someone to do this." He pulled down my Jockey shorts, squeezed my hard cock. "Some surly punk from high school who always gave you a hard time."

"There was a guy like that. Brian Hazzard. I was scared of him."

"Why? He probably just wanted to do this."

Pete got down and sucked my cock—really sucked it. Then I pulled down his pants and really sucked his. It was one of the hottest times we ever had.

The first night I'd gone out with Pete he'd worn a Yale T-shirt. He hadn't lied, but he'd strongly implied that he'd gone to Yale for a while. He'd talked about student friends of his, about living in New Haven—that much was true. He'd lived with a young professor for a while in the early eighties, a history professor named Cord. Pete said he and Cord were still friends, Cord still taught at Yale, where he lived with a Ph.D. student now. Pete never really talked about what had happened with Cord, why it hadn't lasted, but you could tell just from his tone that Cord was the one who'd ended it.

Once Pete told me I reminded him of a young professor. "A sexy young professor," he'd quickly added. "The kind you'd like to suck off in the classroom. In front of the class." Another time he told me that when I had a certain kind of puzzled expression, I reminded him of Cord.

Once I'd sucked Pete's cock while he was only wearing his Yale T-shirt. Afterward he'd said, "So do you like me better as a brilliant student or a dumb mechanic?"

He'd said this lightly, but the cynicism still startled me. I'd said what I thought at the time was the truth: "I like *you*."

But since we'd broken up, I'd wondered a lot if it hadn't all just been a sexual/romantic game. I'd remember my thoughts driving home from the Chevron station the first afternoon, before Pete called me, when I'd thought he was probably straight. What a cool guy, what a total fucking doll, what a soulful—and surprisingly intelligent—mechanic. (In my first shot ever of Pete he'd been sitting alone in the Chevron office on his lunch break, his feet on the desk, his shirt unbuttoned, looking moody and smart and shockingly sensuous, reading a paperback of Camus's *The Plague*.) At that point in my celibacy I was heavily into incorporating hot men seen at random during the day into my jack-off fantasies, so I'd considered a few obvious scenarios: Pete delivering my car just as I stepped from the shower, or while I just happened to be jerking off. Or Pete calling me later, saying he'd thought about me all afternoon. So that when he *did* call it was frightening but also seriously exhilarating. When I got off the phone with him, I felt like I was suddenly living again.

We never actually had sex in the Santa Monica Chevron garage, although we once imagined doing it there after hours. We pictured it just the way it would be, with the fluorescent lights on inside, the windows exposing us to the traffic on Pacific Coast Highway, to the pedestrians going to the nearby restaurant. We imagined horrified people banging on the glass—including Pete's boss!—but I'd be fucking Pete against the greasy workbench and he'd be about to jiz all over the tool chest, and no matter how frantically they banged on the glass, we wouldn't stop.

Usually, we imagined these things in bed *after* sex, not while we were having it. But the first time Pete fucked me, it began as a kind of fantasy. I was wearing madras shorts that day, and penny loafers, and Pete had come straight from work, still wearing his Chevron coveralls. He said I looked like a "stuck-up Palisades yuppie husband." "Maybe your wife's still at her yoga class," he said, pulling down my shorts. "And she's not due home for another hour."

"Actually, *Hope* could be walking in any second now," I said, and we both kind of laughed. Then I unbuttoned Pete's coveralls and sucked his cock. Then he came very close to eating my butt, and I got very turned on, and I hadn't been fucked since 1978, and when Pete finally did it, I got so flipped out I came without even touching myself. It's hard to get over something like that.

But Pete wasn't just a mechanic or a rock musician or a cute, butch guy in a Yale T-shirt with a hard-on. If that was truly all it had been about, I probably *would've* tried to fuck him out of my system. I might have found someone else for technically similar *hot sex*. Except I didn't want a fuck buddy. I didn't want to answer an ad I'd seen: "No emotion, no commitment, no candlelit dinners. JUST SEX." I could imagine Pete reading that ad and laughing, saying "candlelit dinners" with just the right embittered sneer. It could be a long time before I met someone else with Pete's sensibility and humor.

*   *   *

"I thought of you the other night," I said as we drove back past Disneyland. "*Maurice* was on cable."

"*Maurice?*" As if he didn't know what I was talking about.

"The film? Don't you remember? We rented it."

"Oh, right." As if he still didn't remember.

This pissed me off. He couldn't have forgotten. Not only had we watched the film together, we'd done joke variations of it later, especially the scene where Scudder the game-keeper climbs in Maurice's bedroom window at night. We did the accents and everything, Pete, of course, playing Scudder. "It's all right, sir," he'd say in a lower-class British voice. "Let me climb in bed with you now, sir. Let me take off your nightshirt. Now just relax, sir." I'd done Maurice, sounding more like a prim Prince Charles: "Oh, Scudder. You're stretching me. My word." We'd both been skeptical of the film beforehand, afraid it would be too tasteful and anemic, which in a lot of ways it was. But despite our parody of it, the bedroom scene—a rare main-stream cinematic instance of homoerotic catharsis—was a genuine guilty pleasure.

"I'd forgotten how slow a lot of it was though," I said. "Certain films are better in your mind than when you actually see them again."

"That's true of a lot of things," Pete said.

The place where Pete's mom worked was about a mile from her home, in a mini-mall set in an empty parking lot in the middle of nowhere. The vastness of Orange County still amazed me, the big-sky vistas, like a corporate Ukraine, mile after mile of flat tracts and malls and chain stores. The last time I'd been down here much, in the seventies, it felt like the future, a vapid new world for white suburban families fleeing L.A. That was still true, but the future now looked like this minimall. Not more than five years old but already seedy, weeds growing along the walkways. Most of the units were bare and unfinished. One had been some-thing for a while. In its window there was still a sun-faded poster of has-been teen pop star Debbie Gibson. Her face was red. Her lips were KS purple. "Electric Youth," it said.

Pete parked and got out. "I'll just be a minute."

I got out, too. "I need a drink of water. I'm going to see if there's a fountain." Which was true, but just to irritate him I said, "And I'd like to meet your mother, too."

"Tim, why don't you just wait in the car."

"Can't I at least say hello? I'm sure you've told her about me. Bad-mouthed me."

He looked angrier than I'd expected. "I don't tell my mom about that part of my life."

"Why not? She does know you're gay, doesn't she?"

"Yeah, she knows. Tim, I have to tell you, you are already starting to get on my nerves."

"Look, I was just teasing. I'm not going to do anything. Relax. I'm just going to get a drink."

We walked into the courtyard, the wind scattering leaves and plastic trash across the concrete. I didn't see a drinking fountain but I saw the office Pete was going to. I thought it was some sort of real estate or insurance office—until I saw the gold letters on the glass facade above the official seal.

"Jesus Christ," I said to Pete. "Do you know who this *is?*"

"Yeah, I know."

It was a U.S. representative's district office. For the Honorable Gerald C. Bryer, Republican.

There was no one inside at the secretaries' desks in the outer office. But for some reason I still whispered, *"This guy is the worst pig in America."*

"I know."

"Jesus." I felt awed and slightly frightened, like a tourist who'd wandered into an off-limits area in a foreign country. But there was no one around, so I cupped my eyes and peered in through the glass. Magazines arranged neatly on the coffee table. *National Review, Christian Life,* a *Newsweek* from last fall with Magic Johnson on the cover. I imagined Bryer's private racist reaction to that news, his cynical suspicion.

On the wall above the sofa there was a large portrait of the congressman beside an American flag. Shoe-polish hair like Ronald Reagan's. Mean leathery face, like a film noir sadist. You'd cast either Robert Ryan or Sterling Hayden. Men with lipless mouths. He had a nasty chuckle, too, as heard on "Nightline," where he was usually pitted against a gay rights activist from New York. He never came right out and said it, but the subtext, in his chuckle, was always: "You goddamn queers are gettin' *exactly* what you deserve." What he *did* say was bad enough.

"Do you know what he's trying to do now?" I said to Pete. "He's pushing a bill to rescind all the AIDS protection laws. He *wants* people fired and thrown out of their homes. He wants them to lose their insurance. This guy's a psycho. He's even worse than Dannemeyer."

"I know."

"How can your mom work for a guy like this?"

Pete didn't answer. He was already opening the glass door. I stepped in behind him. A warm chemical odor rose from the copying machine, which had run out of paper. In the tray, an article: "AIDS: Protecting Decent Americans."

Pete went over to his mother's desk. Her pink vinyl bag was on the floor. There were two framed photos on her desk, one of a little girl, a niece, and one of Pete, circa 1975. His hair was longer than I'd ever seen it, falling down over his eyes.

I picked up the photo. "This must have been right before you went punk. When you were still into wimp-rock, Jackson Browne."

Pete ignored my remark, picking up an accordion-folded computer-printout list. Names and addresses.

"What's that?" I said.

"Oh, just a bunch of people who should have their brains blown out."

A conservative mailing list of some sort. Under the *A*'s I noted the name and home address of a right-wing L.A. County supervisor. And I got an idea. "You know who could use this?" I was thinking of Todd.

Pete was looking at the closed door to one of the back offices. "Do you hear that?"

41

Stepping closer to the door, I did. Music, soft and thin. Bobby Short singing "I Get a Kick Out of You."

Then we heard a woman's voice, a breathy gasp.

I looked at Pete. A crazy glint in his eye, like the joke impression he did of a cracked pit-bull owner. He wasn't kidding now though.

The next thing I knew he was throwing open the office door, and in my mind what followed always looks like a Martin Scorsese blowout scene. I was the jerky hand-held camera following Pete as he charged into the dark room where the flabby-assed congressman was fucking Pete's mother dog-style on the plaid sofa. Bryer still had his undershirt on, his white butt was jiggling, he wore sheer black socks. You could hardly see Pete's mother at first. Then she screamed as Pete pulled the congressman off of her, and there, for a second, was a nasty shot of her butt and glistening vagina. I looked away.

Then you could say that all hell broke loose, as Pete startled strangling Bryer, and Mrs. Schindler grabbed her orange dress, and Pete held Bryer down against the sofa and the congressman tried to pry Pete's hands from his throat, and I couldn't help noticing that Bryer's balls were gray like elephant skin. And Mrs. Schindler, who looked like Angie Dickinson, was screaming, "Oh, my God! My God!" And I could hear Bryer choking to death, so I finally tried to pull Pete off him.

I was saying things like, "Come on, Pete, it's not worth it," when Bryer hit Pete pretty hard across the face and Pete let go.

Then Pete was winded and his nose was bleeding and I was holding him back, and Bryer was grabbing his gray suit pants, and the hard light coming in from the outer office reminded me of a scene in *Blade Runner,* and I caught a whiff of cherry pipe tobacco, which reminded me of my father.

Mrs. Schindler was pulling on her orange dress without bothering to put on her bra and panties as Pete looked at her and said, "You stupid fucking cunt."

"All right now!" Bryer barked. *"All right! You watch that talk!"* And just his voice, his tone—I'd seen him do the same belligerent intimidation shtick on "Nightline," trying to win the argument by drowning out his opponent. And to be honest a part of me wished there *were* some way to kill him, right now, to just do it (to smash his skull in, for example, with that Remington bronze statuette on his desk). And get away with it, of course, not have to stand trial or go to prison.

"Honey, please just go," Pete's mother said to him in a whiny little-girl voice.

"You really are a stupid fucking twat!" Pete said to her.

"Look here!" Bryer barked as he zipped up his slacks. "I don't know who the *hell* you think you are—"

"I'm her son, you fuck! Her buttfucking, cocksucking son! And you're dead meat, you evil pig! You're fucking *dead!* I'm gonna have you *killed!"*

Pete used his T-shirt to wipe the blood off his face. His nose was bleeding pretty heavily.

And Bryer looked down at his own chest and jumped when he saw blood, Pete's blood, a homosexual's blood, in the white chest hairs above his undershirt. With a look of cold terror, he said, "Oh, my God. I've got to get this off—"

Bryer started for the door, and with a sudden ferocious burst Pete grabbed him. "That's right!" Pete yelled. *"I've got it!"*

He pushed Bryer back against the wall, back against the framed photos of the congressman with Ronald Reagan and Robert Dornan and Patrick Buchanan and William Dannemeyer and Jesse Helms and an emaciated John Wayne and various other right-wing slime. And Pete smeared his bloody fingers across Bryer's mouth. "I've got it and now *you've got it, too!* See how it feels, you vile fuck! You're gonna *die! You're gonna rot in an AIDS ward surrounded by fags!"*

Pete kept smearing his blood in Bryer's mouth despite the congressman's groans and pursed-lipped attempts to spit it out. And to be honest, it's an image that on a certain level of justice still does my heart good—though while it was happening I was completely freaked out.

So was Pete's mom. She kept screaming, piercingly, "Oh, my God, what are you doing! *What are you doing!*"

Finally Pete stopped and let Bryer go, and the congressman made a mad groaning dash to the bathroom.

Pete's mom just looked at him for a second and said in a strangely low-key, intimate voice, "You've really done it *now*." Then she went after Bryer, who was spitting and coughing in the bathroom.

"Let's get the hell out of here," I said to Pete.

On our way to the door, I grabbed the mailing list from Mrs. Schindler's desk.

At Pete's car, I said, "Give me the keys," and he did. He was too tweaked on adrenaline to drive safely, not that I was much calmer. I stuffed the mailing list into his knapsack before I pulled out. Pete took off his T-shirt and used it to wipe the blood off his face.

I headed back down Harbor Boulevard past Disneyland.

"Jesus, Pete. I think this could be kind of bad."

"I don't care. I should've fucking killed him. I wish I had. I will though. He's dead."

"Where are we going?"

Pete took a deep breath. "Newport Beach. There's an AA clubhouse there. I think I need a meeting."

FOUR

BY THE TIME we got on the Newport Freeway, Pete's anger had given way to a kind of baffled depression.

"I just can't believe it," he said. "My own mother. What a fucking *nightmare*."

"Has she worked there long?"

"I don't know. Six months."

"Have you ever discussed it with her? I mean, his politics . . ."

"I tried, but she just got hysterical. I mean, she's not even political, that's the thing. I hate to say it, but she's not too smart. She'd been doing temp work. It was just a better job to her."

"That's like saying, 'I just do a little typing for the SS.' She *does* know you're gay . . ."

"Yeah, she knows. But we don't discuss it. We don't discuss anything—except the pot roast when I come to dinner." Pete shielded his eyes from the white freeway glare. "I just can't believe it. That's it. I can't see her anymore after this. I've just lost my mother."

I didn't know what to say. I was still extremely shaken. I knew what I had to ask him about though.

Pete reached into the messy backseat. "We should probably wear shirts at this meeting. Not that you don't still look good without one."

A throwaway compliment.

"Do you have it, Pete?"

He dug out a faded R.E.M. T-shirt. "Do you want this one? You like them, don't you?"

"You told him you had it. Did you take the test?"

"Yeah, I took it. Twice. A few months after you and I broke up. And again last winter." He pulled out another T-shirt, white with ragged red letters: BUTTHOLE SURFERS. "Here, why don't you wear this one? It's cleaner."

"You were positive?"

"I was negative both times."

I couldn't say anything for a moment. I'm not someone who cries easily, but I almost lost it. Finally I said, "Why did you tell him that then?"

"Why do you think? To fuck with his head. Let him see what it's like to live with that kind of fear." Pete saw that I was trying not to cry. "Are you okay?" The gentlest tone he'd used so far.

"Yeah. I'm just so fucking glad you're all right."

"I am, too."

He took my hand for just a second, a reassuring squeeze, as if to say, it's okay, no harm was done (neither of us gave it to the other).

The AA clubhouse was in a white Mission Revival building on the Balboa peninsula with a tony view of the azure bay. It was a little before six when we got there, so the meeting hadn't started yet. People were still milling around, drinking coffee from Styrofoam cups, talking loudly and cheerfully. An affluent group, khaki shorts and Top-Siders, thin, blond wives like Meryl Streep or Michelle Pfeiffer, guys like Michael and Gary from "thirtysomething," a very heterosexual crowd.

Pete was supposed to meet Joey here, the new guy he was sponsoring, and he seemed concerned that Joey hadn't arrived yet. Pete saw a few other people he knew though, including the young actor Jay Sutter. I didn't recognize Jay till Pete introduced us. He'd grown a beard, for one thing, and I wasn't really that crazy about him as an actor or the films he did, lame yuppie romantic comedies with Jay as the leading man—I usually just caught bits and pieces on cable. I did think he was a good-looking guy though, even more so with a beard.

"What happened to *you?*" Jay said to Pete with a bland yacht-club drawl. "Looks like you had a nosebleed."

"Yeah, I did." Realizing he still had some blood on his upper lip, Pete ducked off to use the men's room for a minute and left me talking to Jay.

"So . . . you work at the California Film Archives? You just had that Fassbinder retrospective."

"Yeah, that was ours." I felt distracted, a bit oppressed by all the bright chatter going on around us.

"Yes, I came to one night of that," Jay said. "*Querelle* and *Fox and His Friends*. Liked the latter. Found *Querelle* exhausted *and* exhausting. His last film though, what can you expect? And Brad Davis. Sad. Wonder if that's where he got it. Doing drugs with the Fassbinder crowd. Like your T-shirt, by the way. They're great. You catch them on the Lollapalooza tour last year?"

I looked down at the Butthole Surfers logo, having almost forgotten what I was wearing. "No, I missed that," I said. "I had tickets that night for Liza Minnelli at the Greek."

Jay's smile kind of froze, like he wasn't sure what I was up to. I didn't know myself. I wasn't sure what *he* was up to. I'd heard a rumor that he might be gay, but it struck me as a classic case of wishful thinking.

"Well, you missed quite a show," he said, his tone turning intimate. "So, are you and Pete together?" His eyes glistened with homoerotic desire.

"Well, we came together." I watched him resist a cheap joke.

"I know that. I mean, are you boyfriends?"

"Nnnn . . . not right now."

He laughed. "Not right now. I'm going to have to think about that."

It was then that they called the meeting to order. I sat down in one of the folding chairs where Pete had left his cigarettes and keys. Jay took the free chair on the other side of me. I looked back at the foyer and saw that Pete was using the pay phone.

"You're in the area?" Jay whispered as a woman began reading Chapter Five from the AA Big Book.

"No, Santa Monica."

"Whereabouts?"

"The canyon."

"You're kidding. What street?"

"Sage."

"This is incredible. I'm right above you. On Amalfi. We've got to exchange phone numbers."

I hesitated. "Okay."

To be honest, I did start thinking things. Jay was not unattractive, not at all. Amazing green eyes. I glanced at him, at his pink mouth, imagined kissing him. *Oh, Jay.* If this had happened a week, even a day, earlier I would have been dazzled. A chance, at the very least, to wipe Pete out of my mind with some seriously rowdy sex. Something I should've done a long time ago anyway. This guy was obviously *ready*. But that in itself gave me pause, the sense that he might *always* be ready, coming on this strongly all the time.

"Are you going to be home later tonight?" he said.

I saw Pete coming back. "I don't know."

"I'd like to come by if you are. You're a very hot guy, you know that?"

"Thanks. So are you."

Pete sat down next to me as they introduced the first speaker, an attractive woman in her midforties, blond hair pulled back tightly, a smart gray suit that seemed a bit formal, but I knew that the speakers often dressed up; the men would wear suits and ties, for example, as if to illustrate how their lives had improved in sobriety. "My name is Carol C.," she said in a shy, wispy voice. "And I'm an alcoholic and an addict."

"Hi, Carol," everyone said.

As she began her story, about her alcoholic parents in Nebraska, Pete whispered, "Bryer called the cops."

"How do you know that?"

"I just talked to my mom."

I was surprised, considering what Pete had said earlier. "Did you tell her you don't have it?"

"No. I want him to sweat."

"*Pete*—they could order you to be tested. There are all kinds of laws now."

"I don't care. Fuck 'em."

"The cops came to the office?"

"Yeah. And get this. Bryer fired my mother."

"Jesus. What a pig."

"Yeah. I should've killed him while I had the chance."

"So the cops are looking for you now?"

"For *us*. Except they don't know your name yet. But don't get hysterical. It's not like there's a manhunt in progress or anything. It's basically just an assault charge stemming from a private dispute. Very low priority."

"Are you sure? He's a fucking congressman. They could call in the FBI—"

Some guy sitting behind us shushed us.

"And then I came out to California," Carol C. was saying in a voice so soft and timid you couldn't have heard her without the microphone. "And it was the sixties, so I guess you know what that meant. At first it was just marijuana, then . . ."

Pete kept looking around, watching the door as a few people came in late. "I'm getting worried about Joey."

I looked at Jay. He smiled. "A *very* hot guy," he whispered almost inaudibly.

I looked at Pete. He was getting jumpy. "Damn it, where *is* he?"

"So then we moved to this old movie ranch out near Chatsworth," Carol C. said, sounding more relaxed and confident now. "And for a while it was great. It really *was* like a family. Of course, Charlie was feeding us so much acid *anything* would have seemed great."

Knowing but nervous laughter. Movie ranch, Charlie. I covered my mouth in shock. "Oh, my God, Pete. She was a *Manson girl*."

49

"So?" he said. "We've all got a past." He got up. "I gotta use the phone."

I looked at Jay. He leaned over and whispered in my ear, "I wish I had your cock in my mouth right now."

I didn't know what to say. Coming from someone else that line could easily have seemed crass. But coming from Jay, it made my cock jerk. He was *very* appealing, and I hadn't had sex with anyone in a year, not since Pete. I felt a hot facial flush of embarrassment.

"And then one night in August of 1969 . . ." Carol C. sighed. "This is hard." She was close to tears. "It was twenty-two years ago last summer, and you better believe I went to a meeting that night. In fact, three meetings." She had our attention. "It was a night much like this. Hot. The wind blowing, a dry Santa Ana." A palm frond scratched a windowpane. "We were restless, our nerves set on edge from the wind and . . . from too much acid. And Tex came to us and said . . . he said, 'It's time to do the devil's business.'"

The meeting secretary, who looked like Ginger Rogers, handed Carol C. a Kleenex. She wiped her cheeks. I saw that it wasn't a scowl on her forehead but, under the makeup, an X.

"Then Charlie came and said, 'There's a house . . . a house up on Cielo Drive in Beverly Hills. . . . I want you . . . I want you to go up there and . . .'"

Pete tapped me on the shoulder. "Tim, come on, we're gonna go."

I got up, irritated. As we reached the foyer, I said, "Jesus, she's just getting to the best part. What's going on?"

"I think Joey's got a problem. I just talked to his sister."

"What do you mean?"

"I think he's on his way to score some speed. I'm gonna try and talk him out of it."

Jay came out. "What's going on, guys?"

"Nothing," Pete said. "I've just got a newcomer problem."

"Anything *I* can do?" Jay said.

"No. I can handle it." Pete had his car keys out, eager to go.

50

Jay put his hand on my arm. "Well, look, can I give you a lift back to Santa Monica? You're not on the program, are you?"

"No."

"I didn't think so. I can always spot a normie." Engaging laugh. "So you'd only be in the way on a twelfth-step call. I'd really like to, you know." Jay looked into my eyes as if Pete weren't there. Behind him in the hall Carol C. was sobbing at the podium.

I looked at Pete but couldn't read his mind at all. I said, "Would I be in the way?"

"No," Pete said mechanically, as if he resented having to say it. "Actually, I could use someone with me. You never know what you're going to walk into in situations like this."

I gave Jay a regretful look. He gave me one of good-natured disappointment. Pete was already out the door, so I just said to Jay, "Last name's Fowler. Nineteen ten Sage. It's listed."

"Hey, you don't mean that Spanish place on the corner, do you?"

"Yeah, that's it."

"I'm going to wake you up in the morning," Jay said. "After my run, when I'm all sweaty. Think you'd like that?"

I knew I would, a lot, but I said, "Let's talk first."

In the car Pete said, "I hope you know what I just saved you from."

"Yeah, a mind-shattering fuck. What's going on?"

"That guy's the biggest sleaze in California."

"You're jealous."

"I don't think so—"

"I mean, of him. If that's true, he's taken your title."

"Fuck you. You were a bigger sleaze than I could ever hope to be."

"I never played in the bushes in Buena Vista Park," I said.

"No, you were up on the lifeguard station at Venice Beach with a dick in each hand."

I knew where this could go. Rubber bullets now, but we both had flamethrowers. "Okay. I'm sorry. Let's not do this."

"You started it, with your bitch mouth."

"I said I was sorry."

"That was one of the problems with you," Pete said. "You're basically a bitch. And all your stupid fucking friends are bitches, too."

"Todd's not a bitch."

"No. But Gregory is."

"Gregory's not a bitch. He's a sweet, harmless guy."

"He's a bitch. He trashed me, didn't he?"

"I think he felt threatened, Pete. I'd been hanging out with him a lot until I met you."

"Well, now you can hang out with him all you want. And be bitches together."

"I haven't been spending all my time with Gregory, you know. Contrary to what you may think in your puerile narcissism, my life's been extremely full since I dumped you."

"I don't think that's quite how it came down, Tim."

"No, it isn't really, is it? That's very important to you, isn't it, who rejected who. How many guys have you blown off since me? You know what you should do, to be really safe? You should just reject everybody right now for all time. Then you could live the rest of your life knowing you'd dumped *everyone* before they dumped you."

"You're crazy," Pete said. "And I don't want to talk about this anymore. This is exactly the kind of abstract bullshit I didn't want to get into."

I watched the surfers in the ocean off Huntington Beach, the cheap new condo buildings along the highway. "Where are we going, by the way?"

"Long Beach."

We came to the open stretches of Bolsa Chica Beach, which I'd seen go from a field of rusty tin cans in the fifties to pure white sand dunes in the sixties to the long parking lot and string of cinder-block toilet buildings it was now. I looked at the ridge in the distance and thought about the afternoon in 1970 when I'd driven back there with Robbie, my first boyfriend, to explore the abandoned World War Two artillery bunkers. In one of the empty concrete gun slots, we'd begun making out and got so turned-on just from kissing each other that we'd both come in our white Levi's jeans.

"So you think Jay's a real sleaze, huh?" I said to Pete.

"That's what I've heard. Frank Booth."

"He'll fuck anything that moves?"

"You got it."

"*You* move. Has he fucked you?"

"That's none of your business." Pete looked at me. Smiled grudgingly. "No."

"Seems like a nice guy though. And just a few blocks from my house."

"It's your life."

FIVE

"LONG BEACH," Pete said we parked at the foot of Pine Avenue by the strand. "The town that doesn't count."

I knew what he meant. A large but dowdy city—Des Moines by the Sea—that always seemed lost and forgotten in the shadow of Los Angeles. "I had some good times here in my teens," I said as we got out.

"Yeah, I know. You used to get your cock sucked at the Pike. This was it, right?"

"Yeah."

We started walking down what had once been the amusement park's midway arcade. Only one building remained, a moldering blue stucco structure a couple of blocks away. Everything else had been leveled over a decade before. There were just the foundation grids, old tile floors, weeds growing up through the pavement. Above us on the bluff, high-rise office buildings lined Ocean Boulevard, where there'd once been dumpy 1920s apartment buildings, in the late sixties filled with bikers and sailors and sluts and queers. "You should stay away from there, Timmy," my mom had warned me. "That place has a bad reputation."

"I'm having a nostalgia rush," I said.

"Yeah, I'll bet. You getting a hard-on?"

"It really *was* pretty cool. I could write a dirty boy's adventure story about the summer of 1969. When my parents went round the world on the love boat and I came to

Long Beach to stay with my evil right-wing aunt. And discovered a crude, intoxicating wonderland of cheap, lurid thrills." I pointed as we walked. "There were booths all along here, with barkers. Milk-bottle/Kewpie-doll places. A shooting gallery. That was the house of mirrors over there. Insane, creepy, like the one in *Lady from Shanghai*. Smelled like piss. That was the fun house over there, with a cackling mechanical lady in front."

"What did that smell like? Shit?"

"No. That smelled like piss, too. And this was the salt-water-taffy place right here. Jeez, I can still taste it."

"A piss taste, huh?"

"Come on. Quit trashing my memories." We came to an expanse of brown, tile-patterned linoleum. "Oh, God, this was the *freak show building!* Talk about pure Americana raunch! There was this barker, totally sleazed out, greasy pompadour, pencil mustache. You'd pay your quarter and go in and there'd be this dancing snake lady, but not quite the luscious figure pictured on the canvas poster. She was sixty, I'm not kidding, somebody's grandmother, in torn fishnet stockings, staggering about to this grungy forty-five of Dave 'Baby' Cortez's 'The Happy Organ' with a half-dead boa constrictor over her shoulders. And the Human Pincushion! The Sword Swallower—this bald, mustached pirate type, like the torso guy in *Freaks!* The Headless Sailor—"

"Tim, come on."

I caught up with him. "The Cyclone Racer was down there. The most horrendous roller coaster on the West Coast. So I heard. I never had the balls to go on it. They used to take girls off of there limp, or in hysterics. Had to hose the piss off the seats between rides."

"What's all this about piss? Do you have a bent we never explored?"

"No. I can't help it if that's the way it was down here. Those were the smells. Greasy corn dogs, piss, salt air, and . . ." I stopped as we came to what had once been a walkway between two buildings. "Oh, God."

"What?"

"Never mind. It's not worth going into."

"Let me guess," he said. "That's where the tearoom was."

"Did I tell you about that?"

"Yeah. More than I wanted to know. The smegma monster."

I winced. He was referring to the story of my first encounter, at age sixteen, with dick cheese. "God, I told you a lot, didn't I?"

"Too much."

"I still can't eat goat cheese," I said as we kept walking. "No Wolfgang Puck pizzas for me. The graffiti in those days was pretty incredible though. In the stalls, I mean. Short stories. Better than anything in *The New Yorker*. Nothing precious about *that* prose, not with opening lines like: 'Last night I sucked off a sailor . . .'"

Pete wasn't smiling. I realized I'd touched a nerve. He'd had a bad experience with a guy right before me: Carlos, a Chilean science student at UCLA. They'd gone together for three months and Pete had let his guard down, but Carlos turned out to be "an emotional ax-murderer," who, Pete learned shortly before they broke up, was also into tearooms. Acting on a tip, Pete had caught him in one at UCLA.

"Of course, that was twenty years ago," I said to distance myself from Carlos. "It was all different then. Innocent in a way. Not that it wasn't ultimately a sign of oppression. But for a teenage homo there weren't many options. Hitchhiking, of course."

"Spare me your hitchhiking stories."

Our destination was coming up, the sea blue stucco building with a cherry red neon sign: THE DIVING BELL.

"Used to come to this place in the midseventies," I said. "When I was at Cal State Long Beach. Pretty cruisy on weekends. Otherwise depressing. Drunks singing along to 'Ain't No Mountain High Enough.'" I looked down what had once been another side street. "The carousel was down there. And the Ferris wheel. A dance hall for sailors. Disneyland killed this place though. A shame. Hard to get your rocks off in the Magic Kingdom."

"Wasn't for me," Pete said. He'd worked there several summers in his teens.

"Oh, right. After hours in the cave on Tom Sawyer's Island with . . . what was his name?"

"Ted."

"Right, Ted. Actually, there was a gay night at Disneyland in the late seventies that was very strange. The thing I always remember is the gas chamber joke."

"Gas chamber joke?"

"Yeah. We were all crammed into a room in one of the attractions. The Haunted House or something. All these armpit-hair lesbians and guys who looked like the cowboy in the Village People. And this guide who was leading us through said, 'Don't worry, folks. We're not going to gas you now.' "

"That's witty."

"Yeah. I think he went on to write one-liners for Reagan. Had a sex change or something. Became Peggy Noonan."

We reached the blue building. Next door to the Diving Bell there was an abandoned tattoo parlor. I stopped to look at the curled photos in the window of a chunky bald man covered from head to toe.

"You haven't taken the test yet, have you?" Pete said.

"No. But you know something?"

"What's that?"

"If you're all right, I probably am, too."

"How do you figure that?"

"Well—we were careful," I said. "But I think there were still a few slip-ups."

"You mean your pre-come?"

"Well, that, too. But I was thinking about the time I got some come in your eye."

"Oh, right." He looked embarrassed.

I caught a whiff of stale beer from behind the curtain over the bar door, heard the Chris Montez oldie "Call Me."

"To be honest, that really worried me at the time," I said. "That you had to go wash your eye out because it stung. But I didn't know if it was really dangerous or not. It's not something they mention in the guidelines."

"No."

"I mean, I couldn't call the hot line. 'Look, I was jacking off in my boyfriend's face the other night, and when I came, a stray dollop of jiz caught him right in the—' "

"*Tim.*" He cut me off, as if—it startled me to realize— he didn't want me making light of our lovemaking. He said, "I thought about it, too, if you want to know the truth. Later, I mean. I repressed it at the time, I guess, because I didn't want anything to . . ." He drifted off, something bothering him. "Look, you might as well know, as long as we're on the subject. One time when I was fucking you, a rubber broke."

"*What?*"

"Yeah. It was the last time actually. After we got back from France. I didn't realize it'd happened until I pulled out. It'd just broken. It was down below the head of my dick."

"Good God. Why didn't you tell me?"

"I don't know. I was in shock, I guess. I was horrified. What good would it have done? It was too late."

"Oh, man," I said. "With God as my witness, I am never going to let anyone fuck me again, ever, not in this life."

"That's why I took the test," Pete said. " 'Cause we'd been having safe sex, but obviously things can go wrong. I just wanted to know if I'd—"

"If you'd been positive, would you have let me know? I mean—left a message on my machine or something?"

"I don't know," he said. "Would you have wanted me to?"

"I'm not sure. Probably not. That's why I haven't taken the test myself, 'cause if I were positive, I think I'd flip out. I'm not someone who'd handle it well. . . . But I *must* be all right if you are."

"Maybe. Assuming you've been careful since me."

"Yeah, I have." I looked out across the vacant lot where the roller coaster had been. "I've been incredibly careful."

Pete parted the filthy red curtain. "Come on. We gotta see if little Joey's still sober."

* * *

It was a long, narrow bar with black walls, large hand-painted signs advertising a drag contest for emperor and empress (and for the dowager-identified gentleman, queen mother) of Long Beach. The place was dead, just the bartender, one customer on a stool, and on a spotlit platform in the back an incomplete Latino transsexual lip-syncing Chris Montez's wispy falsetto voice. I say *incomplete* because the pointy breasts under his red tank top were obviously *real*—that is, silicone as opposed to falsies—and the dick and balls in his sheer pink nylon panties looked real, too. He appeared to be rehearsing for a later performance. The customer at the bar, a gaunt, fiftyish individual in an aqua jumpsuit, was ignoring him and staring into the mirror behind the bottles, taking drags off a long, thin cigarette.

Pete approached the bartender. "Hey, Buddy."

"Oh, boy," Buddy said with a nervous laugh that hit a mildewed memory chord. "I know why *you're* here."

It couldn't be but it was. Twenty-three years had passed but it was. Buddy had to be in his fifties now, but his outsize Tom of Finland pectorals were still bulging under his tight white T-shirt, much the way they'd bulged under his tight white sailor suit the night we met at the trough in the men's room a block away when I was sixteen and sexed up and scared and he was the Headless Sailor. His face was lined now, a kind of wizened cuteness that, joltingly, reminded me of the evangelist Pat Robertson. I recalled his lewd Jiminy Cricket grin as he'd whispered at the urinal, "Sure like to wrap my lips around *that*." He did, back at his place in one of the dumpy apartment buildings up on the bluff, giving me the first in a series of the meanest blow jobs I've ever had.

"Joey been around?" Pete asked him.

"Yeah, you just missed him," Buddy said.

"Is he drinking?"

"Not here. No way." Buddy laughed. Turned out he had been in and out of AA himself. "But it doesn't look good, Pete."

Buddy glanced at me nervously, as if he were trying to place me.

"What do you mean?" Pete asked him.

"Well, he left with Mother Dwayne."

"Who?"

"Mother Dwayne," Buddy said. "The Queen Mother of Long Beach. And I'm afraid she's become something of a crystal queen in the final days of her reign. And I'm not talking Baccarat, as I'm sure you know." He kept glancing at me, troubled now.

"So they were tweaked?" Pete said.

"Not yet. I think they were on their way to connect with someone at the baths."

The baths? I knew there were places like that still open, but the idea of going to one of them made my skin crawl.

"He left you a message," Buddy said to Pete. "He thought you might come by."

I looked at the Latin transsexual as the music changed to the other Chris Montez hit, "The More I See You." I'd never been *into* Chris Montez, except as a kind of camp joke; the quintessence of lamé. But I recalled the singer's popularity with the other "gay kids" I knew in junior high. I had a vague memory of Chris lip-syncing this song on a *Shindig* beach, doing the same sort of limp nelly dance the transsexual was doing now.

"He said he's sorry," Buddy told Pete over the music. "He knows you tried to help. But he doesn't really see the point in staying sober now. All things considered, he said, he'd much rather . . . I'm trying to remember his exact words."

The transsexual did a cheesy Joey Heatherton butt wriggle and winked at me.

"Oh, right," Buddy said, "I remember. He'd much rather go out in one final blaze of infernal glory. That's it. 'Infernal glory.' It's a shame, isn't it? Such a doll. So young, so blond. I tried to talk him out of it, but he already had *that look* in his eye. His heartbreaking, to-die-for blue eyes. And Mother Dwayne." Buddy sucked in his breath. "Well, I hate to speak ill of royalty. But she is one sick lady."

Pete looked disgusted and angry. Without saying anything more to Buddy, he dug out some change and went to use the pay phone in the back of the bar. Buddy started washing glasses, pointedly ignoring me.

"I think I know you from a long time ago," I said.

"I don't think so." He didn't look up.

"Yeah. Twenty-three years ago. You lived up on the bluff."

He came over, furtively glancing at the gaunt customer, speaking low. "Look, that was another lifetime. I don't do that anymore."

I didn't quite understand what he meant. "Well, I realize it was a long time ago, but . . ." To me, it was just a pleasant memory.

"Yeah, but I got caught. I was in prison for seven years. That was not fun."

I was surprised, even though I'd realized at the time that he liked young guys, high school guys like me. I'd never thought of him as a chickenhawk though. He didn't have that fussy, creepy quality at all. In his early thirties, he'd been boyish, easygoing, masculine, like the coach you *wished* you'd had. Instead of stinging paddle swats, you got your jockstrap pulled down and your cock sucked till your eyes teared up.

"I'm sorry to hear that," I said.

"*You* were okay though." Mechanical wink. "Mike, right?"

"Tim."

"I was close." He went to refill the gaunt customer's beer glass.

I went to take a leak.

I was standing at the trough in the smelly men's room when the door opened and I jumped, thinking it was Buddy. But it was the Latino transsexual. He stepped up beside me and whipped out his dick and, thankfully, began to take a piss. He looked at me, at my face.

"What do you do?" he said.

"I'm a ballerina."

"No, I'm serious. Don't be stuck-up."

"I work at a film archives."

"What do you do there?"

61

"We restore and preserve old films."

"What's your favorite movie?"

"Umm, I'd have to say *Touch of Evil*."

"I don't know that one."

"Orson Welles."

"Oh, *Citizen Kane*."

"Yes, actually, that would be my official favorite film. But since everybody says that . . . What's yours?"

"Old films, *Now, Voyager*. Recent, *Women on the Verge of a Nervous Breakdown*. You know it?"

"Sure. Almodovar. He's great."

"Look at our cocks," he said. "Mine's a bit larger than yours, it seems."

"Maybe. Mine gets a lot bigger though, when I, you know . . ."

"Mine goes next month," he said. "What do you think about that?"

"To be honest, I don't really understand it. Can't you express your feminine side without actually . . . ?"

"I've tried. It doesn't work. You're very sweet. Is that man out there your boyfriend?"

"I don't know. I guess not. He was for a while." I shook off, pulled my trunks up.

"You're still in love with him."

"What makes you say that?"

"It's obvious. In your eyes." He stuffed his cock back in his panties.

"What do you see in his?"

"He's unsure."

"Do you think he still loves me?"

"Oh, yes. The way we all of us secretly love one another, or long to."

"So what's the upshot?" I said. "Are we going to get back together?"

He stepped to the mirror, touching his breasts with reverence and wonder. "I don't know. How would I know?" He avoided my eyes in the mirror, a wall going up. "Good luck to you."

Back in the bar, the music had changed, Whitney Houston replacing Chris Montez. The gaunt customer had grown animated, singing fiercely along to "The Greatest Love of All," addressing himself in the mirror behind the bottles.

"Are you ready?" Pete said.

"No, I'd like to hang out for a few more hours. I find it exhilarating here."

As we went to the door, I looked back at Buddy and waved. But he looked away, rinsing glasses.

Outside, I said, "So what's going on?"

"Nothing," Pete said. "I'm going on to the gig. I'm not going to play rescuer. I shouldn't even have come here. Fuck him. If he wants to destroy himself, that's his right. I'm not going to get sucked into his melodrama."

"Who'd you call?"

"A friend of Joey's in West Hollywood. I left a message on his machine. If he wants to deal with it, he can."

As we passed the lot where the freak-show building had been, I told Pete that I'd known Buddy back when he'd been the Headless Sailor.

"The what?"

"I never told you about that? It was the star attraction of the freak show. You paid an extra quarter and they took you back into a special room and drew a red velvet curtain and there he was. Buddy, or someone else, in a white sailor suit sitting in a high-backed chair, seemingly without a head. There were all these rubber tubes sprouting out of his neck and running over to a fake-looking medical machine with dials. The story was he'd stood up on the roller coaster and been decapitated by a crossbeam. And the machine was supposedly keeping his body alive. In reality, of course, behind all the tubes there was a hole cut in the high back of the chair. That's where the sailor's head really went. It worked like a stocks. You'd lean your neck back through the lower part of the hole and they'd fit the top part down over you. I tried it once after hours."

"And Buddy blew you?"

"As a matter of fact he did. It was a little scary in a way because once you were clamped in, it really was like a stocks: you were trapped. You couldn't free yourself without assistance, and you couldn't see a thing, so . . . God, that reminds me of something he told me once. The mystery blow-job story."

Pete looked at me with a vague smile. "Do I want to hear this?"

"Yeah, it's too bizarre. You see, Buddy would be fitted into the chair just before the rest of the freak show began, so for ten minutes for so, he'd be trapped there in the chair behind the curtain. And for a while, he said, during that time, someone was sneaking in and silently digging his cock out of his sailor suit pants and giving him a truly fantastic blow job. But he couldn't see who it was. Someone else in the freak show obviously—"

"The sword swallower maybe."

"A suspect, of course. But over a period of weeks, Buddy eliminated various performers when, for example, the Human Pincushion could be heard doing his act beyond the curtain while Buddy was getting blown."

"Can't be in two places at once."

"Exactly. For a while he suspected the Romanian dwarf knife-thrower, since he performed first and would've had just enough time to get backstage and . . . But one night the dwarf came in to work having lost his dentures, and that night Buddy could tell, as he was being blown, that whoever was doing it had a full set of teeth—"

"This is grotesque."

"In the end, he never did solve the mystery. He got fired the night his worst fear came true. It was often a race against time. Buddy still being blown even as the barker was introducing the act, the danger of course adding to the excitement. But one night the timing was critically off. Not only was Buddy's cock still out when the curtain was pulled, his huge, wet, throbbing hard-on chose precisely that moment to shoot off. Well, there were families out there, women and children, and they screamed."

Pete looked at me. "That's the biggest load of shit I've ever heard."

"I know. But it made me hot when he told me about it."

"No doubt his intention."

"I have to say, he could sure suck cock. Just in terms of pure mean joy, Buddy had no peer. Like all other blow jobs are in black and white, sixteen millimeter. But when Buddy got serious—man, I'll tell you, that screen widened. VistaVision, Todd-AO, Technicolor, 3-D, and Sensurround. The Fox music for Cinemascope."

Pete smiled. "Let's go back."

I thought, if that's what you want, we don't have to go back. "I think that theater's been torn down," I said.

"Too bad."

"Yeah. But you know, as good as it was, there was one serious catch. I had a horrible crush on a straight guy then, Wade—"

"Oh, your Dean Moriarty figure."

"Right. So all this time Buddy was giving me these horrendous blow jobs, I was thinking about Wade."

"Well, nothing's perfect."

"I guess not."

Salt air on the breeze. The orange sun was an inch above the cobalt ocean. The gray Citroën at the end of the bombed-out block.

SIX

AS WE GOT on the Long Beach Freeway, Pete began singing "The More I See You" in a wispy Chris Montez voice.

"Do you mind? I'm already afraid I'm going to be humming that song for the next week even though I hate it."

"Someone should do the Chris Montez story," Pete said. "A bio pic, like *La Bamba*."

"Right. *Call Me*. I wonder whatever happened to him anyway."

"He's probably a K Mart manager in Duarte."

"Yeah. He's probably fat now. Does that ever scare you?"

"What? Getting fat?"

"No. That you might be chewed up and spit out by the culture. That ten years from now people might be saying, 'Whatever happened to Pete Schindler?' "

"Yeah, I worry about it all the time. So did that transie come on to you in the john?"

"No. We talked about movies and compared cocks. He felt his was bigger. It wasn't really. But there was only one way to prove my case, and it didn't seem worth the effort—"

"I liked your cock," Pete said.

"I know, I remember. I liked yours, too."

"The sex *was* good. I could never deny that."

"I don't think it was ever just sex for me, Pete."

"Maybe it should've been."

"That's not what I wanted. I don't think it's what you wanted either."

He dug out a cigarette, punched in the lighter. "I wonder what time it is."

"It must be about seven-thirty. Can I bum one of those?"

He put the pack on the seat. "So how's your cat?"

"He's fine. His AIDS test was negative."

"His what?"

"Yeah, cats can get AIDS, too. It's a different virus though. A feline version. I mean, you can't get it from a cat."

"That's good to know."

"I was concerned. Because he's out there, you know."

"Probably doesn't use a condom either."

"I don't think so. Ever seen a cat's dick?"

"Yeah, but I don't want to think about it."

Pete switched on the radio: Social Distortion's alcoholism song, "Ball and Chain."

"Okay, look," he said. "I'm going to run you out to Santa Monica. I've got just about enough time."

"I wouldn't mind coming to your gig."

"Why would you want to do that? You don't even like my music."

"Come on," I said. "That's not true and you know it."

"You dumped on my songs."

"I didn't dump on your songs. I criticized one or two of them as satirically off-target."

"That's what I mean."

"I gave you my honest opinion."

"That's the problem."

"Well, what do you want? A fawning groupie? Someone telling you that everything you do is an automatic work of genius?"

"I want to be around supportive people."

"I was very supportive."

"No, you weren't. You're a toxic person for me, Tim."

"Oh, is this where we get into the ACA stuff?"

"It's not all bullshit, you know. I scoffed at it for a long

67

time. But I don't think it's any accident that I keep attracting guys like you."

We'd been over this before. "Because I remind you of your father."

"You didn't at first. But you did at the end."

"You mean, when I lost my temper."

An apprehensive look. "Tim, I really don't want to get into all this."

"No, you never wanted to get into anything, that was the problem. *That's* why I started getting angry at you. Because you were shutting down. *Withholding.* Isn't that one of your key ACA words? You were starting to remind me of *my* father."

He didn't say anything for a moment. But he started smiling, amused at something he was thinking. "Maybe our fathers should have become lovers," he said. "That would've solved all our problems."

"Yeah, right."

"We just pushed the wrong buttons, Tim."

"Maybe so."

"See that?" He indicated a section of freeway ramp off to the left, part of an unfinished project: a swerving two-lane bridge up on concrete pillars, chopped off at either end—a transition from nowhere to nowhere. "That's us," he said. "That's the whole story right there."

"You're crazy," I said. But I felt a wave of hopelessness. Maybe he was right. And maybe that was all I was ever going to have with anyone.

I saw a sign: COMPTON NEXT EXIT. "How are you planning to get to Santa Monica?"

"*Shit.* We passed the 405."

"Well, get off and turn around." I saw an interchange ahead. "What's this?"

"I don't know. Maybe if you'd shut up for a while, I could concentrate." He was getting over for the westbound transition lane.

"What are you doing?"

"I'm going to take this."

"This is the Artesia Freeway—"

"No, it's not."

"Yes, it is. It only goes to the Harbor Freeway."

"Let me drive, okay?"

In a moment we were on the new freeway. Endless flat, palm-lined blocks on either side, none of it familiar.

"This is strange," I said. "I don't know where we are." A sign coming up. "Bell Gate? Where the fuck is that?"

"I don't know. I don't like it either. I hate this part of town."

"What part of town *is it?*"

"I'm not sure," Pete said. "But it's bringing back some very fucked memories. I got lost out here once. Here or someplace like it. When I was still drinking. Went home with some guy, and when I left in the morning, I couldn't find my car. Then I couldn't find his place again. Just block after block of pastel apartment buildings, all the same. I spent two hours looking for my car, and looking for his place, completely hung over and panicked, pouring sweat, people staring at me like I was insane. Which I was."

"But you found your car eventually—"

"No. That's the worst part. I never did."

"I'm glad I didn't know you while you were still drinking," I said.

"You wouldn't have. In those days, if you'd come up to me in a bar, I would've blown you out of the water with a couple of words."

I laughed and said, "Why?" instantly wishing I hadn't.

" 'Cause I was even more scared then than I am now."

What the fuck did *that* mean? I looked at him. But he wouldn't look at me.

"You know, I really wouldn't mind seeing you perform tonight," I said. "I actually like your music. I think you know that."

"It wouldn't be a good idea, Tim."

"Why not?"

"Because," he said with a murderous condescension, "I'm seeing someone. And he's going to be there."

I wanted to swallow or clear my throat, but was afraid to. "Well—so what?" I said with pathetic good cheer. "I could still watch the show, couldn't I?"

"It would be awkward."

"Who is he? It's not anyone I know, is it?"

"I'm sure you don't know him."

"Well, is it serious? Or he just a glorified trick or what? Does he have a name, or have you gotten into that yet?"

"Tim."

"I'm just curious. I'm not trying to pry. Is he a good fuck?"

"Let's drop it."

"Has he joined your 'inner circle' yet, of all-time wild-sex partners? Along with Chet and Cord and—who was that guy in New York? And me? Or have I been bumped?"

"Sex isn't everything."

"So he's not so hot, huh? Did you really think you'd hit the jackpot again the next time out?"

"Tim, I don't want to talk about this anymore."

"I think you should dump him and come back to me."

"That's not going to happen. We're in love."

"Oh, really? That's sweet. Have you used that word yet?"

"Tim, you're crossing a line—"

"I mean, have you actually said *I love you*? Have you scaled that height yet? Or are you still in that quaint Alpine cabin at ten thousand feet where you and I lingered so long last year? With '*I more than like you*' carved over the door."

"I never said that."

"You did. I couldn't imagine anything that tacky. I said, 'I like you.' And you said, 'I *more* than like you.' I kept waiting for you to say, 'I almost love you.' But the weeks passed without further declaration. Not even 'I *still* more than like you.'"

"Maybe that's because I'd begun to see reality."

"Yes, I know. You were already starting your descent. I'm continuing the hilariously kitsch mountain-climbing metaphor, you'll notice."

"You think you're being hopelessly clever and arch, don't you? It's just bitterness—"

"Instead of *more than* liking me, you were back to *just* liking me. And then . . . you began to realize that you didn't *even* like me."

"I don't know why you're doing this to yourself."

"I don't know either." My eyes followed a vodka billboard on the horizon. "Maybe it's because I still don't understand why things got so fucked up. We had so much fun for so long. Through France anyway—"

"France was fucked."

I sighed. "Don't trash France. Come on. Leave an old lady a flower to press in her poetry book."

"Tim—it was a *nightmare!*"

Suddenly the engine started making clogged-up, choking sounds.

"Oh, fuck," Pete said. "Oh, no."

"What is it?"

"Sounds like the carburetor. *Shit!*"

We were losing power. Pete got over for the next turn-off. As we came down the off-ramp, the engine died. Pete smacked the wheel. "Fuck! Goddamn piece-of-shit frog car!"

We coasted down the ramp to the street where Pete brought the Citroën to a stop at the curb and tried to start the engine again. No good. He took a deep breath. "Okay. That's it."

We got out. It was a grim, desolate area, a four-lane boulevard of roaring traffic. On one side, open toxic dump fields, a lighted refinery in the distance. On the other, an endless row of windowless industrial buildings with razor-wire-topped fences.

"What street is this?" Pete said.

"I don't know. I missed the sign. You want to call the auto club?"

"No. I'm just gonna leave it here for now. I'll come up and get it next week, assuming I don't decide to become a fugitive." He got his guitar and knapsack out of the backseat.

"You know what?" I said. "We should talk to an attorney. I know a guy who's pretty good. Gay, in Century City. It's

71

too bad we can't say that Bryer was raping your mother. Do you think she'd be willing to say that, now that he's fired her?"

"*Tim!* I can't get into all that right now, it's too upsetting. I mean, she's still my *mother*, for God's sake! I really don't need that image thrown in my face again. *Okay?*"

"I'm sorry. I was trying to think ahead, that's all. So what are we going to do now?"

"Take a bus, I guess. There must be a bus stop up there." He indicated an intersection a half mile to the west: a bright yellow Shell station, a Taco Bell, a Stop-N-Go store.

Pete locked the Citroën and we started walking along the clumpy dirt rim of the highway. There weren't any sidewalks. I cringed as trucks slammed past us, throwing exhaust in our faces. The air had a sweet chemical odor.

"You know what we should do?" I said as we walked.

"What's that?"

"Go back the other way. To Downey. We could break into the Karen Carpenter Museum and steal her '74 Pacer."

"Makes sense."

"It'd be faster than this. And we could listen to her greatest hits on the tape player. And sob." I broke into "We've Only Just Begun," followed by a gut-wrenching sob.

"You're deranged," Pete said, but he laughed.

An especially foul-tempered rig clattered past us. Tom Cruise glistened on the horizon in a lush billboard ad for *Far and Away*.

"Seen that yet?" I asked Pete.

"Sure. The day it opened."

"I'd like to see a billboard for *To Fuck and Die in L.A.*," I said. "With juicy close-ups of William Petersen and Andy Garcia."

"Right." Pete smiled. "Somebody should actually make that."

This was a film-parody idea we'd had based on *mano a mano* cop movies like *Internal Affairs*. Petersen and Garcia would start out as enemies, as macho competitors, and spend most of the film stalking each other, beating each other up. But when the climax came in a burning warehouse, instead of one killing the other, their sweaty-faced struggle would dissolve into the hottest gay sex ever shown in a Hollywood film. We'd come up with this in France, I remembered.

"I don't know why you think France was so fucked," I said. "You seemed to enjoy it at the time."

"I tried to make the best of it. I knew I was going to be stuck there for a week."

"What was so bad about it?"

"Everything."

"Come on, what?"

"It wasn't quite what I'd pictured, for one thing. The place, I mean. A fucking condo with mirrored walls and a sofa bed. It might as well have been in Tarzana."

"Well, the Maugham villa was already leased."

"Constant traffic jams. Rude people."

"That's France. That's French people going to the beach. That's what happens."

"All you did was complain all week about the car killing your back. Or being constipated."

"Well, I'm sorry but I'm a human being with a body," I said. "I guess porno fantasies never get constipated, do they?"

"The day we went to Monte Carlo you looked like a fruit."

"Only in your mind. I was wearing a totally masculine, faded green tennis shirt and a sloppy straight guy's khaki shorts."

"With your collar turned up like a queen."

"You're so insane. That wasn't even intentional. As soon as you mentioned it, I smoothed my collar down."

"Not soon enough."

A couple of grinning German guys had made what *might* have been some antigay remarks while I was taking Pete's picture in front of the casino.

"That was *their* problem," I said. "And yours that you cared. Talk about internalized homophobia! What happened to your *épater les bourgeois?* You're supposed to be so fucking fearless and you care what a couple of dumb Krauts think."

73

"If you want to know the truth, the thing about my dick really spoiled the whole week."

This is what happened. I'd gone over first to attend the Cannes Film Festival on archives business. During that time Pete and I talked on the phone almost every day. This was the period where I thought we were really in love, even if we hadn't used that word yet. My friend Gérard at the Cinemathèque in Paris had given me the key to his vacation condominium in Antibes, where Pete planned to join me when the film festival was over and I could finally relax. By the time he arrived we hadn't seen each other for sixteen longing-packed days. So even though he was severely jet-lagged, we had sex right away. In his punchiness, while masturbating, Pete caused an abrasion on his cock, and by the next morning a serious scab had formed. As a result, we didn't have sex again the rest of the time we were there.

"It wasn't exactly what I'd had in mind either," I said. "A week on the Côte d'Azur watching you wipe salve on your dick."

"I took it as a sign."

"It wasn't *all* bad though. I mean, the mornings were good, when we'd sit in bed drinking coffee and talking. That was the best part, if you ask me."

"Yeah, except that's when I began to feel trapped."

"Trapped?"

"That's when you started talking about your lease being up in August."

"So?"

"You were obviously hinting that we should get a place together."

"So what would have been so horrible about that?"

"Tim, our lifestyles are completely opposite. You're basically an introvert. You like to stay home and read and watch TV."

"So do you, when you're not on the road. We're both basically shy. We talked about that."

"I like *action*, Tim. Adventure. Adrenaline. I don't want to play Ozzie and Harriet."

"Too bad. I really wanted to be your mousy little wife."

"In some ways you *are* very square, Tim. I don't think you can begin to understand what I'm about as an artist."

"That's so pretentious."

"See? You're putting me down right now."

"You're touchy to the point of paranoia."

"No, I just don't want an enemy in bed with me."

"You need therapy."

"I'd *be* in therapy," he said, "if I weren't still paying for that fucking trip to France! Not to mention the phone calls. That's part of why I had to leave Venice, you know. They'd shut off my phone 'cause I couldn't pay for all the time I'd spent sighing 'Oh, Tim' at two dollars a minute. That's another thing you never understood. Not everybody has a cushy fucking job watching von Sternberg films all day. You spend more on one stop at the fucking salad bar at Gelson's than I do on food in a week."

I was really tempted to say something cutting, i.e., "So you're a loser, you have to shop at Food Barn, that's not my fault." I work hard at what I do and I resent people trying to lay an economic guilt trip on me. But I was beginning to feel that things weren't completely hopeless if he was still this upset with me.

"I *know* the trip was an expense for you," I said calmly. "I appreciated that at the time. But I'm sure that in the near future you're going to be making more in one night than I make in a year."

I felt him checking me out, trying to decide if I was being patronizing.

"Maybe," he said.

We reached the intersection. No bus bench, but there was a rusty RTD sign on a post. Pete set down his guitar case and knapsack.

I said, "The night we saw Baby Doc and Madonna was fun."

"Yeah, right."

Fun was not exactly the right word. It was more like creepily poignant. We'd seen the exiled Haitian dictator in a seafood restaurant in Juan-les-Pins, but it wasn't the real

Madonna he was with—just a sad, chewed-up French whore trying to copy the pop star's look, circa "Express Yourself." Baby Doc had looked dissipated, as if he were still carrying a torch for Michelle, who'd dumped him. The whore had looked bored, until the real Madonna's "Wrap Me Up in Your Love" came on through the piped-in music system. At that point she'd come to life, snapping her fingers, mouthing the words, until Baby Doc shot her a censorious look. After that she'd gone numb again, sitting there like a rigid white zombie while Baby Doc ate.

"Except that was the night you made the asshole joke about 'our song,'" Pete said.

After dinner we'd gone to some weird gay bar in Nice that was showing bad videos. I mean, the French should stick to theory and forget about rock—they can't do it. The nadir was this guy who looked like Tom Jones with a bad hair-weave doing a hideous, leering techno-pop cover of the Stooges' "I Wanna Be Your Dog." It was so bad it was not even camp. But I'd turned to Pete, who'd looked stunned and vaguely sickened, and done this kitsch "romantic delirium" routine, rolling my eyes like Laurence Olivier in a junk rush or something, saying, "This is magic. Rapture. Fate is making this our song."

"I was kidding," I said. "Come on."

"I know," Pete said. "You're always kidding, that's the problem. You have this way of turning everything into a cheap, ironic joke."

"Wait a second. Are you talking about the same thing? We were standing in a dive, watching a truly bad video—"

"You were shitting on the moment."

"Shitting on it? It was already shit. I was trying to save it."

"You're missing the point. You were *using* the moment to make this big, campy, jaded-fag comment on what was going on between us."

His bitterness startled me. All I could say was, "I'm sorry you took it that way. That's not how I meant it. I was just fooling around, trying to have some fun."

He said nothing for a moment. Then he said, "Okay, look. Maybe I had a weird reaction."

"I think *so*."

"But that song means a lot to me. I mean, the first time I heard it, it kind of changed my life. Don't laugh."

I almost did, until I saw how serious he was.

"Every musician has moments like that," he said. "Where a certain song radically reorders your aesthetic. I first heard that song in 1974. I was in a car with this friend of mine, this guy Mallory, who was a couple of years older. We were smoking dope, but there was nothing on the radio except drivel. Then he shoved in an eight-track and 'I Wanna Be Your Dog' came on and it blew me away. The simplicity, the compression. In terms of where I was coming from, it was a revelation. It's really what made me pick up a guitar."

"I'm trying to remember when *I* first heard it," I said. "Probably when it first came out. In '69. When you were still into Bobby Sherman."

"Look, I know it's weird to be reverent about a Stooges song. But that French version was so vile."

"It's a good song," I said. "I like the Sonic Youth version."

"No, you don't."

"I like the Bryan Ferry version best."

"What Bryan Ferry version? There's no Bryan Ferry version."

"Yes, there is. It's on an early solo album. The one where he's in the white tux in front of the pool."

"You're full of shit," Pete said. "I know that album."

"It's conceivable. In those days he'd do anything. I can *imagine* how he'd do it."

"I can't."

"I wish he'd put out albums more often."

"You sure played the old stuff into the ground."

"I thought you liked Roxy Music."

"I used to." He looked past me. "Okay. Finally."

The bus was coming. Pete picked up his guitar and knapsack. I stepped over and held up my hand but realized almost immediately that the bus wasn't going to stop. It was doing at least sixty with no sign of slowing down. I waved. There was no way the driver could miss us—

except for one thing: I couldn't see anyone at the wheel.

"Hey!" Pete yelled angrily, but he seemed startled, too.

The bus hurtled past us, the loathsome deejay Rick Dees grinning from the poster on its side. Silhouettes of passengers, all normal enough. The bus barreled through a yellow light at the intersection.

"Pete, I don't think that bus has a driver."

"Come on. He's just a dickhead, that's all. In a big rush to get home and beat up his wife."

"Did you *see* him?"

"He had his shade down."

"Are you sure?"

"Yeah. There was a lot of glare, too. Come on, whoever heard of a fucking bus without a driver."

"Maybe he had a heart attack."

"No. Look, he's stopping up there." Pete stepped over to the curb and stuck out his thumb. "We might as well hitch."

I watched the bus barrel through the next intersection. "He's not stopping."

"Will you forget it, Tim? And get your hand off your hip or we'll never get a ride."

I had one hand stuck in the side of my trunks. "You're so insane. John Wayne used to stand like this. I know how to get a ride quick." With my back to the traffic, I pulled up my trunk leg, exposing my genitals.

"Tim, Jesus, come on." He frowned as if I were being a total asshole.

"Just thought I'd let you see what you're missing."

He sighed. "I should've let you go with Jay."

"I wish you had."

Ten minutes passed and nobody stopped. "This is not the right decade to hitchhike," I said.

"Please, no more sixties nostalgia stories," Pete said. "I'm completely burned out on that decade."

"You're envious."

A restored metallic blue 1963 Buick Riviera slammed

past us in a wave of hip-hop music. My father had driven the same make and model, floating through La Jolla to the sleepy tones of Perry Como. I thought of Pete's TV-ad parody for an album of Perry Como singing soothing snatches of grisly Lou Reed lyrics.

"*Perry Does Lou,*" I said.

Pete said nothing for a moment. Then, in Perry's spacey crooner's voice, he sang, "Herrrr . . . oooo . . . in."

We both laughed. Then I said, "How close are we to South Central here?"

"Kind of close," he said. "See way up there? I think that's a burned-out Circuit City."

"You haven't even asked me how I did through all that."

"How you *did* through it? Nothing happened in Santa Monica, did it? Except there weren't any crosstown buses for a few days. So all the anguished liberals had to do their own housework."

"We were worried about the archives at one point. Palms can be a strange area. Josh slept there one night. With a .357."

"Are you serious?"

"Yeah. It was crazy. I've never been through anything like that Thursday. The panic. It was like *War of the Worlds.* People practically crashing their cars."

"That was the worst day, right? When it spread the furthest."

"Yeah. And nobody was stopping it yet. Jane started getting hysterical at one point. 'They're going to blow my head off just because I'm blond.' I came really close to slapping her the way Richard Egan would."

"I saw it coming," Pete said. "I wasn't surprised."

"Who was?"

"I wish they'd aimed their rage better though. Instead of burning themselves out, and burning down Koreatown, they should've gone after Daryl Gates. They should've gone out to the Simi Valley and burned down the courthouse. And the Reagan Library. With the Reagans in it. You know how I feel."

"Yeah, I know."

"I miss the Black Panthers," he said. "At least they knew who the real enemy was."

"Which is why they got wiped out."

We said nothing for a while. The sun was dropping below the horizon, the sky streaked with orange and violet clouds. The cars shot past us. The sweet chemical odor in the air reminded me of tutti-frutti service-station toilet disinfectant, the kind that made you feel that you should lick the urinal.

"Would you mind if I used some of our fantasies?" I said.

"What are you talking about?"

"I've been thinking of doing a comic book with Todd. Or, you know, a graphic novel. A kind of satiric, surreal story about two guys—you know, boyfriends—who have all these different adventures."

Pete watched the traffic. "Just don't use my name."

"No, of course not. But I would like to use some of our scenarios. Some of that stuff was pretty good, I think. And very spontaneous and unconscious, like automatic writing. I was thinking of the Chile adventure the other day."

He shrugged. "I don't remember."

"Oh, come on. The neo-Zorro idea. We'd fly down to Santiago disguised as poofy hairdressers—"

"Oh, right." Pete smiled. "Foppish sweater queens. You'd spell your name with two *m*'s—Timm."

"Right. And we'd botch Señora Pinochet's perm—"

"So she'd end up bald."

"Exactly. And then we'd gut Augusto and spring Carlos from prison and hijack a plane—"

Pete shot me a look when I mentioned Carlos.

"Of course, I'd change his name, too, but . . . I think it'd make a great graphic novel. I could do the story and Todd could draw the pictures. Of course, Todd's gotten so serious lately. I'm not sure if he'd consider it political enough, or political in the right way—"

"Here we go," Pete said as a white Toyota pickup veered over to the curb, stopping hard.

Something told me to shift into a hypermacho personality mode as Pete grabbed his stuff and we dashed to the truck.

The driver threw open the passenger door. "Howdy!" About thirty, sandy haired, with a big florid boyish face, a tight sweaty red T-shirt, sharp-edged pectorals. "Goin' as far as Hawthorne Boulevard," he said with a deep twangy voice.

"Sounds good," Pete said, letting me get in first.

"Name's Jack." Beer on his breath. A silver pint can of Coors jammed between his legs. Garth Brooks on the radio. I shook Jack's big rough hand.

"Tim."

"Pete."

Underarm stink as Jack reached across me to shake Pete's hand. He threw it in gear and bucked back into traffic.

"Musician, huh?" he said to Pete.

"Yeah."

"What do you play?"

"Rock. You know."

"I like that, too." Jack punched an oldies station, which happened to be playing "The More I See You" by Chris Montez.

I looked at Pete. He smiled faintly. "Where are we anyway?" he said to Jack.

"I don't know what you call it," Jack said as we passed two young black women in shorts at the bus stop. "But it *shore* looks like boogie town to me."

Pete got very still. He had a low tolerance for racist talk. He usually called people on it.

As a battered yellow Eldorado passed us on the left, Jack provided commentary out of the side of his mouth: "Check it out. Here comes a tribe in—what else?—a Cadillac. Bet *they* got a trunk full of CD players. From free day at Fedco."

There were two black couples in the car, talking and laughing.

"That's right. Yuk it up, you thievin' coons."

Pete was biting his lip.

Jack burned out quickly on Chris Montez. "Shit. This guy sounds like a fuckin' fruit." He punched a new station: George Michael's "Father Figure."

"That's better."

Pete was sucking in his lips. I could read his mind. Was it worth it to put up with this shit just to keep the ride?

We passed an Arco station. I cringed when I saw a beautiful black woman filling her Honda tank, certain Jack would notice her as well.

"Hey, baby, where's your spear? Long way from Zululand."

"So where are *you* headed tonight?" I said to Jack.

"Me? Well, you might say I'm on my way to fuck some snatch." He chuckled. "You guys in a hurry?"

Oh, no.

"As a matter of fact, we are," Pete said.

"Oooh, man, that's too bad. These babes are dyin' for it. A couple of sisters up here in Lawndale. Two daughters and a mother. Hell, we could flip to see who fucks Ma." He winked and chuckled.

"It's tempting," Pete said, and I almost laughed. "But I got this gig I gotta get to."

"Wouldn't take more than a few minutes, if you catch my drift," Jack said. "One look at you bucks, these gals'll be drippin'. Hell, that's all they do, lay around all day with their pussies on the sofa, watchin' TV. Ma's got a drinkin' problem. Probably passed out by now. Shit, I'll tell you what. I'll take sloppy seconds just to watch you cowboys fuck."

"I've got a better idea," Pete said mildly. "What if we just fuck you?"

Caught off guard, Jack was confused. "Say what?"

"What do you want, a diagram?" Pete said, "We grease up your bunghole—you must have some Bardahl or something under the seat. Then we punch our fat dicks up your ass. Sound good to you, Tim?"

"Well, uh . . ."

"He's shy," Pete told Jack. "But not with a hard-on. Sure

82

used to fuck the shit out of me. Felt great, too. You ever had a man's cock up your ass, Jack?"

Jack pulled over. "I don't know what your story is, but I want you out of this truck."

Pete and I got out, then Pete said, "Last chance, Jack. Maybe you'd just like to suck us both off. Ever had a man's cock in your mouth? Nothing quite like it."

Jack pulled the door shut. "Goddamn queers."

"You're not even a redneck, Jack," Pete said pleasantly. "You're just a piece of shit."

Jack tore out violently.

"I wondered how you were going to deal with that," I said.

"Well, now you know."

SEVEN

"WHERE the fuck are we *now?*" Pete said.

It was a big roaring intersection at the top of a cruddy hill. A Mobil self-service station, a liquor store, an In and Out Burger. Below in all directions, a vast landscape of run-down stucco houses and apartment buildings and streets lined with chewed-up toothpick palms.

"I don't know," I said. "But everything's still here. That's a good sign, I guess."

"This is starting to make me tense," Pete said. "It must be at least eight by now."

"Well, look, that's north." You could see the distant lights of the Hollywood Hills. "If we catch a bus over there, it's bound to take us up to Wilshire."

It was bound to take us right through South Central, too. But I left that out, not wanting to seem wimpy.

We crossed the street to the bus stop. Pete was almost out of cigarettes so we stepped into the liquor store, the kind of mean fluorescent shit-hole that always seems to be on the verge of a holdup. Mostly black customers; grim, tense Vietnamese clerks. Pete got in line. A mustached clerk, who resembled the Vietnam War figure General Ky, kept glancing at an overhead TV monitor, but it wasn't a security shot of the half-empty shelves. It was *Chinatown*, a cassette apparently, dubbed in French—the last scene, where Faye Dunaway tries to drive off with her sister/

84

daughter and the cops open fire. As soon as the car horn started blasting, the signal that Dunaway had been hit, the clerk, obviously seeing the film for the first time, moaned, "Oh, no! *No, no!*"

As many times as I'd seen the sequence, it was still upsetting, John Huston horrendously vile as he covers his screaming incest daughter's eyes with his hand. *"Mon dieu, mon dieu!"* he said in a voice like Yves Montand's.

"What are you doing?" Pete said once he'd bought his cigarettes. "You're supposed to be watching for the bus."

"I am. Relax. It hasn't come yet."

Pete glanced at the movie as we went out the door.

"That ending still infuriates me," I said on the sidewalk. "Why the fuck couldn't she get away?"

"Polanski probably wondered the same thing about Sharon Tate."

"Yeah, right."

Pete set his guitar down against the bus bench.

"She got away originally though," I said. "In the screenplay. It's a well-known change."

"Yeah, if I were doing it," Pete said, "I'd have her blow John Huston's brains all over the wall."

"I know. You like happy endings."

I thought of a Faye Dunaway line in the film that even in 1974 had jumped out at me as a sentiment I could relate to. "I never see *anyone* for long, Mr. Gittes. It's difficult for me."

Pete stared down the boulevard. He seemed depressed.

"What's wrong?" I said.

"Nothing. I was just remembering who I saw that film with."

"Your mother?"

He shot me a look. "No." He looked down the street again. "No, I saw it with Billy. My best friend. He lived across the street. That was his father this afternoon."

"Oh, the old guy who glared at you."

"Right."

"So you and Billy were just friends?"

"For the most part."

"What does that mean?"

"Well—it was more than friendship. But it took us a long time to admit it."

"So you were what? Fifteen or sixteen?"

"Sixteen at the end." Pete lit a cigarette. "Billy was a year older. We basically just hung out all the time for several years. He lived in his garage. He'd moved out there to get away from his father, and I'd go over there all the time and we'd have these incredible talks that would go on for hours. He was extremely intelligent and really opened my mind to a lot of things. It was Billy who turned me on to the Velvet Underground." Pete smiled. "He had a very bizarre sense of humor. I wasn't really attracted to him sexually though. He was extremely dorky and nerdy, you know, like he lived in his mind, completely physically unaware. I already knew I was gay and all that. I was messing around with Ted at Disneyland, but I was never in love with Ted or anything—we were basically just jack-off buddies. I didn't realize I was in love with Billy for a long time, but we got very close. Mentally. I think as close as I've ever been with anyone. And one night his parents were out of town and we were in the den smoking dope, watching 'Saturday Night Live,' and suddenly Billy started sobbing and said he loved me. And I started crying, too, and the next thing I knew . . ."

Pete stopped for a moment as a couple of jock-type black guys came out of the liquor store. He was also checking me out pretty closely to see if I was about to say something jokey or trivializing. I wasn't.

"So we spent the night together," Pete said. "And to be honest, it was pretty cathartic. I mean, I hadn't really been that attracted to him, like I say. But once we were actually having sex, he was like another Billy. It sounds corny, but it's true." Pete smiled. "I remember even being *glad* he was dorky, so nobody else would know what I knew."

"So you became boyfriends then?" I said.

Pete sat down on the bus bench, which had a mortuary ad on it. "For a while, yeah. Until my dad caught us together."

86

"You mean, while you were—"

"Yeah. We were in Billy's garage. My dad had always been suspicious of us, even before anything happened. Like he sensed that we were too close and all that. So one night he came over and listened at the garage door and heard us. Then he lifted the door. It was one of the worst things that's ever happened to me. My dad completely flipped. Started beating on me. And on Billy. He wanted to blame Billy, since he was a year older. Like Billy had corrupted me or something. Then he told Billy's father. Two days later I was coming home from work and I saw these cop cars and an ambulance in front of Billy's house. He'd hung himself in the garage. They were just cutting him down. I didn't really react at the time, I was too devastated. But the next afternoon I tried to kill my father. I stabbed him with a kitchen knife while he was mowing the lawn. That's why I ran away to San Francisco."

"Jesus, Pete. You never told me any of this."

"Well—you can't cover everything in six months."

"What happened to your father?"

"Oh, he wasn't hurt that bad. I got him in the shoulder, cut his hand. He got the knife away from me. I really meant to kill him though. I was in a total rage." Pete flicked his cigarette into the street. "It took me a long time to forgive him. To the extent that I have. I mean, basically he was just doing what any red-blooded American dad would've done. That's why I blame the whole culture now."

"God, Pete." I almost put my hand on his, but that wasn't a good idea, not on the open street. And he might think I was being overly dramatic or patronizing.

He leaned back on the bus bench, staring out at the last of the sunset. "That's how I felt this afternoon with Bryer," he said. "I really did want to kill him. Somebody should. If you hadn't been there . . ."

"I'm glad I was. I feel the same way about him, but I'd hate to see you ruin your life. I really think there are other ways to fight these people." I opened the flap of Pete's knapsack and dug out the mailing list I'd lifted from Bryer's office.

"I didn't realize you took that," he said.

"Yeah, it was too tempting." I started looking through the list. "I'm going to give it to Todd. He's seriously involved in ACT UP now. They do protests at politician's homes sometimes."

"Protests? They should be lobbing bombs through windows. Killing the scumbags' wives and kids."

"That would get us lots of sympathy," I said, instantly wishing I'd phrased it differently.

"Fuck sympathy. Fuck kissing up to straight people. That's like Jews sucking up to Nazis."

"Not all straight people are homophobes."

"Wanna bet?"

I began to recognize some of the names on the list. "You know, I think these may be some fairly powerful people. Isn't this one of the guys who sponsored Ronald Reagan? Oh! And here's everybody's favorite right-wing commentator—"

"Let me see."

I gave Pete the list. While he was looking at it, a corroded silver Saab pulled up and a truly startling young lesbian got out and came around to the liquor store. She had short-cropped brown hair, amazing peach skin, a handsome face that reminded me of Amelia Earhart's. She glanced at me with jolting green eyes, the same edge of craziness that attracted me to Pete. In fact, she was just the sort of lesbian I sometimes had fleeting sexual thoughts about. As if we were so close on the gender spectrum it wouldn't be *that* different from being with a guy. Or I'd think, if *I* were a lesbian, *definitely*, that's the kind of woman I'd be drawn to.

Another woman was waiting in the Saab. Still no sign of the bus. Pete was studying the list. When I saw the Earhart woman coming out of the liquor store, I got up. It was a long shot, given the animosity lesbians often felt toward men. But those attitudes had shifted in recent years, hadn't they? She was young, she might be more open.

"Excuse me," I said as innocuously as possible, but she still glared at me. "I see you're heading north. Do you suppose you could help two gay brothers who are stranded without a car? We're going up to Wilshire but—"

"Save your breath," she said curtly. "It's not happening."

"Oh, Jan," her passenger said. "It won't kill us to give them a ride."

She opened her door. She was beautiful, with a face like Angelica Huston's at twenty, dark skinned, Latina or Native American, her short black hair slicked back in a *haute lez* Weimar Republic style. She wore violet lipstick, a tight sleeveless T-shirt, silver earrings. An elaborate snake tattoo on her shoulder.

"We're not a *bus service*, Ramona," Jan said to her friend.

"Oh, please." Ramona was already pulling back the seat for us. She was cradling a camcorder. "We're all queers, Jan. We're on the same side."

"*That's* debatable." Jan brusquely got into the car.

I took that as a final rebuff until Ramona, still holding the seat for us, said, "Come *on*. Don't be afraid. Her bark's worst than her bite."

I glanced at Pete. He nodded and grabbed his stuff.

As we coursed along the wide ratty boulevard, Ramona turned to us in her seat, introducing herself. I decided she was probably Native American, like the "real" Ramona.

"And this is Jan, my ex-girlfriend," Ramona said. "She's down visiting from Santa Cruz. I've been taking her on a tour of the devastation."

"We're only going as far as the freeway," Jan said tightly, and cranked up the volume on a women's music tape. I caught part of the lyrics—"Sisters united / Against male definitions"—before Ramona said, "Oh, *please*," and switched to Nine Inch Nails on MARS-FM.

"I don't know *what* is wrong with you," Jan said to Ramona.

"*Nothing's* wrong with *me*, Jan. You're the one who's suffocating." Ramona turned to us. "Santa Cruz. That's why we broke up. I couldn't take it. Too many potlucks. Too much flannel. *Much* too much vanilla."

Ramona raised her camcorder, looking at us through the viewfinder. "You don't mind if I do this, do you?"

I shrugged. It was dusk. There were streetlights, but it was hard to imagine that she was going to get much of an image.

"So are you two boyfriends?" Ramona said, aiming her lens at me.

"Not really," I said. "We broke up about a year ago."

"But you're still friends," Ramona said. "That's good. What happened?"

I glanced at Pete. He was staring hard out the window.

"Nothing," I said. "It just didn't work out."

"Come on, *something* happened," Ramona said. "Tell me."

"Ramona," Jan said. "Why don't you mind your own business."

"It *is* my business, baby," Ramona said. "Just because *you're* sex negative—"

"Don't call me *baby*," Jan said through gritted teeth. "I'm not your *baby* anymore."

"We'll see about that," Ramona said. "The night's just beginning." To us, she said, "I'm taking Jan to the Clit Club. I'm going to get her high as a kite. On whiskey sours, XTC. We'll loosen *this* girl up tonight, believe it."

"Ramona, you're pushing it," Jan said.

To us, Ramona said, "We used to fight. Physically. You know why? Because the sex got boring. We'd only do certain things. Jan had all these 'political' restrictions. What happened with *you* guys?"

"Nothing," I said. "It just didn't work out."

"Why not?"

"It just didn't."

She was starting to bother me. This speak-the-truth-to-the-camcorder shtick was becoming oppressive. What was she trying to do? *sex, dykes and videotape?*

"Can I tell you what I see?" Ramona said. "You guys still want to fuck each other. You want to do it so bad you can almost taste it."

"*Ramona*," Jan said.

Pete finally stopped staring out the window and said to Ramona, as if he meant to close the subject, "Look—I'm seeing someone else. *Okay?*"

"Yeah, but it's not hot," Ramona said with a shrug, and aimed the camcorder at Pete. "You're not satisfied. You're all bottled up. A child could see that."

"Look," Pete said, "I think maybe this is not a subject we should pursue."

"You want to be dominated," Ramona said to Pete, as if she were reading an S&M astrology chart. "You're aggressive by nature. Macho, tight, controlling. Which means that you secretly long to surrender." She turned her lens on me. "Whereas you are passive. You try to slide through life without making waves. Which means you secretly long to take control of someone. Your role is that of the top, the master."

"Look," I said. "I know you mean well. But *I* get aggressive—okay?—when people start telling me what should turn me on."

She said, "I'm losing my light," and switched on the camcorder light, which was blinding. "You guys were too vanilla."

"Ramona," Jan said. "Turn that off. I can't see."

Pete was covering his eyes. He said, "If I were you, I would turn that off. This is not a real cool area. You're making us very conspicuous."

"I'm trying to help you," Ramona said to Pete. "You long to be tied up. Your deepest desire is to be Tim's slave. Why don't you admit it?"

"Ramona," Jan said angrily, *"turn off the light."*

Ramona turned the camera and light on Jan. "And as for you, Jan. As for you . . ."

But Jan had had it. Without saying another word, she veered over to the curb, set it in park, and grabbed the camcorder out of Ramona's hands. Then she got out and smashed it on the pavement.

Ramona jumped out and flew around the car. "You goddamn PC cooze."

Pete looked at me as Jan and Ramona scuffled on the street. "This is too crazy. Come on, we're getting out."

"Pete, I don't know."

We were on a block of burned-out storefronts. In sloppy black letters on the cinder-block wall by the car were the words FUCK THE WHITE MAN.

I was still hesitating when Jan leaned over to the car and said, "Out. Both of you. *Right now.*"

"We're going," Pete said, pushing the seat forward. Jan and Ramona were still standing there, arguing, as Pete and I started walking up the street. I kept looking back, hoping they'd cool off and offer us a ride again. But they were into their own drama. "Do you know what you've become?" Jan was saying to Ramona. "Do you have any idea?"

"Do you have a plan?" I asked Pete.

"Yeah, I'm gonna call the club and have somebody come get us. There must be a phone up ahead there."

He meant the next major intersection, which was four or five blocks away, at the top of a hill. It was reassuringly bright up there and it looked intact: a gas station, a mini-mall, a classic hot-pink-and-aqua Pioneer Chicken outlet. But the street between here and there scared the shit out of me. There was nothing actually going on. In fact, it was so deserted it almost felt like a set. The battered 1920s storefronts, the deep dusk blue of the sky, even the burned-out ruins, had a weird *designed* look, like a soundstage street for a Janet Jackson video. Or a "gritty" background for a black-and-white Guess? ad. But I had the feeling we could come to a cross street and find Tom Skerritt and a wild blonde lying butchered in their blood-soaked vintage convertible.

We walked past a firebombed Winchell's doughnut shop. You could still see where it had been marked BLACK OWNED, but the cop/doughnut connection may have been too indelible. The flames had snagged an overhead billboard for *Lethal Weapon 3*, with some justice charring stupid white homophobe Mel Gibson but sparing warmhearted Danny Glover. Shattered glass crunched under my huaraches.

Finally a few cars started passing us. I cringed when I heard one coming up violently behind us. But it was just Jan and Ramona, ripping past us in the silver Saab.

"I don't think I liked her," I said.

Pete shrugged. "She's young. She's just trying to be provocative."

"You think she's full of shit then? About the domination stuff?"

"Let me put it this way," he said. "I don't think it's worth discussing."

"I thought about tying you up once. Like a western thing. But serial killers always tie up their victims. What if I snapped?"

"Tim, I don't want to talk about this."

"Okay."

We said nothing for a while. We passed a burned-out Jack in the Box, its drive-through menu unscathed. I tensed every time a car came along, expecting a squeal of brakes when they saw that we were white, but it didn't happen. I was starting to think the storefronts were all closed when I heard music and black male voices. I saw the beat-to-shit bar coming up on the other side of the street, a group of men standing around out front. Their voices were slurred. My heart started pounding.

"Are you scared?" I said.

"Not at all," Pete said. "My heart is pure."

"So is mine. But I'd still rather be home in bed right now, reading *Jane Seymour's Guide to Romantic Living*."

This was a kitsch coffee-table book we'd seen on a discount shelf and laughed about, until it seemed a little cruel to make such easy fun of romance-reading housewives. Jane's best advice had been on spicing up your sex life: "Try leather. It works for Tina Turner."

"You should order copies of that in bulk," Pete said. "Pass it out down here."

"Right. I think these guys might enjoy it."

We were opposite the bar now, but the guys still hadn't noticed us, or at least they weren't reacting. A couple of them were arguing. Maybe they were all caught up in that.

I recognized the music, Aretha Franklin's "Chain of Fools."

"I like that song," I told Pete.

"Wanna stop and go in? Do your campy go-go boy routine? It might be underwear night."

"I'm not wearing any underwear."

"I know. I think they know, too."

"Don't."

"What's the matter, Timmy? Do you want your mommy?"

"Maybe I do. At least I'm man enough to admit it."

We'd passed the bar by this point and the guys still hadn't reacted to us. The argument had turned into a yelling match and I began to realize what Pete already knew.

"Those are older guys," he said. "They're too wet-brained to come after us. They're too used to taking it out on each other. Like certain fags I've known."

If that was a shot, I chose to ignore it.

"Well, you can relax," Pete said as we closed in on the intersection. "This looks like the Cosby Mall here."

I saw what he meant. The postmodern Italiante mini-mall was so immaculate it could've been in Brentwood. The cars in the lot were upscale, the black people going in and out of the video store as casually middle class as shoppers at the Westside Pavilion. A young buppie dad was leading his son from the Baskin-Robbins, both of them licking ice cream cones. The dad beeped off his Lexus alarm.

On the other hand, the gas station was gutted, yellow crime-scene ribbons fluttering in the wind. The phones had been destroyed there, so we crossed the street to use the one at the Pioneer Chicken outlet.

The customers there looked middle class, too, black moms and dads with their kids. We caught some startled double takes as we walked to the pay phone by the patio.

Pete set his guitar and knapsack down and dug in his pocket for change. That's when I noticed the three young black guys sitting at one of the tables. I saw the guy who looked like gay-baiting rap asshole Chuck D. first. He was biting into a juicy drumstick when we made eye contact and he froze. Then I noticed his friends, a guy in an X cap

94

and UCLA sweatshirt, and a tall guy in glasses and a Raiders cap. I found the guy in the X cap very appealing—compact, tough, intelligent looking. But he was glaring at me as if I were David Duke.

"Ever had sex with a black guy?" I asked Pete.

"Yeah, but I don't think this is the time to talk about it." He stuck a quarter in the phone and punched information.

"I knew a guy in college," I said, talking low. "Mark. A fellow film student. Astonishing body. You know how some black guys can do ten sit-ups and get a washboard stomach? Mark was like that. And not the least bit femme either. You know how a lot of gay black guys tend to be femme?"

"That's not true."

"I didn't say *all*. That's my point. Mark wasn't. He had a beard, and one night, God, in the editing room, he was showing me his rushes when suddenly we just started kissing, and the next thing I knew he had his—"

"Would you shut up," Pete said under his breath. "I think those guys can hear you." He asked information for the Club Mabuse number.

I looked over my shoulder. The three guys were watching us, but they were too far away to have heard me. I didn't feel that threatened anyway, at least not physically. I'd already decided they were college students. They weren't glaring exactly. They were looking at me with a kind of withering moral contempt. I almost felt like explaining that I wasn't there out of choice, I wasn't slumming, I wasn't going to report back that I'd seen them eating fried chicken.

But what did they know about me anyway, just because I was white? Did they know I was gay? Did they know what *that* felt like, any more than I knew what it was like to be black? And who were *they* to judge *me* anyway?

To Pete, I said, "Fuck 'em. They look like hip-hop pigs to me. Sexist, misogynist, homophobic anti-Semites. A pig is a pig, I don't care what color his or her skin is. I'm not playing guilty liberal this time. I'm not validating all their fuck-up shit just because they're black."

"Goddamn it," Pete said. "You made me forget the number. Will you *please* be quiet?" He punched information again.

The three black guys got up, ignoring us now, as they walked to the lot.

"It's too bad," I said. "The guy in the X cap is cuter than fuck. I could see being boyfriends with a black guy like him. No problem."

"Why don't you go tell him?"

"Maybe I will."

Pete got the club number again and punched it. I watched the three guys as they got into a sparkling red Toyota 4-Runner. That's when I saw the logo on the tall guy's T-shirt: CATCH ONE. The interracial homo dance club.

"Jesus," I said. "They're gay. They're queers of color."

Pete ignored me. "Shit, it's busy." He hung up and thought for a moment.

As the 4-Runner slid past us, I made eye contact with the guy in the X cap, but I couldn't read him. Did I see hatred, lust, fear, yearning, or a mix of all of these? The same question often came up with queers of no color.

Pete picked up the phone again.

"Who are you calling now? Your boyfriend?"

"No. Look, why don't you go get us something to drink?"

"I don't have any money."

He dug out a few dollars.

"I'd better get two drinks," I said. "It might look fruity if we shared a straw."

He did a big exasperated sigh.

I went up to the window and ordered two diet Pepsis. While I was waiting, the patio emptied, except for a love-bird couple: a muscular black guy in a tight T-shirt holding hands across the table with a woman who looked like Patti LaBelle. I watched Pete talking on the phone. At one point he stepped out to the curb so he could see the street signs. I was startled to hear "Chain of Fools" again in a blur from a passing car. What was this, "Chain of Fools" Weekend? Had something happened to Aretha Franklin? I watched the wind beat a palm tree.

When I came back with the drinks, Pete was just ending the conversation. "Thanks, I really appreciate it. Okay, I'll watch for you."

He hung up and I handed him his Pepsi.

"Who was that?"

"Danny. He's an old musician friend. He only lives a few minutes from here."

"Why don't you call your boyfriend? He'd come get us, wouldn't he?"

"I'm sure he's already at the club." Pete sat down on one of the aqua plastic benches.

"So what does he do?" I sat down on the same bench.

"Tim, I really don't want to discuss it."

"It's not that you don't want me to meet him, is it? Is he a geek?"

"You're much geekier."

"You're kind of geeky yourself, you know. At certain times. I've got some pretty funny mental snapshots."

"Tim, please just shut up."

"What's his name?"

"I don't want to say! It has nothing to do with you. I don't want any aspect of it contaminated with your bitch mind."

"That's kind of paranoid."

"I don't think so."

"So is he like your father?"

"Tim."

"Or is it too soon to say? You're probably still at the *nice* stage, where he's all good-natured innocence and you've decided he's different."

"Tim."

"But sooner or later, being human, he's going to lose his temper over something."

"There are ways to calmly and constructively express anger."

"Some of us have flash points, Pete. We can't all go around in a low-level rage all the time like you."

He looked at me. "You said some things I can't forget."

"I apologized. Several times."

"You called me a selfish pig."

"You were pulling away."

"That's not all you said either."

"I know. Please don't repeat it."

"I'm not going to. But you really hurt me, Tim."

Out of nervousness, or guilt, I broke into a falsetto rendition of Timi Yuro's romantic masochist's classic "Hurt." I noticed Pete peeling the plastic lid off his Pepsi. The next thing I knew the drink and ice were in my face.

He yelled, "Why don't you shut your glib fucking mouth—*I've had it!*"

I was jolted. And angry. My face and shirt were drenched. I got up and took off my shirt and wiped my face. Then I let him have it.

"You cold little fuck. Don't tell me about being hurt. Fuck you and your cheesy little feelings. I was *suicidal* the night you dumped me. Todd had to come over to make sure I didn't do anything. You were proably down at the beach getting your cock sucked fifteen minutes after you got off the phone. You wouldn't even tell me to my face, you gutless snake. You had to blow me off like some trick. That's all I was to you anyway, let's face it. A six-month fucking one-night stand with a few stale endearments thrown in to make sure I fell for you so you could fuck me over later. That's all you're good for, isn't it? You don't know shit about a real relationship. You're a fucking vampire, that's all you are. Sucking people dry to feed your sick little narcissistic ego. You wouldn't know love if it shit in your face. I hope you get AIDS and die."

My outburst drew the attention of the muscular black guy, who was dumping his food debris in the trash can. "Hey, watch it!" he called to me.

"Fuck off, breeder!" I said. "We listen to your shit all the time."

Not smart, but at the moment I didn't care. The black guy just looked at me, shook his head like he thought I was crazy, and got into his Nissan. As he backed out, his woman friend called, "Take it back to West Hollywood!"

I was still looking at Pete. He was shaken.

"I take back the last line," I said. "I wouldn't wish that on anyone. Not even you."

"You're really too much, Tim," he said softly.

A part of me already wanted to apologize. But I wasn't going to.

"It might interest you to know," Pete said, "that it hasn't exactly been easy for me. Far from getting my *cock sucked* the night we broke up, I haven't even been with anyone since."

"What about your boyfriend?"

"I don't have a boyfriend." There were tears in his eyes. "I've spent the last year trying to get over you. I think what you've just done has finally accomplished that."

Damn it, fuck. Me and my fucking mouth.

Pete picked up his knapsack and guitar case and stepped over to the curb to wait for Danny.

I watched him for a minute, not sure what I was going to do. I was still mad, and feeling like shit that I'd done it again, done the very thing that had scared him so much before. I was certain this was really it. And I felt a little panicky, too. As soon as Danny came, Pete would get in the car and they'd drive off, and I'd be left on the torn lip of South Central L.A. with a quarter in my pocket. I'd hitchhike, I'd get a mercy ride from a racist white motorist or a warmhearted black person. I'd get home somehow, I'd probably be okay, I usually was. But maybe I should have gone home with Jay, then none of this would be happening. I'd be in bed with a smooth-skinned Hollywood movie star right now. Except not really. Jay would've shot his load after fifteen minutes, made an excuse to leave, and I'd know I was never going to see him again. Or maybe I should've stayed with Victor. *We'd* be in bed now, or lounging in our caftans, watching *Funny Girl* on cassette. Then I'd excuse myself to go use the bathroom. I'd be in there a long time, he'd hear water running. "Tim? Are you all right?" He'd try the door. It would be locked. "Tim?"

From where I was standing I could see the vast shopping plaza that took up the next block to the east: a gutted Boy's market, a charred, collapsed Thrifty drugstore, what may have been a Home Depot. It looked like George Bush had ordered in an air strike.

EIGHT

SEVERAL minutes passed and Pete ignored me as he watched the street for Danny. I could see that I'd really hurt him and I wanted to do or say something. He seemed so raw and vulnerable as he stood there, anxious and jumpy, watching the traffic roar by. There'd always been a sense that Pete was missing some sort of neurological defense system that most other people have. I wondered if that was why he'd become alcoholic, because his nerve endings were so frayed all the time he'd just wanted some relief. I felt a great tenderness for him, and insanely, considering what I'd just done, a desire to protect him. From what? From people like me? It made no sense at all, it was no doubt fucked up, but I finally just said what I was thinking. "I still love you."

He looked at me as if I'd hit him.

Then a car was sliding up, a shiny white Oldsmobile. "Come on," Pete said as he picked up his guitar case and knapsack. So at least I wasn't going to be left there.

Pete stuck his stuff in the backseat and got in beside Danny, making room for me. The first thing that hit me was the reek of pine air freshener, then the gospel music on the radio, and the white leather Bible on the dashboard.

"Danny, this is Tim."

"How do you do?" Danny said with a smile and a winning, good-natured laugh. He was about thirty, thin, with short-cropped hair, deep black skin. With his horn-rimmed glasses and crisp white shirt and narrow tie, he looked as if he'd stepped out of a Martin Luther King documentary.

"You caught me just in time," he said to Pete. "I was on my way to church."

We pulled out, heading east past the gutted shopping plaza. I liked the gospel music on the radio, a live church broadcast with people yelling refrains. But the air freshener was too much, as if someone had spilled a bottle of Pine Sol on the floor of the car.

"Are you okay?" Pete said to Danny. "I tried to call you a bunch of times during the riots. When I finally got through, there was no answer."

"I'm *fine*, Pete. The Lord protected me through that time of trial, as I knew He would. Let us not dwell on what is now past. The question tonight is, how are *you?*"

Danny laughed infectiously, but this time for some reason it disturbed me.

"I'm basically okay," Pete said. "This hasn't been one of my better days. So you're living with your mom now?"

"Yes, I am, Pete. You know, she broke her hip last year and she needs a lot of help."

"I was sorry to hear about Ray."

"It's good to *see* you!" Danny said jarringly, and squeezed Pete's hand for just a second. "You know, I've thought about you. You've been in my prayers."

"That's good. I appreciate it," Pete said uneasily.

"It's been a joyous time since I accepted Jesus Christ into my heart. A-men and a-men. Thank you, Jesus. I love you." Infectious laugh.

Pete looked straight ahead. I could see that Danny's conversion was news to him, and I knew Pete had a very low tolerance for Christian fundamentalism. I already felt a kind of numb sadness, realizing that Ray must have been Danny's boyfriend.

"I wish I could describe to you the happiness He's brought me," Danny said, and looked at me. "Tim, isn't it?"

I nodded.

"I'm still not very good with names. My memory was harmed by all the drugs I used to take. Cocaine. Angel dust. Why they call it *that*, I don't know." He laughed. "But I have been released. Thank you, Jesus. I looked for love in many grim places. *Pete* knows. He could tell you stories. And I tell them myself when I give witness. Because I'm not the only one who searched in vain for the one true love. Do you believe in Jesus, Tim?"

"Well, in a sense. I mean—"

"Do you believe He died for your sins?"

"Well, to my mind—"

"Danny, leave him alone," Pete said softly.

Danny laughed. "All right. Let's talk about *you*."

"I don't think that's a good idea, Danny."

"You've got a few things to answer for, Pete," he said good-naturedly. "If you know what I mean. And I'm sure in your heart you do."

"Danny, I really don't think this is a good subject for us to pursue."

"Some of those songs you sing," Danny said wryly. "And I'm sure you know which ones I'm referring to. Pete, I love you as a brother and a child of God. But if you continue to blaspheme the Lord, there will be a terrible price to pay."

A reference, I assumed, to Pete's blistering, surreal "Jesus Had a Hard-on (On the Cross)." In which, according to the first verse, "God lopped it off 'cause *He* wanted to be Boss."

"Danny, look," Pete said. "I'm glad you're off drugs. I know you had a problem. And I really don't care what people believe—"

"Oh, I think you do, Pete. Or you wouldn't stoop to belittling the faith of others. A faith you know nothing about."

"I have my own faith. My own God."

"There is only one God."

"I don't believe that," Pete said. "I don't believe in your God."

"Then you're serving Satan," Danny said. "You may not know it. But when you speak of our Lord nailed to the

Cross on Calvary with . . . It is an unspeakable blasphemy."

"Don't you think Jesus ever got a hard-on, Danny?"

"*No!*"

Pete sighed. "Then there's no point in discussing this further." He looked at me. "It's just like all that shit about *Last Temptation*. You either think He was a human being or you don't. And if you don't, as far as I'm concerned, the whole thing is drivel. Jesus is everyone who's ever suffered. Otherwise it doesn't mean shit. It's just a fucking Sunday school story for prudes." Pete looked at Danny. "Anyway, your God is a piece of shit. Jehovah, I mean. Fuck Him. That's my attitude. I'm not afraid. He can't hurt me 'cause I think He's shit." Pete gave a finger to the ceiling of the car. "Fuck you, Jehovah, you vicious old fuck! Fuck you in the *ass!*"

Danny pulled over—I was certain, to put us out. But he maintained a steady calm as he turned to Pete. "Let me ask you something. How can you be so angry at something you don't believe in?"

"Because I'm angry about what's happening. About what happened to Ray. I can't believe in a God that would let that, or cause that, to happen."

"Pete, who are we to question God's way?"

"Oh, fuck that," Pete said. "I think that's so much bullshit. I don't think it's God's way."

Danny took Pete's hand. "I understand your anger, Pete. I spent many dark days in a rage at our Lord. You don't know how close you are, this very moment, to accepting Jesus Christ into your heart."

Pete took a deep breath. "Look, I'm sorry I lost my temper. If you have a faith, I really don't mean to—"

"Let me tell you a beautiful story," Danny said softly. "You mentioned Ray. And if he were here, I know with all my heart he would affirm what I'm about to say. For the year that Ray was sick, we tried many ways. The doctors first, of course. The drugs. AZT. We attended Louise Hay, which did provide a degree of spiritual sustenance, though in the end not enough. Ray quit taking the toxic drugs. We tried the natural approach, the wheat-grass juice. For a while he was better. Then they discovered the lesions in his brain. They prescribed chemotherapy, but his insurance had been canceled. Which meant we had to go to County. But it was there in that hellish place that the miracle occurred, thanks to John and Scott—who I'd like you to meet, because we all of us have a great deal in common. John once sang in a Southern rock group, whose name you would know. Scott was a drug addict, who sold his body, in New York City. Both men have known the homosexual hell. The first time I met them, they were talking to Ray in the hospital ward. He'd lost his hair by then and at first I was angry. I said many hateful things, not unlike the things you've said tonight, cursing God for Ray's plight. Then I fell to weeping. For there was finally no denying the light of Christ's love in their eyes."

There were tears in Danny's eyes now. I was both appalled and moved. I could see that Pete was, too.

"I accepted Jesus into my heart that night," Danny said, "and Ray did, too. We asked God to forgive us our sins, to remove our depraved feelings for one another. And He did. And as we admitted our wrongs, we were reborn. And Ray was transformed. A light, a radiance, enveloped him. I thought at first it was a divine healing. How I prayed for that to be so, with all my heart. I offered my own life up to the Lord, if He would only let Ray live." Tears ran down Danny's cheeks. "But I see now that was *my* will, not God's. And so, as we prayed, and I held Ray's hand, his soul left his body and rose up to heaven. I still don't know why! Maybe God needed him for an angel! I know he was saved! His last words on this earth were, 'I love you, Jesus. I love you!' " Danny sobbed.

"Oh, God, Danny." Pete put his arms around Danny and held him as he wept. Pete looked at me. There were tears in his eyes, too. "Why don't you leave us alone for a minute?" he said to me.

I got out of the car and smoked a cigarette on the sidewalk. We were in Koreatown, alongside a bright, intact mini-mall. People clogging a video store. In the window a life-size poster of lizard-faced cretin Arnold Schwarzenegger. Behind the counter a Korean clerk with a flattop and a gun holstered on his hip.

At one point, I heard Danny say through his tears, "I did love him, I did! But it was sin!"

"Danny, it wasn't." Pete's tone was gentle. "I know he loved you, too."

In a few minutes Danny started the engine. I expected Pete to wave me back into the car, but instead he reached for his guitar and got out. "I'll call you tomorrow," Pete said to Danny.

"No, Pete, I don't think so." Danny was wiping his face with a white handkerchief. "I'd like to bring you to the Lord, but I know you're not ready. And I must protect my faith."

"All right. I understand," Pete said. "You take care."

"God bless you, Pete." Danny peered out at me. "You, too, Tim. Remember, God may hate the sin, but he loves the sinner. May you both find the joy I've found."

The spotless white Oldsmobile slid off into traffic.

"Jesus," I said.

"I know." Pete looked up and down the junky commercial street. "Okay, so we're on Vermont. That's Olympic back there. This must be Wilshire up ahead here."

It was only a few blocks. We started walking.

"What a nightmare story," I said. "I've heard of that happening, those Christian guys coming in, laying a guilt trip on AIDS patients."

"Fucking ghouls," Pete said. "If I ever caught anybody doing that, I'd kill 'em."

"How long had he and Ray been together?"

"About six years. Ray was a musician. A good one."

"It's so awful."

"I know."

Then silence as we walked. Pete was still mad at me. Not that I blamed him. He had a wall up. In a few more minutes he'd be rid of me. As Wilshire Boulevard came into view, he dug out his wallet, took out a five. "This enough for the bus?"

"I'm sure it is. I haven't taken a bus in a long time, but . . ."

"Well, tonight you can see how the other half lives."

"I feel like I already have in a way. It's been kind of an adventure, hasn't it?"

"Yeah, right. It's been fun."

"No, but I mean—"

"Okay, look—" Pete stopped. We'd come to the alley below Wilshire. "I'm going up here. So take it easy, okay?"

"I will. But listen, we're going to have to talk. About the Bryer situation—"

"I don't know why."

I held in my anger. "Because I was there, Pete. I was part of it. You're going to need me to corroborate your version of—"

"Tim, I can't get into this right now."

"Well, call me if you need to."

"I will." He started to go.

I took a step toward him and opened my arms. "Let me have a hug, will you? I'm really—"

"No, I'm late. You take it easy."

I watched him walk up the alley toward the pink buildings of the Ambassador Hotel.

"Fucking withholder," I said under my breath.

NINE

A FEW minutes later I was sitting on the bus bench in front of a high-rise bank building on Wilshire Boulevard, feeling like a total piece of shit. I wished like anything I hadn't gone by Pete's place. I should've just hitchhiked home. I would have been there by now, curled up in bed with Jefty and *City of Quartz*, spending a quiet, lonely Saturday night by myself, no doubt with thoughts of Pete in the back of my mind just from having spotted him at the Chevron station in Laguna. But the thoughts would have been like a soft FM radio, bearable, containable. And by the next morning they would have been only a murmur. But now, after all that had happened, I was going to have to go through major withdrawal all over again.

Maybe ten minutes passed. If the bus had come, I would have taken it. But it didn't come, and as I sat there, my emotions grew more and more confused. I was still angry at Pete, at his coldness, which was so much like the way he'd gotten toward the end of our affair. But I also thought of how he'd looked standing by the Pioneer Chicken place as we'd waited for Danny, how I'd wanted to put my arms around him, that's what I'd really wanted to do, even though it was not something I could've done at that particular location, or probably anywhere else for that matter, after what I'd just said. I felt awful and creepy about my explosion, especially the line about hoping he'd get AIDS

107

and die. The worst thing I could think of, obviously, but I was still astonished that I'd been capable of such hatefulness. Of course, I'd instantly taken it back, but that was like shooting someone in the head and immediately apologizing. I was going to have to make a much more sincere amend at some point. When he called about the Bryer situation. Assuming he did. But he'd have to. Or I could always write him a letter. But I didn't know his address. I considered going over to the club now, but that felt all wrong. He'd been late, and he always got crazy before a gig anyway, and if I showed up now— No, that would be too obsessive, he'd really think I was Glenn Close, and if he didn't accept my apology graciously, which he probably wouldn't, I might well lose it again. So let go of it (I heard Todd's voice telling me). I'd held on far too long as it was.

A car pulled up just past the bus stop, a white Honda with an Alamo rental sticker on the back. And Kevin got out, beaming.

My first reaction was shock, followed quickly by guilt, even though I tried to beam back. He was an old friend of mine, an independent film maker from San Francisco.

"I *thought* that was you," he said as he came over. "How *are* you?"

We hugged. He felt thin—although he'd always been thin.

"I'm fine," I said. "How are *you?* God, you look great." Too much surprise in my voice. But it was true. He was tanned and looked years younger without his beard. His pale blond hair was long again, almost as long as it had been when we'd first met in San Francisco in the early seventies. I'd heard that he'd been *diagnosed* (a term that always smacked of voodoo to me), but he didn't look sick at all.

"Well, I just spent a month in Morocco," he said, still beaming. "Plenty of sun there."

"I'll bet."

"This is incredible, this is amazing." So were his eyes, as always: a shocking pale blue with the intensity of a Scientology recruiter. "What are you *doing* here?" he said. "Are you waiting for the *bus?* Where's your *car?*"

"Oh, I got stranded in Laguna. It's a long story."

"Stranded in Laguna? Jesus. That's a long way from here. So where are you headed? Are you still in Santa Monica?"

"Yes."

"*That's* a long way, too. I'd give you a lift but . . . Are you in a hurry? I'd really like to talk with you."

"Well, I don't know—"

" 'Cause I'm going to a club up here. In the Ambassador. There's this incredible group I want to see. Drunken Boat. I don't know if you've heard of them—"

"I think I have."

"You want to join me?"

"Well, I don't have much money—"

"Don't worry about that." He waved me to the car. "Come on. God, it's good to *see* you!"

I got into the car, feeling that this was obviously meant to be. I knew this could well be my last chance to be with Kevin, and I still felt bad that I hadn't called him since I'd heard. And seeing Pete perform, I decided, couldn't make me feel any worse than I already did.

"This can't be an accident," Kevin said as we pulled out. "I've been thinking about you lately. More than usual, I mean. Part of the natural process of reviewing my life, as it were. Seeing certain things I wish I'd done differently. I don't know if you heard, but I had some pretty grim news last winter."

"Yes, I did. I've been meaning to call you, but—"

"It's all right. Don't lay a guilt trip on yourself. You may not have known it, but you were doing me a favor. The last thing I needed was anyone else treating me like a victim. So many people did that up north it nearly *killed me.*" He laughed boisterously as if he found this extremely hilarious.

"I just—"

"I know, you just didn't know what to say. You're too self-aware to bring off lines like 'Kevin, you can lick this thing, you're a fighter!' " He laughed again.

"You're right. I'm not very good at saying things like that."

We turned up the driveway that led back through the seedy grounds to the Ambassador Hotel. "You might have at least sent me a card though. 'Get well soon.' " Kevin laughed at the absurdity of that. "Someone should start a line of AIDS cards. 'Glad you beat that oral thrush. And the toxo, too, before your brain turned to mush.' "

He laughed again but I couldn't. I'd felt the same way after issue four or five of *Diseased Pariah News*, the "HIV humor" 'zine, when the pus-and-retinitis jokes reached critical mass and collapsed back into horror again. Kevin saw my expression.

"Oh, no, Tim. Don't tell me you've lost your sense of humor, too. That's become a major problem up north, let me tell you. Not that San Francisco's ever been a yuk fest exactly. Not with all those PC dykes running around, hissing every other image on the screen. But absolutely no one got *Mexican Face Lift*." His last film. "Of course, it was far too male identified. Too phallocentric . . . according to the phallophobes. Ever heard a lesbian say the word *penis?* And the guys are just as bad. All this shit about positive gay images. Who's going to decide what that means? And how dare they? It was a black fucking comedy, not a goddamn training film. It's hellish trying to get a chuckle out of *anybody* up there these days. I felt like Shecky Greene popping flop sweat at Belsen."

"I liked *Mexican Face Lift*," I said. "I think it's the best thing you've done so far."

"Thank you." He shut off the engine and said, knowing it would startle me, "Why didn't you and I settle down in '73?"

I'd had this conversation more than once in recent years with other men like Kevin, where we'd had a brief affair before deciding to just be friends. It still embarrassed me.

"We lived in different cities," I said.

"That's true. And I could never live in L.A. You could've lived in San Francisco though."

110

"If I'd quit college. If I hadn't gone to film school at UCLA."

"There's San Francisco State—"

"It's provincial, Kevin. San Francisco exists in another dimension."

"It probably wouldn't have worked anyway, would it? There was always an undercurrent of competition. I mean, you had filmmaking aspirations then, too. I still think it's too bad you never pursued that. I mean, I know you did for a while in Hollywood. But you never really belonged there. Let's face it, you're not John Hughes. A slight difference in sensibility."

This was beginning to bother me. "I like what I'm doing now." I opened the car door.

Kevin got out, too, breathing in the night air extra deeply. "Look at this place! I'm not sure it's safe to enter. God forbid there's an earthquake."

He had a point. The hotel was monumentally dilapidated, the salmon pink walls crumbling, eaves sagging. It had been closed for several years.

"I think it's set for demolition," I said.

"That figures. Nothing lasts in the city. Wonder how it survived the riots. It's a tinderbox."

We walked toward the main entrance where a thin young man in a Drunken Boat T-shirt was taking the cover money.

"This place is just brimming with history, too," Kevin said. "Charlie Chaplin, Gloria Swanson. Charles Foster Kane used to finger-bang Norma Desmond behind those hydrangeas, I think. Judy Garland singing 'The Man That Got Away' in the Coconut Grove. Sirhan Sirhan singing 'I Don't Know How to Love Him' in the kitchen."

Kevin paid the cover and we walked back through the gutted lobby and down a long, grungy livid pink corridor to the Club Mabuse.

It was in a large ballroom—I'm pretty sure the ballroom where Robert Kennedy made his victory speech right before he was shot. I was relieved to see how dark and crowded it was. Once the stage lights came up, there'd be

111

no way for Pete to see me, especially if we hung in the back, where we were headed. There was a bar on a slightly raised level back there.

"Want something to drink?" Kevin said.

"Yeah. A club soda's fine."

"Why don't you grab a table."

I sat down at one of the cocktail tables across from the bar. Most of the crowd was below on the dance floor, a typical Drunken Boat audience, nuevo-beatnik college students, art-scene types, cool young guys, both gay and straight, bi- and a-, soulful young women in black.

As I waited for Kevin, I had a mild alienation attack. All around me at the other tables there were couples, both straight and gay, who seemed committed, with an intimate shorthand rapport, as they joked and laughed. The sort of rapport I'd had for a while with Pete. I still didn't think I could find that again that easily, even if I'd been looking.

On the sound system a Japanese band with a female singer was covering "Rikki, Don't Lose That Number," a song that had always seemed gay to me, evoking images of bar pickups, one-night stands in the seventies, phone numbers on matchbooks, lost hopes. My whole life seemed like a lost hope. She sang, "Sen it off in a redder to you sef."

A voice, with a slight Mexican accent, interrupted my self-pity. "What the fuck are you doing here?"

Pablo. I got up, surprised by his harsh tone, which I almost thought was a put-on at first. He looked as good as ever, shirtless, smooth brown chest, handsome Latino face with classic cholo, as opposed to trendy, mustache-and-goatee, silky, short black hair. He'd barely changed in ten years.

"How are you?" I said, still thinking that we might hug.

"I'm fine. But you must be crazy."

"I take it Pete told you he saw me."

"Yeah. He said you came by his place in Laguna. Why did you do that?" His tone was gentler now but exasperated.

"I don't know. I wish I hadn't now."

"You should've left him alone, Tim. He was almost over you."

"I know. I was almost over him."

Pablo sighed disgustedly. "It's all such bullshit. What are you *doing*? You don't even *want* a relationship."

This startled me. "Yes, I do."

"No, you don't. You're an affair queen. Just like Pete. He doesn't want anything to last either. He gets too much mileage out of a breakup. I can see you're milking it for all it's worth, too, in your own suffering masochist's way. Why don't you go home and watch a Joan Crawford picture?"

I laughed incredulously. "Pablo—why are you doing this? I've always liked you—"

"You liked having your dick in my mouth ten years ago, I know that."

We'd had an experience one night on Venice Beach. I'd lived on Ozone in those days, just a few blocks from the cruising area, and I'd sometimes step out for a blow job and a pint of Häagen-Dazs vanilla.

"That was a two-way street," I said. (I'd blown him, too. Then he'd given me his phone number, saying, "I don't usually do this, but you're really hot." I'd never called him though, being scared of any involvement at all in those days.)

"You use people, that's all," he said. "You're a fucking narcissist."

"If you're still referring to ten years ago, I think we used each other."

"You represent everything that almost destroyed me. It took me a long time to get over all that, but I did. And I've got a boyfriend now."

"Bully for you."

"But it's too late for you. You're too selfish to ever share your life with someone. You're just going to keep getting hurt again and again by more guys like Pete till you finally give up and become an old male spinster."

"Why don't you fuck yourself?" I said. "You're still just mad that I didn't call you ten years ago."

"If you believe that, you're really pathetic. Why don't you go back to Santa Monica, huh? Or better yet, why don't you stay, since you obviously love emotional pain. You're going to have a real orgy in a few minutes."

With that, Pablo took off and I still couldn't believe it. The first time Pete had introduced us at a Drunken Boat rehearsal had been somewhat embarrassing, Pablo remembering me well before I placed him. But he'd been cheerful about the memory—he'd even been discreet, implying for Pete's benefit that we'd met on the beach respectably during the daylight instead of disreputably at night. I'd eventually told Pete the truth anyway, another thing I'd liked about Pete, that I didn't have to pretend I'd never done anything raunchy. But I didn't understand Pablo's anger, unless it was just as he said, that I reminded him of a period he wanted to forget. He'd gone too far though. He hadn't really made peace with his own past or he wouldn't have felt the need to attack me that way.

But what if he was right? What if it was too late for me? Maybe I should just resign myself to being a male old maid, a gracefully aging celibate quietly masturbating to his memories. No, I'd tried that for a while. I'd wasted years of my life. There was no going back to that. I'd rather be dead.

Kevin came back with the drinks, two glasses with cherries. "No more club soda. Hope this is okay. It's a Roy Rogers."

"That's fine." I took a sip. Hadn't had a Roy Rogers since I was a kid at the Coast Club. "Happy trails."

"You were talking with the bass player," Kevin said.

"Yeah. I knew Pablo in Venice." I hadn't decided yet if I wanted to tell Kevin about Pete.

"Yeah, Pablo's wild." Kevin grinned.

"You know him?"

"Oh, yes. Met down him here about ten years ago. On the beach. Used to be wild down there at night."

"That's what I've heard."

"Well, *you* used to go there, didn't you?"

"Once in a while. A long time ago." I was getting uncomfortable. "So you're down here on business?"

"No, no." Kevin spoke carefully. "It occurs to me that

114

you don't know this or you would've said something about it by now. But Jeff died."

This hit me like a sound wave.

"Oh, Christ."

"I'm sorry. I was pretty sure you didn't know. The memorial was this afternoon. I thought I might see you there, but—"

"When did he die?"

"Tuesday. Someone should've called you."

I'd dreaded this for years. "Well, we hadn't really seen much of each other in recent times."

"I know that. But I think you were still an important person to him."

This is where I should cry, I thought. But I could feel myself going numb. I thought of Jeff's scratchy brown beard, the wiry hair on his body. I saw him laughing.

"So how was it?" I said.

"What?"

"His memorial."

"You want me to say nice things? Or the truth?"

"Whichever you want."

"It was hideous. Cloying, awful. They played Anita Baker music and released balloons. It was supposed to be joyous. Not sad, but a celebration? An approach that always drives me up the wall. I wanted to yell, 'This is bullshit, he's *dead!* The fucker checked out, he *croaked*, he's stiff as a bat!' "

"Jeff would've probably preferred that. The Jeff I knew anyway."

"Well, it was Neal's idea. Did you know Neal?"

"I've met him. He seems like a nice enough guy."

"He is. He's very sweet. And I don't mean that sardonically either. He really is. A typical sheltered USC pussy."

We shared a quick laugh.

"Can't stand his films though," Kevin said. "Makes Spielberg look cynical."

"I know."

"I admit to some resentment," Kevin said. "I could shoot a whole movie on what Neal spends on catering. But I know

115

he really loved Jeff. And they had almost eight years together. Which is more than a lot of people have."

"That's true."

"And most of it was good. They made what? Five films together. Which in Hollywood is moving along at quite a clip. They had the life they wanted, the whole clichéd shot. The house in the hills with the Hockneys, the antique cars, the twinkie errand boys. I'm not putting that down incidentally. I just think it's sad that Jeff had everything, all the best treatment money could buy, and yet when it came to the one path that could've saved him, his mind was closed."

I didn't know what he meant, and something told me I didn't want to know. I really didn't want to hear about wheat-grass juice or the Course in Miracles now.

Kevin sipped his Roy Rogers. "I know it's probably none of my business, but were you and Jeff boyfriends or partners or what? I was never really clear on that."

I looked at him. "I never was either."

People clapped and cheered as Pete and the other guys came out on-stage and plugged in. Frank, the new drummer, was goateed, grinning, and chunky, the kind of body that would run to fat in a few years if he wasn't careful. Assuming he was still alive in a few years. All the guys in Drunken Boat were gay. Joke names they'd considered were The Wilde Bunch ("If they move, say something witty"), Gang o' Gays, the Thrill-Crazy Queers, Death of Pasolini, the Paul Lynde Story, the André Gide Faction, the Hate Boat, Butt-Eaters Anonymous, and Jesus Was a Homo. Frank was shirtless, so were Pete and Pablo. Soren never was. Soren bothered me—he always had. A hyper-intelligent, stuck-up blond with a blond attitude problem. A Tadzio blond, a British-homo period-film blond (*Blondshead Revisited*), the kind of pale, thin, smooth-skinned blond old queens always have in mind when they sigh *a blond*. He was a great guitar player though.

They dove into a favorite opener, a raucous and weirdly ominous reworking of the Beach Boys' "Fun, Fun, Fun." Over a spiky, churning, infernal rhythm, Pete tossed off the lyrics in a rough, slightly hoarse, sarcastic voice that one reviewer had described as a cross between "a youthful Keith Richards and Lou Reed drifting into amphetamine psychosis." Pete had enjoyed that description. It fit this song especially, which was like the Velvet Underground deconstructing Brian Wilson, the mindless sun-drenched imagery taking on an apocalyptic edge. "Daddy" became a spiteful, punishing patriarch—Jehovah—the "T-bird" a symbol of innocent pleasure and joy. I'm not "reading this in" incidentally—it was there. Kitsch and black humor taken full circle back into seriousness—that was Pete's speciality. For a while I was so overwhelmed by the physical force of the music it was hard to think about anything else. But soon enough my mind began playing its memorial film collage of key moments with Jeff.

The first time I'd see him, at UCLA in 1977, in a film-theory class, giving me a snide look, making me feel like a moron about something I'd said. I'd decided he was an asshole. A talented asshole though. I'd liked his student film, a pseudo–home movie about his Jewish family in "the bad part" of Beverly Hills. I remembered him nervously fielding criticism the day it was shown in Melnitz Hall. I'd pointed out a continuity flaw in a jokey way that got a cheap laugh at his expense.

Six years later, in 1983, he'd come into the film archives one afternoon. I could still see his soft, curly brown hair, his green eyes, his blue/green Hawaiian shirt, his broad grin, in the creamy hall light. By then he'd become an independent producer with several films to his credit, art or cult films like *Benzedrine*, his "beatnik film noir," that usually got good reviews and barely broke even. In other words, just the kind of films I'd always wanted to make but by then had all but given up on trying to do within the studio system. Jeff and I had talked a long time that afternoon, and he ended up asking me out. The truth was I'd always been attracted to him, and it turned out it was mutual. The film school hostility had been a classic case of attitude masking desire.

We only slept together twice. Once a few weeks after

we started going out, and again a year later, right before we "broke up." At the time I wasn't having sex with anyone. Back in the summer of '82 I'd become extremely alarmed about the "strange new disease" that was killing gay men and decided to be celibate "till this blows over." I broke that vow to sleep with Jeff the first time. But afterward I was freaked out, even though we'd done little more than fondle one another. But in those days much less was known. The virus hadn't even been identified yet, so there was a lot more paranoia. I told Jeff I couldn't handle it, I wanted to be celibate again, and he said he understood. He was scared, too. So we continued on that basis, seeing each other all the time, talking every day, hatching movie plans. We wrote several screenplays together, for me to direct with Jeff producing. He was tirelessly aggressive in pursuing financing and promoting me. And we were always more than friends, which I sometimes felt later had been the big mistake. It might have been much better if we'd said after the first time, "Let's just be friends." But we didn't (probably because we were already in love with each other), and there was a tacit sense that we were waiting— until some unspecified point in the future when we'd be safe and in the clear. (Meanwhile, they kept extending the incubation period by years.) Jeff told me later he'd been celibate himself for nine months, waiting, until he'd finally said, "Fuck this," and begun having sex with other guys.

When I found out about that, I was crazy with jealousy. And envy. I'd been celibate, except for the one time with Jeff, for about a year and a half and it seemed like forever. I wished like anything I had Jeff's fearlessness, but for me, at that time, the whole idea of sex had been contaminated. And I knew I had no right to be jealous. If I wouldn't sleep with Jeff, how could I blame him for going off with other guys? I *wanted* to have sex with him, but I was terrified. All that year he'd had minor health problems—colds, the flu, a case of thrush, which I only realized much later was an early symptom. But I was afraid even then that his immune system might be compromised.

Finally we did have sex again though, for the second and last time, and this was also extremely safe. He'd mentioned jerking off with some guys at the nude beach near San Diego, and I'd said, "I guess we could do *that*." So we watched a porno tape as an ice-breaking device. But when it came to sex, Jeff was funny. He affected a leering frivolous attitude as an emotional protection device. So we jerked off to *Like a Horse*, which was not my idea of cathartic intimacy. And afterward, still paranoid, I tactlessly questioned Jeff about some of his other recent encounters, and he bragged defensively about being "fucked blind" by several guys "really into fucking," and when he admitted they hadn't worn rubbers, I flipped. "Then you've committed suicide," I said, and he stormed out of my place in Venice. And except for a few angry phone calls, that was it. All our movie plans died, too. That was 1984.

I'd seen him a few times since then at screenings. Read about his success in *Variety* as he'd entered the mainstream, producing Neal's films, which were generally insipid, PG-rated teen and/or fantasy films, though you could always guess the director was gay since inevitably there were cute young guys who took off their shirts a lot. The last time I'd seen Jeff, at a screening of *My Own Private Idaho*, he'd been friendly, as always, even warm (years had passed; we'd forgiven each other). But I'd caught a few jokey doom references: "assuming I'm still alive then," "if I don't run out of time." He could have been speaking generally, in the sense that many of us didn't know anymore how much time we might have. But I knew Jeff. He wouldn't spend years playing mental guessing games the way I had. He'd take the test.

"Paula Abdul ought to cover this," Kevin said with a laugh as Drunken Boat went from "Fun, Fun, Fun," into "Date Night at Dachau."

"Yeah, right. Or Amy Grant."

Wouldn't happen soon. The conceit of this song involved the idea of a "death-camp land" at a Disneyland-like theme park. As the narrator and his date climb off the gas chamber ride:

> *She said: "Gee, it's so real!*
> *I felt just like a Jew!"*
> *I said: "I know. That hiss and everything!*
> *I did, too!"*

The melody itself had a Kurt Weill feeling with a jagged propellant beat.

Gregory and I had had quite an argument about this song. He'd found it extremely offensive. "The holocaust is not something you should joke about." I'd tried to explain that Pete wasn't making light of the death camps, that on the contrary, the song was disparaging the way the holocaust had been trivialized as entertainment. "Those TV movies are truly obscene," I'd said, "because they sanitize what happened. They end up making it thinkable again." Gregory had disagreed. But of course he worked for the TV producer who'd filmed Jane Seymour at Auschwitz.

In fact, Pete and I had come up with an equally dark variation, "AIDS land," where family people could safely experience such attractions as Rock Hudson's Closet, Dead Queer Mountain, the Haunted Hospice, Lesions of the Caribbean. All of which had seemed much funnier a year ago, when Pete and I were laughing in his sunny bedroom, than it did when I thought about it now.

From "Date Night," they went into a new song, "Côte d'Azur," and I got my first taste of what Pablo had meant about Pete getting mileage out of our affair. It had a dreamy, reverb-drenched Chris Isaaks feeling, despite Drunken Boat's generally crude, crunchy sound. For a moment I thought it was going to be genuinely tender, but it quickly turned into a demented Riviera road trip: a psycho loner at the wheel, trashing the insipid romantic landscape on his way to mass murder, to "bloody up some pretty flesh," at Saint-Tropez. I found the chorus weirdly moving though:

> *Your kisses drove me to the brink of delirium*
> *Now I dream of Querelle like Cocteau on opium*

There were other references to things we'd talked about in France: *Detour*, Godard, Jim Thompson, *To Catch a Thief*. One verse had Hitchcock stalking Princess Grace in a Ballard *Crash* scenario, filming her last eroticized gasps in the wreck. The song had a very bitter edge, but as satire I liked it.

From there they slammed into "Bring Me the Cock of John Dillinger," which Pete had written during our affair, after reading the Peckinpah book I'd given him. This was a song with a story, a musical movie, in which the Warren Oates narrator is forced to raid the Smithsonian for the pickle jar containing Dillinger's fabled gargantuan member because a rich Texan has kidnapped his Mexican bride. Instead of the severed head of Alfredo García beside him on the car seat, he drives cross-country "with the outlaw's crank." But after the jar breaks: "Damn! That thing stank!"

The song had a good-naturedly rowdy danceable groove, and the people on the dance floor were really getting into it. Pete was, too, ripping out riffs on his Rickenbacker, dancing around. He was slick with sweat now, the hair on his chest matted; he had a grinning glow. It made me think of the first time I'd seen him perform, after we'd been going together about a month, the realization I'd had then that any number of people, both men and women, would give anything to be with him, but for some reason I was the one. But the one he'd loved? Or the one he'd picked as an easy victim, a fresh sacrifice to his ego?

Of course, he himself had been just that sort of victim not long before. The next song reminded me of that, a pulsing, hypnotic song called "Seventeen Lies," which I knew was about Carlos. There were lines that seemed to tell the whole story, as Pete addressed Carlos:

> *He broke* your *heart*
> *So you had to break* mine
> *Now it's* my *turn to hurt someone*
> *Pass the pain down the line*

If that was reality, maybe it *would* be better to just give up. A hundred Xanax washed down with Absolut. Or slit wrists in the bathtub. I could see why people chose that option. Maybe the best people, the most perceptive, leaving the world to the vicious and stupid. How long could you go on watching people torture each other before you finally said "Fuck this"? But that kind of suicide still seemed petulant, especially now, when so many people were dying without choice.

I thought about Jeff, about how much was being lost, that he was only thirty-four, he should've had a whole life ahead of him. But in a way I felt I had no right to grieve for him as if we'd once been lovers, since we hadn't been really, even though we'd loved each other.

"Tim?" Kevin said.

"What?"

"Jesus, you're spacing out. I said, I just took the AIDS test again last week."

"You did?"

"Yes. I felt it was important to confirm, even according to Western science, what I already knew."

His cheerful tone baffled me.

"You should have seen my doctor's face when he had to tell me I'm negative now. And that all the backup tests confirmed it."

"What—"

"It's gone. There's no more virus in my body."

"That's great," I said. What else *could* I say? But I was certain it was some form of extreme desperation.

"We should talk about this later," Kevin said above the music. "This is not the most conducive atmosphere."

He was right. I had to shout as Drunken Boat went into their jackhammer "good-time version" of "Sister Ray." "Well, I'm just glad you're better!"

"Not better. *Well! Cured!*" Kevin moved his chair closer so he could talk in my ear. "I've gone back to a plane I left some years ago and in the process discovered what all this is about. AIDS, I mean. Like everything else, it begins on the spiritual plane. The disease is just a gross physical manifestation."

I didn't mistake this for typical New Age talk, which Kevin had always ridiculed. But in the early seventies, during the period of our affair, he'd been living in a Haight Street collective, taking mushrooms and peyote at least once a week, immersing himself in the cabala and the occult teachings of Aleister Crowley. That had seemed like a phase though.

"It's the power of thought!" he said through the music. "The power of negative prayer! The waves of hate aimed at us for so many years finally manifested on the physical plane."

I should've let it go, but I said, "What about the blacks in Africa?"

"They're hated, too. Devalued. It's the same psychic virulence at work. The same people who want us dead want to clear the Third World. But in the process they're going to kill the planet and themselves. It's the suicidal gasp of the Christian Aeon."

This was definitely Crowley talk. The Christians were holding on to their power, the line went, even though their time had passed. The next aeon, the Age of Horus, the liberating, anarchic child, was struggling to be born. But the scared, repressive Christians would rather destroy the world than allow the child free reign.

"But's it not too late," Kevin said. "The power of white magick is still infinitely stronger. I was very sick, Tim. I had KS." He rolled up his sleeve to show me his tan arm. "There were lesions and now they're gone. I went to see Lee in Morocco. He's been there ten years now. Do you remember Lee?"

"Yes. Not easy to forget Lee."

Another face from San Francisco, circa '73. Lee, with a full beard and long flowing auburn hair, had worn white robes everywhere—Jesus in a Ford pickup truck, the Savior at the Laundromat on Fell Street, King of Kings at the Alpha Beta. On formal occasions, a gay lib dance or a protest, he'd wear black robes and a demonic headdress made from a wolf's head. A self-described "magus" with X-ray green eyes that made dogs run squealing off across Golden Gate Park and grown clones sweat.

"All the years I spent making movies," Kevin shouted through Pete's guitar, "believing in the redemptive power of art . . . all those years, Lee was there in Marrakesh, remaining true to his school!" Kevin laughed. "Lucky for me! There weren't many who did! Most of the others, who *dabbled"*—he looked at me—"are dead now!"

"I wouldn't say I ever *dabbled* in the occult, Kevin," I said. "I found it interesting from an intellectual point of view at one time. The cabala and all that. As an alternate spiritual tradition."

"It's much more than that. It's the way out. The *only* way out now. I invoked the sun."

"You what?"

He held a finger to his lips. Despite the corniness of the gesture, I found myself moved by *his* reverence. Whatever had happened, *he* believed in it. And maybe that was finally all that mattered. I always thought of Western doctors as high-tech voodoo men anyway: "Lab test say: you die."

"We'll talk later," Kevin said.

For a while we watched Drunken Boat, still into "Sister Ray." They transformed this quintessentially demonic junkie anthem into a pounding euphoria machine. When Pete sang of searching for his main line, it sounded like a phase in a cracked Disney song. He was dancing around, pushing his boyishness way over the edge, Lou Reed replaced by an unhinged Jonathan Richman.

"He's something," Kevin said.

"Yeah, he is." Partially to brag, and also because I needed to talk about it, I said, "Actually, I know him. We were going together for a while. Last year. I was with him earlier this evening. Thought we could patch things up. That's why I was up here." The music got louder as Soren went into a battering distortion barrage, so I just shook my head to indicate the hopelessness of the situation with Pete.

"I know how you feel!" Kevin shouted in my ear. "We had a thing for a while, too!"

I was both surprised and not surprised. Sometimes it seemed as if everybody had been with everybody at some point—which was probably true. The music dropped to a level we could talk through as Pablo's bass took over.

"Pete never mentioned that," I said to Kevin.

Kevin shrugged. "Oh, well, it was a long time ago. 'Seventy-five. He was lying about his age, as it turned out. Sixteen. I could've ended up in prison. He was writing poetry then. Living in some dump in the Mission District. Still have some of his poems. God, I was in love with him. He was crazy then though. But you know how it is. When you look like Pete, you can get away with anything. It was classic though. I made a total fool of myself. I was twenty-four and followed him around like a goddamn dog. He was vicious, too. A mean little drunk. *Dérèglement de tous les sens* and all that. I thought I'd never get over him. I guess in a way I didn't. That's probably why I'm here now. What happened with you?"

"About the same thing. Except he was sober."

Kevin laughed. "Speaking of which, I could use another drink. Looks like you could, too."

While Kevin was at the bar, "Sister Ray" squealed off down the road and they began a new song, "Driving with Tears in My Eyes," which I quickly realized was about Pete and me. It was a slow, spare song with an underlying country feeling, which, like X, Drunken Boat could bring off without slipping into stickiness. It was addressed to me, with so many real-life details, it was like watching a movie of our affair, e.g.:

> *The tostados were cold*
> *But your eyes were on fire*
> *I got a hard-on just holding your hand at*
> *Law of Desire*

(Our first *date*.)

> *Making out on the edge of the Mulholland Highway*
> *Till the dirt bikers came*
> *And called us names*

125

(Pete had called them names back and there'd nearly been an altercation.)

The third verse really got to me in the way it described his feelings since we'd broken up. Despite what he'd said about trying to get over me, it was still hard for me to believe he'd gone through as much as I had.

So I pick up the phone, punching only six numbers
Although once I got your machine
Only last night I drove by your house again
Where I was afraid I'd be seen
My friends all say you were just an addiction
That in time the longing will die.
But tonight I still miss you so much
I can taste it
I'm driving with tears in my eyes

Kevin came back, handing me my drink, as Soren did a eloquent silvery lead riff through the break. "Sounds like you broke his heart," Kevin said.

I decided he was only guessing that the song was about Pete and me. Or being flip.

"I know. And I always thought he broke mine."

Kevin sipped his drink. "He still loves you, you know."

This startled me, especially Kevin's matter-of-fact tone. It also irritated me. I hate people making intuitive pronouncements about my life.

The next song set off a strange memory rush. "When Jesus Came to My House," one of Pete's several Jesus songs. But unlike "Jesus Had a Hard-on (On the Cross)," this was one even Danny might have liked—I think. It was inspired by a 1950s children's book of the same name that depicted a little boy leading the Robed One by the hand into his suburban home. I had only a vague memory of this book, but Pete had seen it more recently; a friend of his collected fifties childhood mementos. Through the crunchy beat, the mood Pete created was ineffably innocent and sad:

> When Jesus came to my house
> I introduced him to my folks
> We drank Cokes in the rumpus room
> Swapping parables and jokes

It was classic Pete: both funny and serious, the song finally evoking a wrenching sense of childhood loneliness.

> And when I get afraid at night
> Jesus is my friend
> Mom and Dad don't like me now
> But Jesus' love will never end

I don't know what it was really, it wasn't just the song. But I started to cry. It was the mood of the song, I guess, the way it triggerd dormant childhood memories, the same way my mother's death had. Images that for no rational reason I associated with grief. The bronzed bell at the elementary school. A papier-mâché pueblo in a fifth-grade classroom. My cowboy outfit. Cap pistols. Cub Scouts. Mom as a den mother.

Jeff. A sense that Jeff hadn't done anything, he was innocent and shouldn't have died. Jeff lifting himself out of the swimming pool, the hair on his chest and stomach dripping water, his wet, glossy, pink-lipped grin.

"Are you okay?" Kevin said.

"Not really. I still don't understand why any of this is happening."

"I've tried to explain it to you. I'm sorry you're so skeptical about certain things."

"I don't know, Kevin." I really didn't want to hear any more of his occult shit. "I just don't know."

But he started in again. "The secret chiefs of the Christian Aeon have the world in a death grip. It's too late for art to

127

make a difference now. That's why I've given up filmmaking. The battle must be waged now on the astral plane. We've got five years . . ."

I found myself tuning him out as Drunken Boat began a new slow narcotic blues song, which I realized was also about Pete and me. Pete sang:

> *Like film noir lovers*
> *We were trapped by the plot*
> *We looked for perfection*
> *And found only rot*

> *We once had the freedom*
> *To make our own fate*
> *We could've saved each other*
> *But now it's too late*

I knew the song was about us, inspired by what had happened with us. But it was just a conceit, I decided. It was like Pablo said: Pete would rather miss me, he'd rather plumb his own emotions after the fact for musical material than actually deal with *me*. The next verses scared me though, and made me feel like I was going to start crying again.

> *I still remember*
> *The things you'd say*
> *The ways I try to forget them*
> *I know will kill me someday*

> *But it's not all hopeless*
> *No matter what was said*
> *We'll forgive each other, I'm certain,*
> *After we're dead*

"You've got to go to him," Kevin said into my ear. "He's still in love with you."

I was startled, angered. More intuitive shit. I've learned the hard way never to take advice. "No, he's not. It's just a song."

"He's singing to *you*."

"He doesn't even know I'm here."

Kevin leaned over to me, put his hand on mine on the table. "*Go to him*. He still wants you. That's all you've got to do."

"Kevin, you don't know what you're talking about. I spent the whole evening trying to make up with him. Listen to the *song!*"

Pete was singing:

> *Up in heaven*
> *We'll forget these nights in hell*
> *Up in heaven*
> *That's where I'll love you well*

"Kevin, that's his way of saying it's not going to happen!"

"No, no, you don't understand anything. God, no wonder you've had problems in this area. It's a *plea!*"

"It's not a plea! He doesn't even fucking know I'm here!"

"I'm not disputing that. But it's a prayer! My God, you know what a prayer is, don't you? *Go to him*."

Pete was singing:

> *Up in heaven*
> *When everything is done*
> *That's when I'll finally tell you*
> *That, yes, you were the one*

"*No!*" I said to Kevin. "He'll only reject me again. He spent the whole day rejecting me. Fuck him." I drained my glass. "I shouldn't have come here. This is fucked up. I'm going to go." I got up.

Kevin got up, too. "Tim, you *have* to go to Pete. You don't have any choice."

"Kevin, look, I know you mean well. But I really don't want to hear it, okay? You don't know what happened. I was there, I do. I'm going to go. I'll see you later, okay? I'm glad you're better. I'm glad you're well."

I started to leave. Kevin caught up with me. "Look, I'll give you a ride, but first I really think you should—"

"*No,* you stay. I want to be by myself. I want a nice long bus ride across Los Angeles with no more bullshit from anyone. You take care. I'm not mad at you."

As I made my way down through the hot, sweaty dance crowd, the blues song ended, and on a much higher pitch the band roared into "What This Country Needs (Is a Baader-Meinhof Gang)." At the door I stopped to look back at Pete, flailing away at his Rickenbacker.

This was one of the songs I'd criticized. It had upset me the first time I heard it, the violent imagery, and the sense that it was openly advocating political terror. Pete had defended it by saying it was a catalog of fantasies a lot of people had but usually censored, a suppressed rage that the wrong people were dying. When he'd put it that way, I'd seen his point, but the images were still extreme:

> *The Reagans let their friends*
> *Turn this world to crud*
> *That's why I'd like to drench them both*
> *With AIDS-infected blood*

We'd joked about Whitney Houston covering that—she needed a hit. Or George Michael or Michael Jackson. My favorite verse had been and still was:

> *Like to see that Jeane Kirkpatrick*
> *Machine-gunned in a revolving door*
> *The death-squad dead won't be avenged*
> *Till someone smokes that right-wing whore*

Now, as I stood watching from the door, I had no more moral reservations about the song. The music itself was pure, brilliant, cathartic, surging through wave after wave of ecstatic guitar configurations. "If you guys would do something about your lyrics," an A&R man had once told Pete, "you could be as big as U2." An insult to Drunken Boat. Pete sang:

> *It's time to go down to Carolina now*
> *Before it's too late and I'm dead*
> *I want to see the look in the senator's eyes*
> *Right before I blow off his head.*

I couldn't believe how good Pete looked. Sweated out, soaked down into his faded black jeans, shining in the light, iridescent. He'd added some new lyrics, however, which did make it hard to believe he didn't mean to incite. He sang:

> *This isn't therapy*
> *This isn't art*
> *Make this real*
> *Go out and start*
> *Pick up a gun*
> *Kill a right-wing pig*
> *Kill as many as you can*
> *Kill someone big*

Pete yelled the chorus:

> *I'm sick of watching the wrong people die*
> *with a victim's whimper instead of a bang*
> *What I'd like to see*
> *What this country needs*
> *Is a Baader-Meinhof gang*

I took a long last look, certain it would be the last time I saw Pete in the flesh. I might see him on TV, in a video. I might see him being interviewed by Kurt Loder. A year ago that had seemed improbable. But that was before Nirvana. It might still be improbable. This was not the safe "anarchy" of "Smells Like Teen Spirit." This was not anarchy as marketing hype. Then again it was no more inflammatory than rap songs like "Fuck tha Police," was it? Or *was* it? Who knew what could happen? American culture had proven many times that it could absorb almost anything.

From where I was standing, the scene was like a wide shot in a video. I was already home in bed, watching Pete on "120 Minutes" on my thirty-two-inch Sony XBR.

131

TEN

MY EARS were still ringing as I crossed Wilshire Boulevard and sat down on the bus bench in front of the Jack in the Box. The night was warm but the wind had died down. I watched the traffic and thought about Jeff, how if I hadn't been so scared, if we'd become boyfriends in '84, *we* might have been together eight years. Then I thought, Jesus, do I always have to think of everything in terms of myself? I'm such a fucking narcissist no wonder I'm alone. Pablo's probably right, it's too late for me, I'm too selfish.

I tried to imagine what Neal must be going through now. That had to be the worst of all, I had no idea what that was like. I'd seen friends in the hospital, but that wasn't the same as living with someone, going through the long, escalating nightmare day after day.

But I imagined Jeff and Neal having had long periods of contentment before things got bad, years where they'd been happy while I'd been safe and alone, and I did wonder if I'd made a mistake, if it wouldn't have been worth it to be with Jeff all that time, whatever the risk. I really had loved him. Of course it wasn't that simple, it hadn't just been up to me, there were no doubt many other reasons, even if AIDS hadn't existed, why Jeff and I wouldn't have lasted together. But I still wondered if eight years ago I hadn't blown my one chance to be happy with someone. In some bizarre way I could *see* myself living with Jeff, it was easy to imagine, while it had always been hard to picture that with Pete.

The smell of greasy bacon-burgers drifted out of the Jack in the Box. I watched the traffic and thought about Kevin's occult explanation of why AIDS had happened and recalled other crackpot theories I'd heard over the years. One of the weirdest—from Sidney (New Year's Eve, '89)—was the God-as-gourmet theory. It's not a matter of divine punishment, just a simple desire for gastronomic variety. God gets hungry for souls, that's all, and in the 1940s, it was kosher fare. In the 1980s He developed a craving for queers. *Bon appétit*, Lord. And by all means, have another African—you prepared way too many. Guess your eyes were bigger than your stomach.

I began to feel odd—a buzzing sensation in my solar plexus. Of course, I hadn't eaten all day. The buzzing moved up, through my chest, down my arms, up the back of my neck. My scalp tingled. Headlights began smearing, leaving colorful trailers. I rubbed my eyes. I wanted to believe it was just exhaustion. But my nerves were too charged. Sounds—car engines, brakes—were turning shrill, Dolbyized. My heart was pounding. I was jacked up. Someone had slipped something in my Roy Rogers.

"Goddamn you, Kevin. Shit."

I hadn't taken anything like this since . . . 1975. In San Francisco. Psilocybin. With Kevin.

"You asshole. You fucking dick."

There was no point in fighting it though. That could make things bad. So I tried to stay calm. And after ten or fifteen minutes, when I could still tell it had *been* ten or fifteen minutes, and the high-rise insurance buildings along Wilshire hadn't melted or been sucked off into outer space, I felt a guarded sense of relief. It was either mescaline or a fairly weak dose of acid. So I wouldn't be disintegrating into the Wilshire District. I wouldn't be ending the night in the USC General psych ward. If I avoided eye contact, I doubted that anyone would know I was losing my mind.

A short, dark Hispanic woman approached the bus bench and with some hesitation sat down as far from me as pos-

sible. Indian. Guatemalan or Salvadoran, I guessed. Like
the maids who waited for the bus along Channel Road in
Santa Monica Canyon. I could feel her checking me out,
not fearfully, but as if she didn't want to get involved in
anything weird. I realized I was tapping my foot compulsively. I tried to stop but couldn't. I considered saying
something to her but decided against it. She was turning
into an ancient wise matriarch whose sons had been butchered by death squads. What did she care what some nervous
Anglo guy in a Butthole Surfers T-shirt thought about anything? It was a shame that people didn't talk to each other
more though.

A yellow Corvette slid up to the curb, a man with styled
blond hair at the wheel leaning over to the passenger window. Early thirties, handsome in a plastic Texas kind of
way, a gold wristwatch, Herb Alpert on the radio, "This
Guy's in Love."

"Need a lift?"

"No, thanks."

Blue eyes. Looked a bit like that late porno star, Casey
what's-his-name, whatever his real name was. Huge dick,
no doubt. A voice in the back of my mind, like a friend
imposing his tastes on me: Are you *crazy?* You're passing
up a chance to—

"Are you sure?" he said. Fuck-film eyes. Come back to
my condo, poppers, this guy's in love, with himself, with
cologne, ask you to spend the night, but—

"Yeah, I'm sure. I'm waiting for my mother."

"Okay." A shrug, a wry smile. He slid away. Corvettes.
Tacky cars. Yellow. Tacky color.

I looked at the Hispanic woman. Blank, stoical, couldn't
see her eyes. Could she tell from that exchange that I'm
maricone? Should I have been firmer? Fuck off, homo. No.
He's still my gay brother, even if he's tacky. Fuck what she
thinks anyway, fucking Catholic homophobic spicstress.
Son's probably a gay-basher. Don't lay your death-squad
guilt trip on me, baby. I'm not some bleeding-heart westside yuppie. You're sitting next to a *queer*, señora, and
we've got our *own problems*.

134

"You know what time bus come?" she said to me.

"No, I don't."

She sighed. "Long wait."

I felt like a turd. She was just a sweet old woman putting up with a lot of shit that I couldn't even imagine. Life wasn't easy for anybody.

Were *was* this fucking bus though? I was starting to lose track of time. It seemed that at least a half hour had passed. I could see cars leaving the Ambassador. Maybe I should hitch. What if Kevin came along? I was going to have to be mad at him. It really was fucked up to dose someone. I watched apprehensively for his white rental car, hoping like anything the bus would come first.

Then I saw a car I knew: Pablo's 1956 Mercedes convertible, the fat grill with the emblems, the primered olive green paint, the canvas top down. I got up as it swept over to the curb. *Definitely* had to still be mad at Pablo. But it was Pete at the wheel.

"If you're coming, come on!" he called. "There's traffic!"

I got in and he pulled out. It happened so fast I didn't have to time to decide what it meant. The car had a raunchy mildewed-leather smell I remembered from the year before. On the boulevard ahead of us the high-rise buildings were starting to sway, as if a silent earthquake were taking place. I found it hard to look at Pete. The mescaline was stripping away some sort of polite perception barrier, and I saw more pain in his face than I'd ever been aware of. He looked as if he were about to cry, or as if he had just cried hard. I realized this was one of the subconscious reasons I loved him.

"I guess you didn't like the song," he said.

"Which song?" Pablo must have told him I was there, but he didn't seem angry.

"The encore."

"I didn't hear any encore. I left during 'Baader-Meinhof.' "

He moaned. "Oh, Tim! *No!* You missed one of the key epiphanous moments of your life."

"What do you mean?"

"I did our song. I did 'I Wanna Be Your Dog.' Except I did it like I've never done it before. I did it exactly the way Bryan Ferry would do it. If he were insane or something. On crack. Or in rapture."

"Like my idea—"

"*Of course,* like your idea. That was the whole point. It was amazing. At first the other guys didn't know what I was doing. Then they got into it completely. Pablo and Soren doing this weird Chili Peppers thing. Except it was more like Sonic Youth backing Bryan Ferry foaming at the mouth."

"Foaming at the mouth?"

"I went way over the top, Tim. And that's not all. I made up all kinds of new lyrics, new verses. Stuff aimed directly at you. It got so intense it was like this huge magnet. I almost expected it to suck you right up to the stage."

"It sounds interesting. I'm sorry I missed it."

"*Interesting?* Jesus Christ, I was laying my fucking heart on the line!"

I didn't know what to say. I hadn't prepared for this. And visually he was starting to *look like* Bryan Ferry, shockingly handsome, suavely romantic, the wind blowing through his shiny black hair as we made a sudden, sweeping turn off Wilshire.

Then we were streaming down a cool, quiet street lined with stately 1930s apartment buildings, pictorialized by the mescaline into a stunning von Sternberg set.

"I laid it all out," he said. "The whole thing on me and you. In one tight verse right after the other. I don't know how I did it, Tim, off the top of my head like that. Except I felt it was my last chance to get it across to you. And by the end I was *begging.*"

"Begging? For what?"

"Oh, come *on!* You know the song. Do you need it in block letters? *I wanna be your dog!*"

I got it in block letters, big translucent, three-dimensional block letters floating out of his mouth: I WANNA BE YOUR DOG. When his features started changing into a Pluto-like cartoon-dog face, I looked away.

"Are you okay?" he said.

"Yeah, but I don't understand. What do you mean, you wanna be my dog? What does that *mean?*"

"It means I give up. It means I roll over."

"*What?*"

"Okay." He sighed. "It means I've missed you a lot, Tim. It means you still really get on my nerves, but at least when we were together, we also had fun a lot of the time."

"It doesn't mean you want me to keep you in a dog collar, does it? Like an S&M scene."

"Not unless you want to."

"No! I mean, I don't think so. I mean, that stuff scares me."

"Tim, I was kidding. It's an *expression*, that's all. A metaphor. I don't want to be kept in a dog collar. It wouldn't work out. I've got too many things to do. If you'd heard the song you'd understand."

"Okay."

He pulled over at the top of a rise by a golf course. "Tim, look at me."

I did, and he looked human again, but illustrated: a compulsively detailed realistic drawing, every whisker meticulously dotted in. The smooth slopes of the golf course looked illustrated, too: the black-green of the grass and trees, the black-blue of the star-filled sky. An animated biplane buzzed across the downtown skyline.

"Look, I don't believe in magical solutions," he said. "We're both flawed. We both have character defects. I *know* I'm passive-aggressive. I'm well aware of that. And you've got a mouth problem. You still really irritate me . . . at times . . . But we might as well be together, 'cause at least there's some fun then. Otherwise, we're both just alone and thinking pissed-off thoughts about each other, which seems like a waste. I've missed you a lot, and I don't know, I'm probably deranged, but even today, even though you said some really fucked-up, unforgivable things . . . I don't know. We're both gonna have to try a lot harder."

He was giving me exactly what I wanted, but instead of being elated I almost freaked.

"But what if it doesn't work out again?" I said. "I don't think I could go through that again."

"Okay." He was breathing hard. "You're going to make me say it, aren't you? I love you. There, I said it. Are you satisfied?"

"Yes. I love you, too."

"I know."

The next thing I knew we were kissing, making out like you wouldn't believe. And for the first time ever we were kissing deeply. I'd never really understood why we'd drawn the line on that before, sticking to the dry, safe-sex approach, since we'd been seriously blowing each other. It probably had less to do with health risk than some feeling about emotional intimacy. But that line was crossed now, and kissing Pete like that completely leveled me. I felt as if my brain, my heart, my entire body, was on the verge of an orgasm. It was so astonishing I got scared for a second, until I looked in Pete's eyes and knew it was "real," that however much the drug might be enhancing what I felt, I wasn't just lost in some private delusion.

Looking in my eyes, Pete said, "Tim, are you on something?"

"Yes. I think it's mescaline. I think Kevin dosed me."

"Kevin?"

"Kevin Saunders. I didn't realize you and he—"

"Oh, yeah," Pete said. "We go back a long way. Are you okay? Jesus."

When Pete touched the curve of my chest, it felt so good I had to groan. My cock was so hard it felt like it could shatter.

"I'm fine," I said. "It's been a while, but I can handle it. I used to toss back tabs of Blue Cheer with my breakfast juice. Ever seen a homeroom teacher turn into Vishnu?"

"Are you sure? This isn't the Summer of Love."

"Neither was the Summer of Love. I could tell you some very grisly stories."

"We could have one of our own tonight." He gave me a final wet kiss and turned back to the wheel.

"What do you mean? Where are we going, incidentally?"

Pete pulled out. "If all goes well, back to your place soon. If I'm not being presumptuous."

"That's a thirty-minute drive. I don't know if I can last that long. I'm kind of close to shooting off right now."

"Oh, yeah?" He grinned and squeezed my cock through my trunks.

I groaned and removed his hand. "I'm actually not kidding."

"Look," he said, "I'd like nothing better than to drive straight back to your place and, once we got inside the door, press you back against the wall and pull your trunks down and—"

"Stop. I don't want to talk it, I just want to do it. I want to be with you so bad I feel like I'm panting."

"I want that, too, Tim, believe me."

At a red light he gave me a long, horrendous kiss. When I squeezed his denim crotch and felt his hot, fat erection pressed against his groin, it shocked me so much it was like I'd never touched another man before.

"But I'll feel guilty," he said, "if I don't check on Joey first."

Oh, no. "Joey?"

"Yeah, he called the club and left a message. Soren took it. I'm not sure what's going on. But it sounds like he scored some speed and shot up but it's not working."

"Not working?"

"He wishes he hadn't done it. I shouldn't give a shit, but I do. I know how hard he tried to stay clean, but it's a very addictive drug."

"So what are you going to do?"

"I'm just going to talk to him. If he really wants to stop again, we can take him by Brian's. A guy he likes on the program in West Hollywood. He can stay there. Don't worry. I'm not going to invite him to come back with us."

"Why not?" I leaned back in the seat, trying to cool down. "Is he cute?"

"Extremely. Too cute. That's part of his problem."

"We could have a three-way. You, me, and a cute speed freak. With blood dripping down his arm."

Pete took my hand. "Look, I'm sorry. But I have to do this."

"I know, I'm just kidding. I understand."

In a while Pete took a left, heading north up Larchmont, through a deserted business area that set off a memory jag of walking the same empty street late at night after a dance in 1971. When we came to a small bright café that was still open, Pete pulled into one of the diagonal parking spots. "I'm gonna run in and snag something to go. You eaten anything?"

"No."

"You wanna come in and look at the heterosexuals? Might be fun on mescaline."

"No. I'm bored with straight people. It's always the same old shit. I'll wait here and listen to the radio. I feel a nostalgia binge coming on."

I watched Pete go into the yuppie café. I sat up and played with the radio dial till I came to "Brown Sugar." Perfect. One of the songs we used to dance to at . . . Jesus, was that it right there, two doors down from the café? It had been a long time, but I kind of remembered the glass door, the stairway. I was almost positive—yes, that had been Larchmont Hall. I got out and walked over, the Rolling Stones song bringing back a flood of images of men dancing, stomping, shaking the floor upstairs. Some of what I saw was slightly embarrassing. The long, stringy hair of 1971, the striped bell-bottoms. But I saw other images— a blond-bearded kid's wet erection jutting up against his tie-dye T-shirt—that made me glad I'd been eighteen then instead of now.

The hall was some sort of Hindu-sect place now. The glass door was unlocked, the stairs inside bright and clean. What harm could it do to take a look?

"Brown Sugar" faded as the glass door swung shut behind

me. As I climbed the stairs, I smelled sandalwood incense. Suddenly my mind seemed loud and raucous.

At the top of the stairs I saw the hall itself. Light and airy now, spotless cream-colored walls. Rows of meditation pillows on the floor where young men had once sweated and yowled. There was a shrine in the back with flowers and a photo of a bearded swami where the huge speakers had once stood. To the left in 1971 there'd been a small lounge with old sofas. This was a bookshop now, displaying spiritual texts with serene sky-blue covers. I remembered making out with a young Jewish guy in the lounge one night, making out for hours. His full, sensuous, creamy mouth, his soft, curly brown hair—like Jeff's. We'd had no place to go, both of us having straight roommates. So we'd ended up having the make-out party we'd missed when we were fifteen.

An Indian woman in a blue sari came out of what had once been the bar, where men in genderfuck, beards and dresses, had struck poses for a *Life* magazine photographer. She recoiled as our eyes met. "We're closed now."

"That's all right," I said as gently as I could to reassure her. "I was just taking a look. This place used to be something else."

This seemed to bother her. "You have to go."

A dark Indian man came out of the same room, scowling angrily as if we already knew each other, as if I'd done something to him. "Go!" he said. "Leave. Get out!"

"Okay. Take it down a notch." I couldn't help but laugh at his cartoon anger. I hadn't done anything, after all. I went down the stairs.

Pete was waiting at the car. "What were you doing?"

"Just looking." I got in the car and he handed me a croissant stuffed with something that looked like chicken and semen. I indicated the hall. "That's where the gay lib dances used to be." I looked at the croissant. "This isn't jiz, is it?"

"Yeah, they've got a bunch of Syrian guys beating off in

the kitchen," Pete said. "No, it's chicken divan or something."

I took a bite, trying not to think about the Syrian guys. Pete started the engine.

"The people up there were very strange," I said as we pulled out. "Do you think physical locations contain the vibrations of past events?"

"Yeah, sure. We've talked about this. Like taking acid at Auschwitz."

"Right." The first time he'd thrown that idea at me I'd cringed. We'd agreed that you wouldn't have to be on acid to feel what had happened at Auschwitz.

"Because they're meditating up there now," I said. "It's some sort of Hindu place."

"They're probably seeing visions of a lot of sweaty guys with hard-ons."

"That's the way it was, you know. But it was really pretty ecstatic."

"I know. You've told me," Pete said. "Whitmanic."

"Well, it was. There was a different energy then. There was a lot of sex but it wasn't jaded."

"Dionysian?"

"That's a trick word. No, I'd say it was a lot of people feeling good about themselves for the first time in their lives. That was the best time, really, the early gay lib days. There was a bohemian spirit, you know. In a sense, it was still the sixties."

"Blakean, huh?"

"In a way it was," I said. "The end of repression. Making love in the sun-drenched ruins of the church. You wouldn't understand. You were still getting a boner over David Cassidy in the 'Partridge Family.' "

"I believe you," Pete said. "It was like that in San Francisco at first. Till the second wave came. The clones."

"So I hear you played Rimbaud to Kevin's Verlaine."

He smiled. "Yeah, I guess. I was pretty crazy then. It was scary though. When you're sixteen a lot of things can happen. I was lucky to meet Kevin. I don't know why he put up with me as long as he did though."

"He had it, you know."

"Had what?"

"AIDS. But he told me he's cured. He went to Morocco and invoked the sun. Don't ask me what that means."

"Sounds like Crowley stuff," Pete said. "I thought that was just a phase he went through."

"He seems to be back into it again. He said he'd tested negative, after having been positive. Do you think that's possible?"

"I don't know. Maybe. Who knows?"

"He said the whole thing was caused by people's bad thoughts. Hatred aimed at gays like negative prayer."

"I can see that in a way," Pete said. "If people allow themselves to be magnets for that kind of shit. But the best defense is an offense. That's what still pisses me off about most homos though. ACT UP and Queer Nation don't go nearly far enough. I agree with Larry Kramer. They're just putting on street skits. It's Mickey and Judy in pink-triangle shirts. They should've gone into Saint Patrick's with sub-machine guns. Here in L.A., they should kidnap Mahony and gut him. They should go into the Vatican, remove the fag art, and dynamite the place. Douse the pope with gas-oline, set him on fire. But most gay men are still suck-ups. They're still into playing victim and martyr, which is just what people want to see. Be a good little faggot and mince on off to the hospice and pay the price for your sins. Fuck *that* shit. Why should *we* always be nonviolent? That's why I've had it with these fucking AIDS vultures like Louise Hay and Marianne Williamson. Hug a teddy bear, boys, and visualize Bambi, till you're too weak to cross the room, let alone pick up a gun. George Bush couldn't come up with a better containment plan."

Normally this kind of rant wouldn't have alarmed me. I'd heard most of it before. But this time the mescaline began changing his features so that he looked like a were-wolf—murderous, psychotic.

"Am I upsetting you?" he said.

"Kind of."

"Sorry." He smiled and—*magically*—the craziness went

away. He was a blue-eyed seaman in need of a shave now, a fresh young Jack London, as portrayed by Jason Patric, in a glistening, sublimating Joel Schumacher film.

"I think you're being a bit unfair about Marianne," I said.

He shrugged. "Look, I know she does good work, schlepping meals to people. But I still think all those Hollywood power fags who are into her are vile flesh-eating slime."

"I can't disagree."

Pete switched on the radio: New Order's euphoric "True Faith," a song I'd played obsessively in my car during the celibate years.

"The Day the World Went Queer," he said. "I was thinking of that the other day."

"Oh, right. That was funnier a few years ago though. Before the word *queer* got sucked dry."

"It's still funny," he said. "If you see it as a fifties film title. Searing red letters against an L.A. skyline."

It was a science fiction parody based on the paranoid right-wing notion that if homosexuality were "condoned," it would spread like wildfire through the entire population. So all these Ozzie Nelson–type dads would suddenly start mincing and cruising each other over their lawn mowers, and June Cleaver would turn into a ducktailed lesbian, and Wally would come down to dinner wearing nothing but a cock ring, and so on. At a certain point, of course, they'd have to call in the army—but all the officers and soldiers would turn out to be fags.

"Yeah, I pitched that idea at Disney once," I said. "That's the real reason I got thrown out of Jeff Katzenberg's office."

"Kevin would do it."

"He's quit making films. He thinks it's too late for art."

In a moment, Pete said, obviously quoting, " 'I dragged myself through stinking alleys. And, eyes closed, I gave myself to the sun, God of fire.' "

"What's that from?"

"A Season in Hell. That's probably what Kevin did. Gave himself to the sun."

I didn't know what to say except, "Yeah, it sounds like it."

* * *

Candy-colored lights on the trendy strip of Melrose. Morrissey on KROQ, "Girlfriend in a Coma." Pete wanted to change it, but I said, "Come on, I like this. This song was the 'Georgy Girl' of the eighties."

Pete sneered. "He needs to sit on a dick."

"Come on. He was my idol during the celibate years."

"Who's your idol now?"

"You."

"That's sweet." His sardonic tone reminded me of Jeff, of once discreetly trying to hold Jeff's hand on a plane. Jeff, embarrassed, making a face.

"Jeff died."

"The guy you had the celibate thing with."

"Yeah. Kevin told me. The memorial was today."

"I'm sorry."

"I am, too." I saw Jeff making coffee in his Venice kitchen in '84, recalled the conversation we'd had. "It's strange."

"What?"

"I remember Jeff saying the same thing you used to say. That if he ever got it, he'd take someone with him."

Pete was silent. I could tell he was censoring himself.

"Of course, that was a long time ago," I said. "I guess it's one thing to say that when you're fine, but . . ."

"I think a lot of guys have those thoughts," Pete said. "It's like the Kübler-Ross thing about the different stages of reaction to a terminal diagnosis."

"Oh, right. Denial, anger, bargaining . . ."

"Right. But most guys are talked out of acting on their anger."

"Which isn't necessarily a bad thing."

"Well, I can't speak for anyone else," he said, "but I know what I would've done if my test had gone the other way."

A measured response. But he sensed correctly that I was not in the mood to hear him go off on how Jeff should've driven back to Washington, D.C., with an Uzi.

145

*　*　*

I was still thinking about Jeff as we crossed La Cienega, about the trip to Puerto Vallarta right before our breakup. He'd gone down a week ahead of me with a buddy of his who was supposed to be leaving as I arrived, so I'd thought Jeff and I were going to be spending a week alone. I'd been all psyched up to overcome my fears and sleep with him again, so I was picturing a breakthrough hyperromantic idyll. But it turned out his friend was staying on. Not a bad guy, but it changed everything. Instead of two boyfriends, we were three gay buddies commenting on all the cute guys—except that I went in and out of a sullen pout all week and Jeff was sarcastic and cutting. We each had our own room in this condo Jeff had access to, and one morning I looked in on Jeff in his bedroom and watched him sleeping naked on his stomach. I'd wanted like anything to lie down next to him, to wake him up, for us to make love. But by then I knew he'd been fooling around with a number of other guys the week before I got there, doing God only knew what.

I thought about the first time I'd had sex with Jeff, at his place in Venice, a hellhole "investment house" in the Oakwood ghetto, the yellow afternoon light coming in through his barred bedroom windows. I remembered his soft brown beard, his smooth back, his hard cock, as we'd rolled around. A stray line of his from the *last* time we'd fooled around, after he'd briefly gone down on me: "I don't know how you feel about saliva." We'd never kissed at all. I'd been too paranoid to do that then.

Pete and I were in West Hollywood now. At night this empty stretch of Melrose, lined with lighted antique-store windows, set off another memory. Twelve years ago, walking to my car at two in the morning in a state of sated dejection, from . . . the white two-story building on the corner up ahead, empty now, posted with blue Coldwell Banker FOR LEASE signs.

"Know what that used to be?" I said.

"A mortuary?"

146

"No. The 8550. The most popular bathhouse in West Hollywood."

"No kidding. It looks more like a mausoleum to me." Pete took a right on the next side street and pulled up beside the building.

"What are we doing?" I said.

"This is it." He looked up at the building as he shut off the engine.

"What do you mean? This place has been closed for years."

"Yeah, but people are still using it. Homeless people, hustlers. This is where Joey was sleeping before he went to stay with his sister. You wanna wait here?"

I looked up at the building, a streetlight casting quivering palm-frond shadows against its chalky, windowless white facade.

"You're going inside?"

"I don't know. I've never actually been here before." He got out.

I hesitated, having some idea how the place might affect me on mescaline. Knowing how it made my skin crawl driving past it in broad daylight with a clear mind. But for some reason I decided it was a piece of my past it might be good to confront. I got out. "Wait up."

We tried the battered red front door first. That was locked. The wind was picking up again, scattering leaves along the sidewalk by the rusted, empty *Advocate* news rack.

"God, I remember when there used to be lines around the block here on weekend nights," I said. "Men in tight T-shirts and 501s waiting for other men to leave—"

"Other men in tight T-shirts and 501s."

"Right. With their schlongs stuffed down their pant legs. Nobody does that anymore. Unless they've been in Yuma for the last ten years."

"They do in Silver Lake," Pete said.

"Yeah, I know. That's where old clones go to die. God, did I say that?"

"I think old clones are dying in West Hollywood, too,"

Pete said. "New clones, too. Come on, let's try around back."

Pete tried a door on the alley. Locked. A stairway led to a second-floor door. "Let's try up there."

"Speaking of West Hollywood," I said as we climbed the stairs, "you know who owned this place, don't you?"

"Yeah. *Mister* West Hollywood. Talk about scumbags. He kept this place open *for years* after people knew what was going on."

"I know. I think it sent out the wrong message at a very crucial time."

"It was unconscionable," Pete said. "The greedy pig."

"Denial, too, I'll bet. The end of a way of life."

"Yeah, his last chance to devour twenty or thirty more young guys. Fucking vampire."

"Pleasant guy in person though," I said.

"Oh, no. Do I want to hear this?"

"I met him once socially, that's all. A rather stiff, pretentious West Hollywood dinner party. A too-tasteful apartment on Hayworth, Firbank/Virginia Woolf literary chitchat, you know the scene."

"No, I don't, thank God."

"Anyway, Mr. West Hollywood was charming and mildly flirtatious and sang a slew of Noel Coward songs at the piano after dinner."

"Sounds like my kind of evening."

"Actually, it was a bit precious."

"He got what was coming to him," Pete said. "God only knows how many men were infected here. Occasionally there's some justice. I spit on his grave." He tried the door at the top of the stairs. It was unlocked. He opened it.

The first thing that hit me was the smell. Rot. Mildew. Rancid shortening.

"Jesus, it still smells like stale Crisco," I said.

"Are you getting a hard-on?"

"Give me a break."

It was pitch-black inside. Water dripping somewhere.

"What's that?" Pete said.

"What?"

"I thought I heard something." He called, "Hey, Joey? Joey?"

No response, just the water dripping. Pete called Joey's name again.

A snort in the dark, like someone imitating a pig.

"Did you hear that?" Pete said.

"Yes."

"Joey? Hey, Joey!"

Nothing.

"I'm sure I heard someone." Pete dug out his Zippo lighter and flipped it on. "Come on."

We stepped inside. The carpet felt squishy under my huaraches. And I began to feel afraid. I took Pete's arm. "I really don't like this," I said. "Anyone could be in here. Most homeless people are harmless, I think. But every once in a while there's a crazy with a knife."

"Don't worry," Pete said. "I think that guy's crouching outside Nancy Reagan's window tonight, watching her undress to take a bath."

We were moving slowly up a wide black-walled corridor.

"Do you remember the layout?" Pete said.

"Sort of. It's been a long time. I quit coming here in 1980 after I found out about the deaths."

"Deaths?"

"Guys dying in their rooms. I was pretty naive, I guess. I knew there was dope-smoking—you could smell that. But once I talked to a guy who worked at Cedars and he told me about all the men who OD'd. The attendants would find them dead in their cubicles, but not do anything till dawn when the place cleared out. You know, so they wouldn't bring down the other customers."

"That was considerate."

"Yeah, after that, it was hard to think of this as an innocent pleasure palace. Not that I ever did, really. I always had very mixed feelings about it. A lot of cruelty here. Rejection. Everybody looking for the perfect body, the biggest cock. A lot of psychic damage."

"Sounds like a fun place." Pete held his Zippo up to an open cubicle door. A stained single-bed mattress, a smudged mirror on the wall, a yellowed jar of Elbow Grease.

"It wasn't," I said. "It was actually pretty awful. The way people treated each other. As objects. Things. I don't know, I've got nothing against spontaneous sex—"

"Spontaneous?"

"You know what I mean. Anonymous—but that's so pejorative."

"You mean, like swapping blow jobs with Pablo at the beach?" Pete said.

"Yes. I don't see anything wrong with that. Morally, I mean. Sometimes, depending on the context, that sort of thing can be incredibly ecstatic and warmhearted. But something about this place always . . . I don't know, it wasn't joyful. It seemed to bring out the worst in people. It wasn't sex as catharsis or redemption, but sex as a drug. A crazed, compulsive abuse of what sex can provide. Cynical and loveless. Sex as ego gratification, as ephemeral validation. Sex as a product, something you need to feel better about yourself for a while. A new shirt, a new car, a new fuck. Capitalism. I didn't like the music either."

"Ooooh," Pete moaned sarcastically, and sang, "Love to love you, baby. Ooooh." He held his Zippo up to a wall painting: a cartoonlike illustration of a huge cock stuck in an asshole.

"I know where we are now," I said. "That's the butt-eating room up there on the left."

"The what?"

We stepped to the door. In the flickering Zippo light we saw a row of doorless stalls with low outhouse-style wooden seats.

"The butt-eating room," I said. "See, one guy would crawl down under there under the seat and—"

"I get the picture. I just don't believe it."

"Come on, spare me your Gidget routine. You know about butt-eating."

"Yeah, but this is *mass* butt-eating. There are *six stalls*."

"Yes, and there were six queues running all the way down to Robertson on Saturday nights. It *was* a bit like an as-

150

sembly line, I'm afraid. Monitors with stopwatches. *Bing*. Your ten minutes are up. Move 'em up, clean 'em out. Keep those butts arollin'."

Pete laughed but said, "That's deranged."

"I thought so, too, actually. I wouldn't admit this to a lot of people—they'd think I was a prude. Well, maybe not now. But I've never actually eaten a butt."

"I have," Pete said as we stepped back into the corridor. "But not recently. And I was in love."

For a moment I thought I smelled perfume. That didn't make sense though. I tried to get my bearings. "I think that's the glory-hole room up there on the right."

"Is that where *you* camped out?"

"Be nice to me, will you?" I said. "I'm in a delicate state. And this place is already starting to give me the horrors."

We stepped up to the glory-hole room and suddenly the lights came on, weak, buzzing overhead fluorescent lights.

"Jesus," I said. "Did you do that?"

"Yeah, there's a switch here." He pocketed his lighter.

I'd never seen the bathhouse in this much light before. The stalls in the glory-hole room were hospital green, the carpet rust colored, badly stained. Crud everywhere, trash, a decomposing orange condom.

"Still romantic though," Pete said.

One of the lights was flickering severely, setting off a wave of translucent hallucinations, colorful, busily moving Keith Haring designs.

"This reminds me of UCLA," Pete said.

"What do you mean?"

"The men's room in the student union. Where I caught Carlos."

"Oh, right."

Pete had paid Carlos a surprise campus visit at lunchtime, but Carlos wasn't on the patio where he usually ate. An "odious queen" friend of Carlos's had tipped Pete off: "I think I know where you can find her." In the men's room, which Pete described as "bright but filthy, like the gutted housing project in *A Clockwork Orange*," he'd caught Carlos fondling another man at the urinals. "You scum-fuck!"

Pete had yelled at Carlos. "You sick beaner slime!" And had started hitting him, finally chasing Carlos out through the study hall. Later, Pete said, he'd tried to take a more compassionate view, realizing that Carlos was addicted to that kind of sex the same way Pete had been addicted to drugs and alcohol.

"Have you talked to Carlos at all?" I said.

"No." Pete looked away. "He's dead."

"Oh, Jesus. AIDS?"

"No. He was murdered."

"You're kidding."

"No. Last fall. Right before I moved to Laguna. The cops came to see me."

"Are you making this up?"

"No. I wish I were."

"What happened?"

"He was stabbed. Something like nineteen times. At his place in Mar Vista. With one of his own kitchen knives. Apparently by someone he knew. Like a crime-of-passion situation. That's why the cops came to see me."

"Did they know about your song?"

"No, no. There're only a few people who have any idea that song's about Carlos."

"Jesus, Pete. That's actually kind of terrifying. I mean, the prescience."

The song, "Seventeen Lies," which Pete had written at least a year *before* Carlo's death, had a verse that went:

> *You broke seventeen hearts*
> *You told seventeen lies*
> *Now somebody's stabbed you seventeen times*
> *I fell in love with you*
> *I'll bet that he did, too*
> *Now you're dead at the scene*
> *Of your seventeen crimes*

"I know," Pete said. "I was very freaked when I heard about his death. I wouldn't sing that song at all for a long time. But then I decided, it wasn't like I'd *caused* Carlos's murder by writing that song. If anything, I think I just picked up on something in the air around him. The way he treated people, he inspired that kind of murderous rage. *I* wrote a song about it. But I think he finally fucked over someone who didn't have a creative outlet."

"They don't know who did it?"

"No. I have some theories. This guy Bill, right before me—he got it a lot worse than I did. At least I had some warning. I mean, Carlos and I had been having problems for a while before the UCLA incident. But with Bill it was very sudden. Everything was great—perfect love and intimacy. Then he came home one day and Carlos had moved out. No note, no explanation, nothing."

"Jesus. Why was Carlos like that?"

"Well, I know he'd been fucked over himself really bad once. So I guess he was just passing it on. It took me a long time to believe this, but I don't think Carlos was even intentionally evil. I think the better part of him wanted to be close to someone. But at a certain point he got scared and had to fuck over the other guy before he could be hurt himself."

"I felt like that's what you did to me," I said. "I thought about killing *you* once, you know. I drove by your house one night about a month after we broke up. I wasn't armed or anything, but I was pretty overwrought. Jealous. Wondering if you were already with somebody else. Your house was dark though. Your car wasn't there."

"It was probably the night I drove by your place."

"Yeah, right. We probably just missed each other. What was on *your* mind?"

"I had this huge knife under the seat." Pete slid his hand across my back. "No, just kidding. I don't know. I missed you. I felt like I'd made a mistake."

"You had."

"I *know* that, Tim. And I was ready to admit it. I had this idea that you'd open the door, and without saying a word, we'd just start kissing."

"I wish I'd been home."

Pete shrugged. "Yeah, but I decided I was deluded. It seemed like too much of a fantasy. I thought *you* might've met someone else. I would've felt like a dork if you'd opened the door and there was some other guy there."

"What would you have done?"

"Probably the same thing I did anyway. Cry all the way home." He said this as if it were a joke, but I thought of his song, and I wanted to kiss him, but not here.

That's when we heard something in one of the stalls—it sounded like clothes rustling—and I felt a rush of embarrassment, imagining a homeless person huddled in there, listening to our conversation.

Pete opened the squeaky stall door and I quaked. The stall was empty, but for one demented moment I thought someone was in the next stall, dangling his limp cock through the glory hole—his limp gray cock, like Gerald Bryer's, his limp, gray, twitching cock with something hanging from the end of it, like a swaying tail. It was *a rat!*

"Whoa!" I jumped back. Pete did, too. We scrambled out to the hall. I was completely freaked. Pete was laughing.

"Oh, God, oh, Jesus," I said, still cringing. "I hate those fucking things."

"Come on, Tim. That could be Mr. West Hollywood reincarnated."

"That makes sense. Or Carlos."

"That makes sense, too, unfortunately." Pete put his arm around me. "Are you okay?"

"Yeah, I'm fine." My heart was still pounding. "But I'd like to move on soon. This place is really starting to bother me."

Pete walked over to the stairwell at the end of the hallway and called down, "Joey? Hey, Joey!"

It was dark at the bottom of the stairs.

"What's down there?" Pete said. "The fistfucking room? Thirty bathtubs in a row for piss and scat?"

"No, this wasn't that kind of place. Just the showers, as I recall. And the entrance to hell. I want to go."

"Yeah, okay. I still think there's somebody here though."

We started up the corridor, the flickering lights setting off cartoon Egyptoid designs now. The black walls looked wet. I could *feel* them oozing decade-old despair.

"This place should be razed," I said. "That's Todd's idea. They should level it and put in a park with a plaque like they did with that McDonald's in San Ysidro where that guy killed all those people."

"Or turn it into a hospice," Pete said. "Plenty of beds. Name it after Mr. West Hollywood."

A snort in the distance.

Pete stopped. "You hear *that?*"

"Yes. But let's just go."

Another snort. But not a snort exactly. A snore.

Pete looked down a side corridor. "It's coming from over there."

"The orgy room."

We made our way through the dingy mirror maze into the room where there'd always been just a single weak red overhead light. Now, under the fluorescent tubes, the black walls were streaked with frosted semen trails, the carpet wet and spongy, and on the king-size mattress where thousands of men had fucked, a huge fat man in a cream-colored jumpsuit was sleeping on his back, reeking of Chanel No. 5. The scent was overwhelming, a bottle spilled or broken. It reminded me of my mother. The man had a fat, fleshy face, a fifty-year-old baby face, and thin, wispy hair like you'd see on a chemotherapy patient.

Pete nudged his shoulder. "Hey. *Hey.*"

He opened his eyes and moaned. "Oh. Oh, my."

"Hey, come on. Wake up."

I finally realized what Pete already knew, that this was Mother Dwayne from Long Beach. His brown eyes were watery, his jelly face quivering. He sat up. "Oh, my God, where am I?" He spoke with a soft Southern drawl.

"In the Flamingo Hotel," Pete said. "Where's Joey?"

Mother Dwayne put a small pudgy hand to his brow. "Oh, what happened?" He sniffed. "Someone's been into my Chanel." He looked around the mattress. "Where *is* my bag?" He found it, a white Leatherette bag, its contents, including the perfume bottle, spilled on the floor. He leaned over to pick up his things and almost lost his balance.

"Look, do you know where Joey went?" Pete said.

"Oh." Mother Dwayne reeled back onto the mattress, fingers to his temples, as if his head were spinning. "Please, I never want to hear that name again. This is all her doing. And I fear now I've been robbed as well." He touched his head. "Where's my hairdo? My Elizabeth Taylor wig. Why would they take *that*?"

Pete was disgusted. "Look, Joey left a message for me around ten saying that he was coming here with you. Do you have an idea of what's going on? I'm really tired of these fucking games."

"Oh. Please don't shout, darlin'," Mother Dwayne said. "Can't you see I'm not a well woman tonight? I'm a fading flower of the South in great distress." He tried to focus on us. "I sense that you men are not evil, unlike the others."

"*What* others?" Pete said, bored and pissed off.

"I shudder. The last thing Mother Dwayne recalls is that awful pack of beasts, young brutes, appealing though they might be on a purely physical plane. Which only goes to show what appearances are worth."

"These were friends of Joey's?" Pete said.

"If that evil child can be said to have friends. She tricked me. She used me heartlessly, I see that only too well now. She promised me things which she did not deliver." A stagy gasp. "*You* must be Pete. Yes, he spoke quite lovingly of you. Yes, you *are* on the side of good in this world. I still believe there's some goodness in everyone, despite the mounting evidence to the contrary." He looked at me. "And what's *your* name, my noble young prince?"

Translucent worms in his rubbery face. "Almo."

"*Almo.* Oh, darlin', I sense you're having fun at Mother Dwayne's expense. Please don't do that. So many have."

The Chanel was becoming unbearable, setting off a chain of childhood impressions. Cackling housewife canasta parties, the sharp reek of the perfume meant to mask another, ranker bathroom odor. "Mom, what's that *horrible smell?*" "Shush, Timmy. Mildred's had an *accident* with her *period.*" "Her *what?*" And then for one truly ghastly moment Mother Dwayne *became* my mother. It was all I could do not to cry out: Oh, no, God. Not here.

"Where were you when Joey called me?" Pete said to Mother Dwayne.

"Oh, a house. A horrible house. A dreadful Hollywood bungalow on De Longpre. The abode of a hideously reptilian Latino. Mother Dwayne was reminded of the Night Stalker. But she took out her lavender billfold and produced two hundred dollars, and he returned with the crystal. And that, I fear, is where the real trouble started. For no sooner had Miss Josephine injected herself than she began to behave most erratically. At first she blamed our host, disparaging the quality of his wares. Voices were raised, which Mother Dwayne always abhors. Then Miss Josephine excused herself to use the facilities, where she could be heard retching quite severely. And then, it would seem, she used the telephone in the bedroom to call you. A call which was cut short by an angry reptilian Latino who reminded Mother Dwayne of a man who slashed window screens and the pale throats of women. Soon thereafter we departed. In Mother Dwayne's cream-colored Cadillac Seville, on Santa Monica Boulevard somewhere between LaBrea and Fairfax, the girl who had by now fully revealed herself to be the Bad Seed pitched the works out the window. *Well.* Mother Dwayne is above all else a lady, despite her occasional poor judgment in the choice of companions. And a lady, it is well known, does not inject *herself* with crystal Methedrine. And so as the works flew out the window, on their wings flew my dream of stolen bliss. A lady never snorts a drug, it's unbecoming. Words were exchanged in Mother Dwayne's cream-colored luxury car. In a gesture of appeasement—a false gesture I now see—the Bad Seed assured Mother Dwayne that a new hypodermic syringe could be procured. A blessing, it seemed. For in truth, in the rush of desire at the reptile's abode, Mother Dwayne might well have exposed herself to unsanitary conditions leading to an eventual illness too dire to name."

"That's quite likely," Pete said.

"We stopped at a phone booth. Then we came here. The evil one produced a pill, which she claimed was a mild tranquilizer. I vaguely remember the wild ones' arrival. All were quite appealing, each in his own boyish, bare-chested way. Though Mother Dwayne could only recoil at the harsh butch words uttered by their hairy-chested scoutmaster. A mature and achingly handsome stud, though clearly over the edge on an ungodly cocktail of Methedrine and testosterone."

"Shit," Pete said under his breath. *"Glenn."*

"I fear they've stolen my cream-colored dream car. As well as my dreams for tonight."

Pete dug some change out of his pocket. "Look, is there someone you can call to come get you?"

"I suppose. If I can think of a good enough reason for certain so-called friends to come all the way up from Long Beach. Perhaps I'll simply tell them the two of you are waiting here. Like angels in this pit of hell."

"I think there's a phone across the street," Pete said. "Are you okay? Do you want us to call for you?"

"No." Mother Dwayne turned wistful. "No, I'm in no hurry. I suppose I should be gloating that here I am at last. You know, Mother Dwayne once tried to gain entry to this establishment in the long-ago times, and a cruel young man turned her away. A reference was made to her then merely plump full figure, a remark which, due to its brutality, I shall not repeat. But those thoughtless words are still etched in my heart like a scar. Mother Dwayne fled down the stairs in humiliated tears through a gauntlet of sniggering perfect young men. Still, I hold no grudge. With poignancy, I reflect tonight on the fate of many of those who laughed at me. I would not wish that, even on them. But perhaps they will return to me tonight. Mother Dwayne believes in such things. Perhaps they're sorry now for the way they behaved. Perhaps they will return and plead my forgiveness. Which, with an open heart, I will gladly grant." He lay back down on the stained mattress, a hand shielding his eyes. "Do me one favor, honey lambs. As you take your leave, do shut off these frightful lights."

We made our way back to the door. Despite Mother Dwayne's request, Pete left the lights on. "Otherwise, he'll never find his way out of here."

From the top of the back stairs we saw Mother Dwayne's cream-colored Cadillac parked in the alley below.

"Should we tell him it's still here?" I said.

"I don't think he can miss it."

We looked back down the flickering corridor as we heard Mother Dwayne softly singing to himself the old Donna Summer disco hit "I Feel Love." Pete gently closed the battered black door.

ELEVEN

IT WAS good to get out of there, to be moving again, back
in the comfortably caved-in leather seat of the surging convertible. We headed south on Robertson, streaming past
the designer shops filled with Southwestern and Chinese
furniture, out of West Hollywood. The warm night air
rolled over me, wiping away the memory of the smothering
perfume.

"What a character," I said. "*Mother Dwayne*. It's guys
like him who made me want to go straight. You know, back
before gay lib, when I thought that's what it meant to be
an older gay man."

"Mother Tim." Pete laughed mock-sarcastically.

"Mother Pete." I did the same laugh. And thought of
Victor in his purple caftan. I pictured him dead drunk by
now in a Santa Fe armchair, "Send in the Clowns" still
playing. Or perhaps he'd gone out and picked up a trick.
Or hired a hustler. Yes, I could see that. Victor passed out
naked on the Navaho bedspread, River Phoenix—no,
Kevin Bacon—going through his wallet.

"So who's Glenn?" I said.

"He's an artist. Taught at CalArts until recently. He got
fired a few months ago. He lived in Venice for a long time."

"Is that where you know him from?"

"Yeah. We had an affair in 1980. Then we were friends
for a long time after that—up till '84, when I came into

160

AA. We had kind of a falling out at that point, because Glenn was still using tons of drugs, with no thought of stopping. As much I liked him, I couldn't be around that."

"Was he using speed then?"

"Yeah, but he wasn't shooting it yet. I think he just started doing that a few years ago. His boyfriend died. Rick. They'd been together ten years. After that it was like he just didn't care anymore. Then about a year ago, I guess right after you and I broke up, he showed up at a meeting. With Joey."

"So he and Joey were involved at that point?"

"Yeah. The three of us hung out together a lot last summer. Going to meetings and all that, before I moved to Laguna. The thing is, I still really like Glenn when he's sober. *I'd missed him.* His sensibility, his humor. Aesthetically, we were very good for each other. Glenn *incites* me. You know how some people tend to be censorious? Always saying, 'Oh, no, you can't do *that?*' Well, Glenn's just the opposite, which I need sometimes."

"What's his last name?" I said.

"Kunkel."

"Oh, Jesus. The guy who made the exploding madonna. I read about that."

"Actually, it was a baby Jesus that exploded. Yeah, he caught an unbelievable amount of flak over that. That's why he lost his job."

"It was at an art-for-AIDS opening."

"Yeah, that's what flipped out a lot of people—even those who would've understood in a way if the people who got splashed had been obvious enemies. But instead, they felt Glenn was deliberately terrifying and alienating the very people who were already sympathetic."

"Which is certainly a valid point," I said. "Because it was a roomful of rich art collectors, with all of the proceeds going to AIDS research. And then to have a plastic doll explode—"

"It was made of rubber, actually. The head kept expanding like a bicycle tire."

"But to have it explode and drench everyone with what

they *thought* was AIDS-infected blood—that really seems over the edge."

"Well, that's kind of Glenn's specialty."

It occurred to me that Pete's tactic with Gerald Bryer might have well been inspired, if only unconsciously, by Glenn's precedent. I recalled reading that Glenn had yelled the same sort of thing at the horrified, blood-splattered gallery crowd: "You've all got it now! Now you can *really* empathize! 'Cause you're going to die *too*, you smug [expletive deleted in the *L.A. Times*]!"

"Yeah, Glenn's always been pretty radical," Pete said. "He hates all those people anyway—the dealers, the collectors, the whole art-as-investment scene. His main regret was that he had to admit it was only pig's blood, and offer an apology, in order to avoid prosecution. That pissed him off, 'cause he felt it was tantamount to saying he was only kidding."

"Some joke."

"Yeah, I have mixed feelings about it myself," Pete said. "I don't like to say it, I'm not comfortable being censorious. But Glenn does go too far even for me at times."

"I didn't think that was possible."

"Well, music is a different medium. But I do draw certain lines."

"Where? I haven't noticed one yet."

"Be careful. You're getting censorious."

"I'm kidding. *I* incited you, didn't I? Come on. How many other guys would lie in bed with you and develop narratives like *Dan Quayle: Portrait of a Human Toilet.*"

Pete smiled. "That's true."

We stopped at a 7-Eleven to get something to drink. The store was so shockingly bright, the colors so intense, that I felt as if I'd stepped into a Jonathan Demme film. Jacked-up blacks at the video games, cheerful Latino customers, Brazilian music jumping from a boom box. For a moment I was David Byrne, but that passed. Reality turned virulent when I saw Gerald Bryer's face on the *L.A. Times* Sunday

Preview edition. "Bryer Denies Extermination Quip," the story headline read.

Pete saw it, too. "Extermination quip?"

"Yeah, he made some remark somewhere about gassing everybody with AIDS."

"Fine," Pete said. "As long as he personally stuffs Kimberly Bergalis into the oven."

For a moment Bryer's features in the newspaper photo seemed to be moving. Not seemed to—*were* moving. He was grinning sadistically, silently chuckling. For a moment, he was my late father. Then he was William Dannemeyer. Then he was *definitely* Sterling Hayden: the vicious crook in Stanley Kubrick's film noir *The Killing*, the mean-tempered police captain who beats up Al Pacino in *The Godfather*.

"That vile fuck," Pete said as he looked at Bryer's photo (which, with those words, quit moving on me). "I really should've killed him while I had the chance."

Pete's anger as we stepped back outside reminded me of an incident the year before.

"Hey, remember the rubber-buying blowout?" I said.

"Oh, right." Pete grinned as we got in the car. "They only wanted to make love in peace. But their desire ignited an apocalypse."

All that had really happened was we'd gone into a Thrifty drugstore late at night to buy some condoms, and this fat clerk overheard us joking around at the display rack, trying to decide which ones to buy: ribbed or regular, lubed or dry, or the new elaborate two-part adhesive "no-slip" condom: *Caution: Applicator hood must be removed prior to intercourse.* "Like something in a sexual/industrial nightmare," Pete had said. "Robocop fucking the Terminator on an *Alien* set." We'd just been having fun, but this clerk really gave us a hateful glare, and when we went up to pay, he was also manning the register and made a big point of not putting the change in Pete's hand, as if he didn't want to have even glancing physical contact with a homo. I'd experienced the same slight more than once paying for an

Advocate, and Pete had also encountered it before, and leaving the drugstore, he'd been steamed. "If that fat sack of shit had said *one word* . . ." But we'd soon diffused our anger by imagining how the situation might have escalated—from an insult to a fistfight, to a gun being whipped out, to the clerk's brains blown all over the tabloid rack, to screaming bystanders, hostages taken, the SWAT team arriving, tear gas, a fusillade, plate glass shattering, cops blown away, passersby killed in the crossfire, a wantonly excessive Peckinpah slaughter scene—all because two boyfriends stopped to buy a pack of rubbers at one A.M.

"In a way that was kind of prescient," I said. "A lot of Thriftys got hit during the riots. I wonder if we were unconsciously perceiving something that was already in the air."

"Could be." Pete seemed preoccupied. He took a swig off his bottled diet Pepsi. "I think I'm going to go out there."

"Out where?"

"To Valencia. To Glenn's. To try and talk to Joey."

"Right now?"

"Yeah." He started the engine. "And I'm going to drop you off first."

I said, "No, look, really—I do *not* want to be at home alone on mescaline. What am I going to do? Watch some drivel with Tom Hanks on cable? A porno tape? I'd commit suicide. Really, I might do something crazy, Pete. Run naked with a machete down Pacific Coast Highway."

"These people could be pretty flipped out, Tim."

"All the more reason why I should go with you. You shouldn't be walking into a den of speed-tweaked, Derrida-spouting art queers alone."

"They might be spouting a lot more than Derrida," he said. "I don't want you to get hurt."

For some reason I couldn't get scared. "I don't want *you* to get hurt. I'm going with you. It's a long drive out to Valencia. Can I suck your cock on the way?"

He laughed and pulled out. "I'm not sure If you're joking or not."

"I'm not either. Why don't you whip it out and we can both see."

He looked at me with a grin. "It's tempting. But I think I'd rather wait till I can suck yours, too."

"That makes sense, I guess."

"I wish you wouldn't look at me like that," he said, still grinning.

"Like what?"

"Like you really want to fuck."

"I can't help it. I really do."

Pete switched the radio on to a classical music station. "I think we'd better change the mood or we're going to end up whacking off on the freeway."

"I'll bet lots of guys are doing that right now. Driving down the road, slowly stroking their erections. It's that kind of night, Pete."

"That could be the quintessential L.A. image. A languid masturbator in two tons of hurtling steel."

"Having phone sex on the freeway."

"That sounds dangerous," Pete said. "If you had the phone in one hand and your dick in the other, how would you steer?"

"With your cock. Haven't you ever done that? You just press your hard-on against the wheel. It's tricky on sharp turns, but—"

Pete laughed. "You're crazy."

"No, just absurdly sexed up. I feel like I haven't come in about a year."

A severe Bartók concerto leveled out the mood on the freeway. As we passed the lighted monoliths of Century City, I went off on a mental tangent about Ayn Rand and *The Fountainhead*: kitschly phallic skyscrapers, Gary Cooper's sweaty hands on a vibrating jackhammer. Patricia Neal's breathless ride up the erectile elevator to Cooper, astride his monument, the wind whipping his slacks. The mulatto *Die Hard* building (where Ronald Reagan kept his office in the tip of the glassy glans penis) appeared to flex like a living cock. I looked away and rubbed my eyes, which made me see spinning swastikas.

"So why didn't Glenn and Joey stay sober?" I said.

Pete shrugged. "I don't know. I think the truth is Joey wanted to more than Glenn. It was Joey's idea to come to AA. Glenn sort of came along because he didn't want Joey out of his sight."

"Uh-oh."

"Exactly. And I think Glenn realized that if Joey stayed sober, their relationship wouldn't last. It's got an extremely fucked-up dynamic."

"Kind of like us, huh?"

"No. Believe me, we're like Pat and Shirley Boone compared to them."

"God, what an odious comparison. I'm not even going to ask who's who."

"The thing is, on some level, I think they really love each other."

"Pat and Shirley?"

"No, Glenn and Joey. But it's this possessive, obsessive dance-of-death thing. Like *Realm of the Senses.*"

"All's well that ends well. Are they into S&M?"

"Not formally," Pete said. "Not with leather and all that. Glenn would consider that hopelessly lame. But emotionally, yes. I mean, Glenn's forty-two, okay? But this incredibly hot older guy."

"Just like I'll be in a few years."

"You're holding up well, Tim."

"It's my new skin-care system. All my friends think I've had a face-lift. So it's a dad-and-lad scene?"

"Yeah, exactly. Except Joey's real father was a monster. There was a lot of abuse, some very sick stuff. I mean, torture. Cigarettes on his dick, stuff like that. When Joey was five."

"Jesus."

"Yeah. His dad wasn't Ward Cleaver."

"Not unless I missed an episode. 'Beaver, come here.' 'Dad, no! Ouch! Gee!' "

"The thing is," Pete continued seriously, "Joey's already

done a lot with his life against incredible odds. I mean, he came out here when he was fifteen to get away from his father, and he hustled for a while and lived on the streets. Finally he met a guy who took him in and all that, and he went back to school, and then he got this scholarship to CalArts. He's incredibly intelligent and talented as a painter. And going to CalArts was like his ultimate dream come true. And then, on literally the first day, he met Glenn. And they've been fighting and fucking and shooting speed ever since."

"Until a couple of months ago."

"Yeah. Joey couldn't take it anymore."

"Do you think *we* could live together without fighting?" I said.

"I don't know."

I knew this would irritate him but I said it anyway: "Because my lease is up again in August."

He looked at me. "I really think we should just see what happens. Let's not start designing our dream house tonight, okay?"

"No, you're right. I'm just thinking out loud."

"That's okay."

I leaned back in the seat. The warm air felt smooth and liquid.

"Jeff and Neal had a dream house," I said. "In Topanga Canyon. They were building it last year, the last time I saw Jeff. He was very excited about it. Which is odd in a way, because I think he must've known then he was dying. Or at least that his time was running out."

"Well—maybe they had a few months in their dream house."

"Yeah, I think they did."

The hallucinatory aspect of the mescaline was fading, but colors were still intense and highly pleasurable. Even the trashy, junky expanses of the San Fernando Valley seemed strangely exhilarating. We passed an Earl Scheib car-painting outlet: Scheib's crusty, grinning face on the glowing, slowly turning plastic sign against the sky. My mind went off on another tangent: from the concept of the Earl Scheib sign found three thousand years from now (A.D. 4992), mistaken for a religious artifact, to Saint Earl of Pacoima, to the Video-book of Earl discovered like the Dead Sea Scrolls in the ruins of KCOP: Blessed are the meek, for they will paint any car for $89.95. Yea, though I drive through the valley of the smokes to the orange hacienda, I will fear no Indian, for Ramona is a lesbian—

"Introducing the 1978 Ford Schlong," I said.

Pete laughed. "The Buick Clitoris."

This was an old game.

"The 1970 Mercury Buttfucker," I said.

"I can actually see that in chrome," Pete said, "on a mustard-yellow fender. The 1988 Toyota Vagina."

"The 1968 Pontiac Cocksucker," I said.

"Those are worth a lot now."

"Right. They don't make engines like that anymore. Real jiz-guzzlers though."

Pete laughed but said, "That's disgusting."

"Oh, no. Pete prudes out."

"That reminds me of a prank idea Glenn had. You'd call the White House and tell them a chef with AIDS had beat off in the dessert topping."

"That's witty."

"Yeah, we pictured Bush's expression as the Secret Service man whispered in his ear. Naturally, he'd have a mouthful of dessert—"

"Which he'd spit out in a big spray."

"No, he'd do it in a napkin. But when he told Barbara what was going on, *she'd* spit it out in a big spray."

I laughed but said, "That's an extremely unconscionable joke, you know. You could get some chef in a lot of trouble."

The classical music was becoming oppressive. I switched to the Lightning Seed's "Pure," the catchy techno-pop song I'd been addicted to in France. The song's fruity Popsicle atmosphere had always elated me, but on mescaline it made my scalp tingle with ecstasy. "My God," I said to Pete. "*Listen* to this! This guy is so in love it's embarrassing. Is

168

this song a sweet, juicy candy land of homoerotic love or am I just reading in?"

"I don't know. But Pablo was obsessed with it for a while."

That leveled me out. "Why was Pablo so nasty to me? He was really vicious."

Pete shrugged. "He's having boyfriend problems. He found out that Bob's been seeing someone on the side."

"God, how discouraging. Do you think any gay man can stay monogamous for an extended period of time?"

"He can now—if he knows what's good for him."

"We'll have that understanding again, right?"

Pete hesitated. "Yeah, I guess."

"You guess?"

"Unless I met someone really hot."

I hesitated. "I know you're being facetious. But I have to tell you, that still touches a very primitive nerve."

He took my hand on the center divider. "You're just gonna have to fuck me real hard before I go on the road."

"Okay."

"So my asshole's still throbbing two weeks later."

"No problem." The idea of fucking Pete again made me feel a little crazy. "So did you see anyone at all during the last year?"

"No. I told you—"

"I know. I just thought you might have *dated*—"

"No. I hate that word."

"Yes, I know. Sorry."

"No, I didn't care about any of that," Pete said. "I was very depressed for a long time. After Doug died. And then, when I heard about Carlos . . . I don't know. As much as I came to hate Carlos, I really did love him at one point. He gave me a lot. I was a lot more scared before Carlos than I think you realize. About sex, I mean. I went through some pretty long celibate stretches myself."

"I thought you might have. There seemed to be quite a gap between Cord and Carlos."

"Yeah, there was. And I was depressed about what hap-

169

pened with us, too. I don't know if I should tell you this, but I almost got drunk behind that."

"Are you serious?"

"Yeah, it was this very strange impulsive thing. Completely out of the blue. It was maybe a month after we broke up, and one night I walked down to the beach. I knew there was still a cruising area there, and I thought I might feel better if I, you know, got a blow job or something. But it was too depressing. I saw a few guys jacking off in their cars—that image again—but it just seemed forlorn and abject. I knew I'd feel even worse after something like that, it was so much less than what I really wanted. So I started home, but I stopped at the Trading Post, that liquor store on Horizon."

"Oh, God, that place."

"Yeah, it's pretty grim. But I was very depressed, and I was just going to get some cigarettes, but the next thing I knew I was saying, 'And a fifth of Jack Daniel's.' I was just in a very Charles Bukowski/*Exile on Main Street* mood."

"Sounds like you were trying to self-medicate," I said.

"Right, I should've been on Prozac. But I wasn't, so I walked home, and at the time I just didn't care. I really missed you a lot, and I just felt like, what's the point, I'm never really going to have anything that lasts with anybody. So I was pouring myself this huge drink when the phone rang. And it was this guy Reese, a guy I knew from AA, whose boyfriend had died about a week before, and he was feeling suicidal. So I went over to his place in Palms and spent the night with him. You know, just holding him. But before I left, I poured the Jack Daniel's out in the kitchen sink. The whole fifth. I can still remember the smell of the sour mash fumes as it gurgled down the drain."

"I'm glad it turned out that way," I said.

"I am, too. I'm really a total alcoholic, Tim. It's not cute, it's not funny. When I drink, I turn into what's his name in *Under the Volcano*."

"Albert Finney."

"Right. It gets terminal fast. I have no illusions that I

could ever control it. Maybe it's genetic, I don't know. But once I start, it's anybody's guess when or if I'll stop."

"I'm glad that didn't happen."

"Me, too. But it was scary. A very close call. When people have relapses, nine times out of ten it's over some fucked-up relationship. So after that I kind of decided to give that area of my life a rest for a while and just concentrate on my music."

"That's pretty much how I felt, too," I said. "I went out a few times, but my heart wasn't in it. I know it's not the same thing as drinking, but I lost myself in my work. We were putting together the film noir marathon, so I got pretty caught up in that, which was fun in a way. We found a pristine print of *The Night Has a Thousand Eyes* in the basement of a building on Yucca. I guess I didn't really expect to meet someone like you again right away."

"You know what?" Pete said. "We should try and be more polite with each other this time. I think we quit being polite."

"Yeah, I know what you mean. We did."

We were moving into the sagebrush hills north of the Valley. The air felt cooler. I could smell the pungent dusty odor of the chaparral.

"Sergio Leone country," I said.

"Right. *The Good, the Bad, and the Buttfucked.*"

A few times when we'd been making up stories, we'd gotten into western stuff: raunchy outlaw scenarios, lonesome uncut cowboys, ramrods and buttholes in the O.K. Corral. But Pete had basically been indulging me. That terrain wasn't charged for him. He was too young to remember the genre at its luminous big-screen sublimating peak.

"That reminds me," Pete said. "I finally saw Guy Madison."

"Oh, yeah?"

He shrugged. "Nice bod in buckskin, but too glossy. Those fifties guys always look shiny, shellacked."

"I know. He was strictly a prepubescent icon. My own

tastes soon changed radically. It's not like I'm still looking for Guy Madison."

"That's fortunate," Pete said.

Suddenly I felt a strange weightless sensation in the pit of my stomach, like being in an elevator. "*Whoa.*"

"What?"

"Nothing, I guess. I just thought for a second that we were lifting off the ground."

"I can do that if you want," Pete said. "If I change stations, we'll go airborne."

He switched to KROQ: the heavy, wet emotions of Concrete Blonde's pertinent "Joey."

"I wish we could really *do* that," I said. "Beam up and zoom the fuck out of here. Make a *Blade Runner* exit. Except they were actually flying into outtakes from *The Shining.*"

"What?"

"The end of *Blade Runner*. The original version. When they're flying out through the pretty vistas and all that? Those are outtakes from *The Shining.*"

"Too bad."

"I know. I still like that ending though. I didn't think it was a cop-out. It's not like they're going to live happily ever after. You know Sean Young's battery's going to run down eventually. To me, it was poignant."

"I think about that film a lot," Pete said.

"Who doesn't?"

"Gay men seem like replicants now. Younger guys especially."

"Right. With memory implants. With photos of their midwestern moms. Don't tell them she doesn't exist. They'll start crying."

"I know," Pete said. "It's true. Black leather jackets and limited life spans."

He said nothing for a moment. Then he said, "We could be in Needles in an hour. We could stop and put a wreath by the roadside where Sam Kinison died."

"Take a dump, you mean."

"We could be in Tucson by dawn. Or Tombstone. You could fuck me in the butt in the actual O.K. Corral."

"Let's do it," I said. "But I want to wait till the tourists arrive. I like an audience."

"Then we could drive up to Scottsdale and gut some rich pigs and steal their rings and Rolexes."

"And hole up in New Mexico for six months."

"Yeah. Fuck our brains out and grow blue corn."

"And when we got tired of that," I said, "we could drive back to Virginia Beach and cut off Pat Robertson's head with a chain saw."

Pete laughed. "Right. And after that, we could go to Spain and play gay lovers in a Pedro Almodovar film."

"Right. An update of *Pillow Talk*."

"You'd have the Doris Day role, of course," Pete said.

"I'll accept that. But that means you'll have to play Rock Hudson all the way and—" I censored myself.

"What? Die of AIDS in the last reel?"

I thought about my outburst earlier that evening. "Incidentally, I don't think I've made a formal amend yet. But I said some pretty awful things to you in Baldwin Hills—"

"Don't worry about it." He took my hand. "You were mad. We both were. I said some nasty things to you, too."

"That's true."

He gave me a look. "So let's just forget it, okay?"

"Okay."

He gave me a quick kiss, his beard stubble scratching my cheek—which set off a memory rush of my father's scratchy face, a birthday-party kiss when I was three or four, something I hadn't thought of in years.

"Where were we?" Pete said.

"Spain."

"Oh, right. So the film's a big hit—"

"But now the FBI knows where we are," I said.

"Right. So one day we're fucking in our beach house—"

"On Mallorca."

"And we're both about to shoot, when suddenly—"

173

TWELVE

VALENCIA was out in the middle of nowhere, after miles of empty black hills. We got off at the McBean Parkway, where a bright gas station was glowing in cheerful yellow/orange tones. We drove past the rustling trees and chalk buildings of the CalArts campus and entered an area of vast bland brown housing tracts. The street was empty. The houses were dark and felt empty, too, as if the area had been evacuated after an industrial accident and no one had bothered to shut off the automatic sprinklers.

Glenn lived in a new upscale tract of large lot-filling homes that came in a choice of nuevo-kitsch architectural styles: Tudor, Château, Camelot, Miami Vice. Glenn's house was classic Taco Bell Mild Mexican, beige stucco with a fake red-tile roof and cheap-looking wrought-iron fixtures. An amber porch light was burning. As we pulled up, Pete said, "His car's not here."

"Then let's go."

Pete keep looking at the house. Then he shut off the engine. "No, I'm going to check around back. I'm curious about something. You can wait here if you want." He got out.

"No. I'm curious, too." I caught up with him. "Are you sure no one's home?"

"We'll know in a minute."

It was hard to feel apprehensive in a neighborhood this

tidy and family oriented. It wasn't as if we were approaching some sort of biker Methedrine factory in the desert east of San Bernardino. I noticed a Volvo station wagon in the driveway of the Camelot house next door, a BABY ON BOARD sign in its back window, and wondered what those people made of Glenn. "Mommy, look at this sticky balloon I found. . . ."

We walked up the driveway. There was a basketball hoop over the garage door, which for some reason seemed like a porno-film setup. I pictured a glossy mideighties tape of slick Tom Cruise, Rob Lowe, Emilio Estevez look-alikes fighting for the ball, before the jump-cut to the three-way on the pavement in *Rim Shot* or *After School Special.*

A gate in the slate fence led to the backyard and the swimming pool. The pool lights were on, the Hockney resonances reassuring until I saw the body of the little girl floating facedown in the water.

I quaked. "Jesus!"

"It's just a doll," Pete said.

It took me a moment to believe that. It was not a toy-store doll but incredibly realistic, its pale skin smooth and seamless. It wore a blue bathing suit.

"It's a special-effects doll," Pete said. "Once some people came over who hadn't seen it before and Glenn did this whole number. 'Oh, my god, *Debbie!*' He raced out to the pool and dove in. 'It's *too late!* She's dead! My precious little angel! *No.'* These people almost shit."

"I would've, too," I said. "I'm not sure how funny that is, really."

"Well, I don't think Glenn's goal is to entertain."

Through the plate glass windows we could see into the living room and kitchen. The place was gutted, as if a gang of criminals had murdered Chuck and Cindi and the twins and taken over their house, deliberately trashing the discount home furnishings. In the living room there was one of Glenn's sculptures. *Contraption* would be a better word: an evil, virulent-looking piece made from junk and scrap metal and crushed toys and appliance parts. On the walls there were paintings, the most prominent of which, over the filthy white cotton sofa, was a large colorful collage work featuring a picture of Ronald Reagan nuzzling Nancy.

Pete tried one of the sliding glass doors. It was unlocked. He opened it cautiously.

"What are you doing?" I said.

"I just want to look around."

We both heard a TV in the other room.

"Hello!" Pete called. "Glenn? Hello! Joey?"

Nothing.

We stepped in. Up close the Reagan painting was considerably more startling. The picture of the cooing leather lovebirds, I realized, had been appropriated from *Vanity Fair*—the Annie Liebowitz photograph that had run just as Reagan was leaving office. I'd been so disgusted by it, and by the fawning tone of the accompanying article, that I'd written off an angry letter, canceling my subscription. Didn't they realize how many of their readers were gay? If we were Jews, would they have run a simpering homage to Heinrich Himmler?

In the original photo, I recalled, the White House had been in the background. Here, that had been replaced with an AIDS-ward photo: emaciated, hollow-eyed men in their deathbeds. Other elements stuck in the messy paint-smeared collage included pictures of dead fish on a garbage-strewn beach and—between Nancy's legs—a dead brown baby that had apparently choked, the way fish do, on a plastic six-pack ring. This was not cool content, or oblique image-text work. In sloppy block letters across the bottom of the painting: GENOCIDE. KILL THESE FUCK-PIGS NOW. Below that: J. BARLOW 1990. The entire painting was splattered with runny trails of red paint, the same shade as Ronnie's cardigan sweater and Nancy's dress. Except it wasn't paint. It was human blood squirted from syringes.

There was an eyedropper syringe, with a baby pacifier tip, resting in a glass of pinkish water on the coffee table beside the art magazines and fast-food debris and overflowing ashtrays, and a Christmas card and a stubby black .38 revolver.

The Christmas card startled more than the gun. It said

MERRY CHRISTMAS in bright spangly letters, but it was a color photo of a waxy-faced bearded man in a coffin. I picked up the card and opened it. Inside, in a grotesque parody of a newsiness, it said: "As you can see, my 'roommate' Rick croaked this year. Oh, well! Nothing lasts forever. Happy Holidays!"

"Jesus." I showed Pete the card. "This was his lover?"

Pete winced. "Yeah. He sent those out a few years ago. To all his straight relatives back in Ohio."

I was appalled. But at the same time I could understand why he'd done it. They'd send him Christmas cards showing their growing families, their new babies, but not want to know about his pain and grief. So he was shoving it in their faces, making them feel it.

While Pete went to check the other room, I took a closer look at Glenn's contraption. It depicted, if that's the right word, a woman with her legs spread, blowing a man who stood over her. The woman's head was a vacuum-cleaner base; her lips, wrapped around an electric knife, were fashioned from a rubber douche bag painted scarlet. The spiky rusted-wire male figure stood with hands on hips and wore a stained, shredded, white South American military uniform and matching peaked cap. His face was a telephone, from which wires ran down to his Brazil-nut testicles. Between the woman's rusty legs, there was a doorbell and a little placard that read: PRESS JEANE'S BUZZER. I was tempted to do it, just to see what would happen, until I saw that I'd have to reach in through an open (labialike?) steel-claw animal trap in order to press the buzzer.

"Joey's been here," Pete called.

I went into the next room, the den, where a TV was showing an old episode of "The Adventures of Spin and Marty" on the Disney channel. Pete held up a Drunken Boat T-shirt. "This is Joey's." He picked up a pair of black Levi's jeans. "So are these." A frayed Bike jockstrap fell out.

"So where would he go without his jockstrap?" I said.

"I don't know."

I looked at the TV where Tommy Kirk and Tim Considine

were talking in a bunkhouse. "Do you think they're in love?" I said.

"Yeah, I'm sure of it," Pete said, preoccupied.

"I wonder if they ever ate each other's butt."

"Yeah, I remember that. Spin and Marty: the butt-eating episode."

"I'd like to eat your butt when we get back to my place," I said.

Pete looked at me. "You're crazy." He gave me a quick kiss. "Come on, let's check upstairs."

As we came back into the living room, I indicated the contraption and said, "I almost pressed Jeane's buzzer but—"

"Oh, Jesus." Pete touched my arm. "You would've lost your *hand*. I should've warned you."

"Well—I kind of figured that out." I was still shaken to have my suspicion confirmed. "What if someone *didn't* see the danger though?"

Pete did a little girl's voice: " 'Mommy, I want to press the—' *Fwomp! 'Ahhhh!'* "

I laughed, but looking at the animal trap, I said, "I think this may actually be genuinely sick though. Not to say meanspirited."

"Well, Glenn likes to get rowdy."

"I'd say Joey has the same tendency." I indicated the painting at the foot of the stairs.

"Whoa." Pete was even more startled than I was.

Using paint and appropriated still photos, the picture depicted a naked young man with a fat, shiny erection blowing the brains out of a real-life Orange County congressman, a fellow every bit as vile as Gerald Bryer. The gay porno photo was cut roughly into the photo of the right-wing homophobe at his desk, a ragged image of a firing revolver placed over the young man's hand. The exploding blood and brains had been painted in. The big sloppy block letters across the bottom of the painting read AIDS CURE.

"Jesus. Can he *do* this?" I said, meaning wasn't there some sort of law against using a real person's likeness this way.

"I don't know," Pete said. "But he's doing it."

There was another of Joey's paintings on the wall at the stairway landing. A well-known conservative senator's head was exploding at a backyard barbecue. The expressions of the other family members, no doubt smiling in the original photo, had been distorted with paint into smeary screams. MAKE THIS REAL the messy text read.

"Is this a *joke?*" I said.

"I don't know. I'm not sure anymore."

Pete continued on up the stairs, as if he didn't want to discuss what he knew I had to be thinking: that these paintings were very much like some of the fantasies we used to spin.

We'd fallen into amusing ourselves with political assassination scenarios once I'd gotten over my initial reservations about Pete's Baader-Meinhof song. I'd seen his point, that anything in art was permissible, that to depict something was not the same as to advocate it, let alone do it, and I felt that our fantasies, besides being fun, were a kind of harmless way of blowing off steam. So we'd imagine, in the most extreme and lurid cinematic terms, the obliteration by gunfire of different right-wing people we disliked. William F. Buckley, for example, might be machine-gunned on his sailboat, or Jesse Helms in the doorway of a Southern church, or Patrick Buchanan might have his head blown "clean off" on TV. Sometimes these events were just passing episodes in wide-ranging fantasy adventures. We liked the idea that we could machine-gun George Will, for example, in Washington, and suck each other off in Mexico in the same sentence. Often though, we'd toss out the images as one-liners. "Dannemeyer with his brains blown out at a Sizzler salad bar," Pete might say. "Smashing the Gipper's head with a sledgehammer and Nancy's reaction," I might respond, and we'd convulse with laughter. Part of the fun came from the sense that there were people who would find our fantasies tasteless and shocking, especially, as Pete said, "the Gandhi wimps." Or the "Sam Waterston liberal/humanists" (the sort of character Waterston often portrayed in films): "Good *God*, man! There's

179

nothing *funny* about *killing* people!" Or the female-identified queens who would say at any mention of violence, "Oh, you boys are just *too* butch!"

Sometimes, however, in a more sober vein, we'd wonder why there hadn't been any AIDS kamikazes yet. And Pete would lament the fact that most gay men were "wimps and professional victims." "We should've learned something from what happened to the Jews," he'd say. This was usually where he'd add, not having taken the test at this point, that if he ever got it, he'd take someone with him. And that was usually where I'd change the subject to something more pleasant.

At the top of the stairs I said to Pete, "Have you seen those paintings before?"

"Not the originals." He looked back down at *AIDS Cure*. "But they made some black-and-white posters of that one. I've seen them up on walls around Silver Lake and West Hollywood."

"Well . . . I guess it's all right to be provocative," I said. "After all's said and done, it's still art. It's not like they're actually *doing* it."

Pete didn't say anything.

There were three bedrooms upstairs. We looked into the first one, the master bedroom, where there was a king-size mattress on the floor. Next to the bed there was a large open jar of Vaseline, a stack of *Re/Search* magazines, several 'zines, and a number of books, including Jean Baudrillard's *Cool Memories*, Larry Kramer's *Reports from the Holocaust*, Susan Sontag's *AIDS and Its Metaphors*, Frantz Fanon's *Black Skin, White Masks*, a scuffed twenty-year-old copy of *The Anarchist Cookbook*, and Eric Knight's *Lassie Come Home* with an illustration of the beloved collie on the cover.

Noting the Vaseline, I said, "I take it Glenn isn't into safe sex."

"He probably figures there's not much point."

Indeed, you didn't have to be too quick to figure out that with Glenn's lover dead, and Joey's past as a hustler, and the sharing of needles, it would only be a fluke or a miracle if they didn't have it.

I still felt a twinge of envy though. Sometimes I really missed fucking without a rubber and resented guys who were still doing it, either because they were both negative, or knew or assumed they were positive and/or just didn't care. After Pete and I broke up, in a despairing moment I'd considered taking the test and if I'd come up positive, going to a scummy Silver Lake sex club I'd heard about and fucking my brains out, drenching myself in anonymous sex for whatever time I had left. But I'd decided that would be too soul-destroying, that even if I *was* doomed, I'd rather spend my last years remembering what it had been like with Pete than having a bunch of crazed sleazy guys mauling me in a black, sticky-floored, amyl-nitrate hellhole at two in the morning.

The second bedroom was empty except for a couple of sleeping bags on the carpet and a few of Joey's older paintings leaning against the wall. Dated '87 and '88, these paintings were in a neo-expressionist style, and in contrast to the violent 1990 collage works, these were almost shockingly tender. My favorite showed two naked young men sleeping on a bed in bright sunlight, one on his stomach, his arm over the other one, who was sleeping on his back. The image had a kind of messy charge that kept it from feeling sentimental. It looked like two guys flaked out after hours of hot, sloppy sex.

Another painting showed a blond-haired young man and a scared-looking dark-haired teenage boy sitting at a bright, dirty orange and yellow Del Taco outlet.

"That's Joey with Gary," Pete said. "They were boyfriends a few years ago, when they were both hustlers. They took care of each other."

"God, I can't imagine anyone being a hustler now."

"I know."

The third painting was a study of Gary asleep on his stomach in a ratty hotel room. It was very reminiscent of the image in my mind of Jeff asleep in his bedroom in Puerto

Vallarta. The painting had a strange mix of tones—it seemed both poignant and angry.

"Where's Gary now?"

"He died about a year ago."

"Jesus." Gary looked about twenty in the painting. "Talk about replicants."

"I know."

For a moment I thought the image was changing on me, turning into Jeff. It wasn't, I decided, not in a hallucinatory sense. I was just projecting. But it was still getting to me. I stepped out of the room, afraid if I didn't, I might lose it again.

The door to the third bedroom had a padlock on it, but the lock wasn't fastened.

"What do you think this is?" I said.

"I don't know." Pete took off the lock. "This could be where we find Joey tied up and strangled with his tongue hanging out."

I knew he was kidding, but I still cringed as I pictured it.

"Did I ever tell you about Clem?" he said.

"Oh, right. The serial-killer buff. Gacy's pen pal."

"Right. He came to one of our gigs last month."

"It must make you feel good to have fans like him."

"He's creepy, there's no denying it. Guess what he showed me."

"Autopsy photos?"

"Close. Jeffrey Dahmer crime-scene photos. Don't know how he got 'em. Brace yourself. The head in the refrigerator. A black cock in an olive dish—"

Picturing that, I covered my ears and said, "*Stop*. You're deliberately playing with my mind and I'm not enjoying it. Will you please just open the fucking door?"

He did, and the truth was startling enough. When Pete switched on the overhead light, the room looked like a news shot of a captured drug dealer's arsenal. At least a dozen automatic weapons were lined up neatly on the orange carpet, submachine guns and smaller machine-pistol-type weapons. There was a box of hand grenades, many boxes of 9mm ammunition, and on a low table, what I thought at first were white kilo packs of speed, until I saw the black letters on the plastic wrap: SEM-TEX.

"Oh, Jesus," I said. "That's plastique. Sem-Tex—that's what the IRA uses. I saw a thing on 'Frontline' about it once."

"I was afraid of this," Pete said, almost to himself. "Damn it."

Seeing the weapons and explosives finally did it. These people were insane and I was scared. "Pete, I think we should get out of here."

But he was picking up what appeared to be several latex Halloween masks. "What the hell are these?"

They were the kind that fit over your entire head, but instead of Frankenstein's monster or Dracula, we saw, as Pete held one up, that they were in the flesh-colored shape of a glans penis—dickheads.

I laughed. There were eyeholes cut below the glans portion, which I'd always felt resembled a helmet—or rather, the reverse: that military helmets resembled dickheads. We saw that they were all different, individual. One was brown—Latino or Asian. Another, with a messy ring of bunched-up skin, appeared to be uncircumcised. One's shape reminded me a great deal of the cock in the porno portion of Joey's assassination painting. It was obvious they'd all been modeled on the real thing.

"This is somewhat demented," I said.

It was then that we heard a car pulling up outside, the ragged rumble of a sixties muscle-car engine.

"Oh, shit," Pete said. "That's *Glenn*."

Pete threw down the masks, and we took off. As we came down the stairs, we could hear the car lumbering up the driveway, its raunchy engine setting off a memory flash of violent macho high-school morons, the kind who'd yell out their 'Cuda window, "Hey, *queer!*" even if you had your arm around a girl. The car's brakes screeched as it came to a stop in front of the garage, several male occupants giggling. We assumed they'd be coming through the kitchen or the back, so we dashed to the front door. But it was locked with a deadbolt.

When we heard them coming up to the kitchen door, we ran back through the living room to the sliding glass door, reaching the patio just as they came into the kitchen. But someone was still out at the car, blocking our escape route. We ducked behind some tropical shrubs by the pool. Crouching there, we could look back into the house through the plate glass windows.

Glenn came into the living room first, and I realized I'd seen him somewhere before, probably around Venice. And I saw what Pete meant about him being very appealing. He was shirtless, and his extremely hairy chest and stomach, and receding brown hair and hyperbutch jock face, reminded me of a gym coach I'd had a crush on in junior high. Glenn looked a lot smarter than Mr. Zalinski though—who'd once appeared to be getting a hard-on while giving my teenage butt paddle swats. Glenn's green eyes had a brilliant amphetamine intensity behind round glasses. He was laughing as he slid his hand across the bare back of the second man.

"That's Dexter," Pete said.

Dexter looked about thirty with a wiry build, silky pale blond hair falling down over his eyes, and a high-contrast reddish-brown mustache and goatee. His torso was pale and hairless, thick veins bulging in his arms. I noticed a bruise inside his right elbow and thought of a William Burroughs line—a junkie observation about having "fun with veins like those." Dexter laughed at something Glenn said, white teeth flashing like a robust young Kirk Douglas in *Lust for Life*. Only Dexter's eyes looked glassy and cranked. He and Glenn went over to the coffee table, where Glenn took a packet of speed from his pocket and, crouching down, began tapping the powder into a bent spoon.

"Mikey," Pete said as the next man stepped out of the kitchen, popping a beer. Mikey was Japanese American, and also shirtless, with a really nicely defined glossy torso and a stunningly good-looking samurai face under short,

184

parted black hair. He reminded me of a Japanese guy I'd been attracted to in college.

Joey came in last and he was just wearing gym shorts, which were loose enough to let his dick hang out. Even though I'm not into the *blond syndrome,* there was no denying that Joey was more or less hopelessly appealing, painfully boyish, appallingly cute, a blond and blue-eyed, pink-mouthed wet dream. He was not a smooth Aryan blond however; Joey was an Irish honey-blond with downy blond hair on his arms and chest and lots of color in his skin, in his face, a kind of golden honey glow. In other words, just the sort of cute little blond guy many men would take one look at and give anything—decades of their lives— to fuck once. I felt that I'd seen Joey somewhere before, too, but wasn't certain. He was a *type* you saw so often, on the streets of West Hollywood, in the floodlit rooms of porno cassettes.

Joey joined the others at the coffee table as they prepared to shoot up. At one point they all had their backs to the window and I looked at Pete, wondering if we were going to take this chance to make a dash for the gate. We were just about to when Glenn turned and came over to the sliding glass door, which was still open slightly. "Who the fuck left this unlocked?" he said as he shut and latched it.

Then we saw that Dexter was shooting up. And I was right about his veins. He didn't even need to tie off. As he tapped the needle in, which caused me to wince (I can't even watch shots like that on TV), I was genuinely jolted to see that Mikey was unbuttoning Dexter's black Levi's jeans. As Dexter squeezed the Methedrine into his vein, Mikey leaned down and began sucking Dexter's cock, which was limp and uncircumcised—I knew which mask was his.

Dexter grinned as the amphetamine washed through his brain. He pulled the needle out and handed the syringe to Glenn, a look of orgasmic bliss on his face as he ran his hands through Mikey's glossy black hair. Dexter's cock was getting hard now, as Mikey kept sucking him.

Glenn squirted Dexter's blood into Nancy Reagan's smiling face. Then he drew up another hit of speed.

I looked at Pete. I felt a little queasy and yet, I have to admit, also strangely excited. There was something going on, I think, for which the speed was only a catalyst, an energy being released, like an odor in the air, the smell of human sacrifice. Pete seemed even more disturbed than I was, no doubt because for a while in his late teens he'd shot speed himself. I'd snorted it occasionally in college, and even that way the rush was impressive.

Dexter pulled away from Mikey, his sloppy half-hard cock sticking out. He stepped over to Joey, who already looked excited, licking his lips with anticipation. Mikey got up and also came over to Joey and pulled down Joey's gym shorts. Joey's cock was already getting hard.

While Glenn watched, holding the syringe, Mikey and Dexter went down on Joey at the same time, both of them licking his cock from either side. To be frank, just as a rowdy sex fantasy, this was something that really put me away—the idea of two guys down on *me* at the same time. I'd only lived that out once, years ago at the beach, and it *had* been pretty wild. And I'd thought about it for jack-off purposes for years afterward, and even though I wasn't really into porno that much, I did have one cassette with a sequence where two guys were . . . And that's when I realized where I'd seen Joey. I'd seen two other guys going down on him at once in *Round-Up*, a tape I'd bought at Drake's during the celibate years mainly because it had a cowboy motif. In *Round-Up*, Joey had worn a blue kerchief around his neck and a straw cowboy hat, and one of the men had held his hands behind his back, just as Mikey was doing now, and both of the raunchy outlaws had sucked Joey's cock and licked his balls and turned him around and eaten his butt, then stuck their tongues out to catch his jiz as he jacked off in their sweaty unshaven faces.

Now Glenn crouched down and also gave Joey's cock a long, slow lick up the shaft. And you could see that Joey was very excited, like he might be about to shoot. But then (and I really wasn't ready for this) Glenn lifted the syringe in one hand and with the other located a vein along the side of Joey's cock.

"Oh, no," I whispered to Pete. "I can't watch this."

But I did. Glenn tapped the needle into the vein in Joey's cock. I winced. Pete looked away. Joey's head rolled back as he swooned in bliss, Dexter licking one of Joey's nipples now, Mikey running a hand over Joey's downy butt. Then, as Glenn pulled out the needle, Joey jerked, his whole body jerked, and he shot off—big long endless streaks of jiz flying up over his chest and stomach. I'm not exaggerating when I say I don't think I've ever seen anyone come for so long or so much. It was hard not to think that it must have felt really incredible.

But it was still, you know, kind of insane. I looked at Pete. "You're right," he said to me. "This is hopeless. This was a waste of gas and time."

In the living room Dexter began licking the semen off Joey's chest. And that was too much. Even in the old days that bit in porno films had always seemed unnecessarily gross. But *now*—dear God.

And yet, in some other way that wasn't even entirely sexual, I was still excited. Watching through the window, it *was* like looking at a silent porno tape (I always turned off the sound anyway, to lose the bad dialogue and music). And even though this was dangerous, disgusting, deadly, unconscionable—shooting speed! Swapping blood! Eating jiz!—these guys obviously just didn't care anymore. They were already doomed, so what did it matter? And there was a terrifying but profoundly seductive freedom in that. They could do anything now, anything they wanted to, anything at all.

Joey was grinning as he walked punchily into the kitchen, Mikey close behind, grabbing him playfully, laughing. And that was another thing. Even if their euphoria was artificial, they seemed to be having an intensely affectionate and genuine good time. There was none of the hard-faced posturing of impersonal sex or S&M.

As Glenn prepared to shoot up, Dexter stepped over to him and appeared to take out Glenn's cock. They both had their backs to us, so Pete and I knew this was our chance. We made a dash for the gate. I looked back. They hadn't seen us.

In the driveway I experienced quite a jolt. As soon as I saw Glenn's car, I remembered where I'd seen him. It was a black 1966 Pontiac GTO, a car eroticized for me forever— because of what had happened with Glenn. One night in 1980, I'd driven down to the Ocean Park lot where men cruised, and Glenn had pulled up beside me. I'd only recently bought my '68 Camaro convertible, and we'd admired each other's vintage cars and talked about our engines, but soon Glenn was looking down at his crotch and I knew he was jacking off. I got very turned on and got out of my car, and the next thing I knew I had my cock out and Glenn was blowing me sloppily, noisily, as I stood at his car window. Meanwhile, he was jacking off, and finally I pulled back and came really hard in his face and down the side of his car door. And it *was* pretty wild, and I never forgot it, but I guess I hadn't placed him at first since it had been twelve years, after all, and the last time I'd seen Glenn's face he'd had his tongue out like a guy in a porno film ready to catch my flying jiz.

THIRTEEN

PETE and I didn't say much as we drove back toward the freeway. We were both pretty shaken by what we'd seen. I considered telling him about my encounter with Glenn, but it didn't seem like the right time for an amusingly raunchy anecdote.

I was also beginning to feel a creepy sense of voyeur's guilt over having been so turned on by a sex scene so fraught with horrific elements. I wanted to blame it on the mescaline, on the drug's aestheticizing effect, but it reminded me a lot of the way I'd felt the afternoon I'd driven up to Griffith Park during the celibate years and watched three men having extremely unsafe sex in the bushes. That was all I'd planned to do, just watch, to get some fresh material for my mental pornography cache, and I'd been alternately repelled and aroused. The unsafe nature of the sex had appalled and terrified me (I hadn't really known what to expect), but I'd told myself they'd obviously made their own decision about it and would no doubt have been doing the same thing whether I'd been there watching or not. But suddenly the man who was getting fucked in the ass had *looked at me*—like a porno actor shattering the screen—he'd looked straight at me with utter contempt, as if to say, how dare you cop a cheap, vicarious thrill when we're actually risking (sacrificing?) our lives to do this? I'd slunk away, feeling small and guilty but still glad I hadn't

189

let anyone touch me. And I'd still used what I'd seen, projecting myself into the action, when I'd thought about it jerking off at home later.

We were almost out of gas, so we stopped at the station by the freeway. While Pete was filling the tank, I said, "You know, I think I saw Joey in a porno film once."

"Yeah, *Round-Up*." Pete watched the digits on the pump. "He showed me part of it at his sister's. He was proud of it. He thought it was hot."

"It was, in a way," I said, thinking of the scene where the two guys went down on Joey. "Except it's hard not to feel funny about porno now, if you think about it very much. I mean, anything made after '82, if the guys are doing everything."

"Yeah, I know. I remember watching a cassette at this awful party in the Hollywood Hills a few years ago. Fred Halsted's *House Party* or something—"

"That was a TV show. Art Linkletter's 'House Party.' "

"*A Night at Halsted's*—that was it," Pete said. "And everyone was standing around raving about what a big dick this one guy had, and I said, 'Yeah, but I think he's got lesions.' "

"Did he?"

"The color was real bad, all smeared and orangey. But it sure looked it."

"Jeez. Fred Halsted's dead now, too, you know."

"Yeah. I know. Suicide at Dana Point."

"Yeah, porno's weird," I said. "But I even wonder about memories sometimes. There was this guy, Joel, I went with in college. A really nice guy and he loved to get fucked. For years afterward he was one of the guys I'd think about when I jacked off. But after I heard that he'd died, I couldn't do it anymore. It would have been too strange or disrespectful or . . . I don't know."

"Yeah, I've had the same experience," Pete said. "I've even wondered if masturbating to a dead person might somehow alert them and cause them to watch."

"God, what a creepy thought."

"Don't you ever think things like that?"

"I try not to," I said. "Once I did have the feeling that my father was watching me. You know, looking down from heaven, shaking his head. 'There he is, jackin' off to that *fag stuff* again.' But I quickly pushed it from my mind."

"What if everyone who was dead was watching?" Pete said. "Like bleachers full of people. Your parents, old boyfriends, teachers, your grandmother—"

"Could we talk about something else? I'm still feeling a bit vulnerable mentally. And after what we just saw . . ."

"Sorry." Pete stared down at the freeway lights. Gasoline gurgled through the hose.

"Look, there was nothing you could do," I said.

"I could've *joined* them. They'd probably have liked that. A five-way." He looked at me. "A six-way."

"They all *are* very appealing. Visually, I mean."

"You want to go back?"

"Not tonight." Again, I considered telling Pete about my encounter with Glenn, again decided not to. "So what's the story on Mikey and Dexter?"

Pete shrugged. "Mikey's a poet. Or was. I don't know what he's doing now. Dexter doesn't really do anything creative in a formal sense. He's like a nuevo–Dean Moriarty figure. Loose, crazed, nonstop libido. Hangs out with a lot of artists. Kind of a homoerotic muse."

"A primitive."

"Right. Like he read Genet in prison or something."

"Prison?"

"Yeah. He got busted for an art prank up north about ten years ago."

"An art prank?"

Before Pete could explain, we heard the rumble of Glenn's GTO. Pete ducked down behind the pumps as the car bounced through the intersection. Joey was grinning, glinty-eyed at the wheel, Glenn riding shotgun, Dexter and Mikey in the backseat. The tape deck was pumping "Date Night at Dachau." One of them giggled as they swerved across the double line to the southbound freeway entrance.

"Come on!" Pete said, jumping into the Mercedes.

"What about the change?" He'd given the guy a twenty.

"Fuck that. Get in!"

A moment later we were roaring down the on-ramp after them.

"Why are we doing this?" I said.

"Because it's fun."

"It's not fun. It's fucked. These guys are crazy, Pete."

"Don't be such an old lady."

"That's a sexist remark. I'm going to report you to Gloria Allred. Pete—they are almost certainly armed."

"I'm not going to confront them. I just want to see where they're going."

They had a good head start. For a minute I thought we'd lost them. Then Pete spotted the Pontiac's taillights.

"There they are."

He changed lanes.

"We should be staying further back," I said. "If they realize we're following them—"

"They're not going to do anything on the freeway."

"Right. No one ever gets shot on the freeway."

"I don't think they'd shoot us, Tim."

"No, maybe not. They'll just lob one of those hand grenades into the car."

"Why don't you just relax?"

"I can't. I'm not enjoying this."

"Maybe some music'll help."

He switched on the radio: My Life with the Thrill Kill Kult's "Sex on Wheels." I'd always liked the song before, but now it triggered pictures of Edie Sedgwick, drugged in a Warhol snuff film, reptilian junkies biting into her flesh.

I said, "I don't want to do this."

"Tim, please don't get wifey."

"Wifey?"

Pete was trembling as he dug out a cigarette. "Pretend we're the Hardy Boys."

"Why?"

"Because I want you to."

192

I punched the radio buttons till I came to "More Than This," a dreamy Roxy Music song that reminded me of France.

"You think the Hardy Boys were in love?" I said.

"Are you kidding? They were obsessed with each other."

"Except they were brothers, weren't they?"

"Not really. They just said that so they wouldn't get hassled at motels in the Midwest."

"Right. But once that door was closed, I'll bet they fucked each other blind."

"That's a funny phrase now," Pete said.

"What?"

"Fucked blind."

"Yeah, a lot of phrases are funny now," I said. *"The dick of death.* That was your favorite expression, wasn't it?"

"Yeah, right. It sounds like a name. Dick of Death. Like Jesus of Nazareth."

"I was thinking about Him the other night. That if He appeared on the 'Tonight' show, the band would play 'He's a Rebel' as He came out in His robes."

"Like *Scorpio Rising.*"

"Exactly."

" 'Jesus, I know you can't stay . . .' "

" 'No, Jay, I can't. I've got a show at the MGM Golgotha . . .' " I thought a moment. "Except He'd be a homo. He'd look like this classic Hollywood Jesus, Jeffrey Hunter, but when He opened His mouth He'd be a total queen. 'Those *awful* butch centurions! I mean, *puh-leese!* And Miss Pilate—*get over it,* girl!' "

"He'd do 'Oprah,' " Pete said, "and reveal something sordid."

"Right. That Joseph molested Him. Or that He hustled for a while as a teenager in Jerusalem. Had a wine problem."

"He'd do a Barbara Walters special. She'd make Him cry."

"Right." I drifted, "He's a Rebel" running through my mind: the Crystals over grainy clips of Christ from De-

Mille's *King of Kings* in *Scorpio Rising*. That film had jolted me when I'd first seen it. Butch homo greasers, phallic chrome Harleys, the teenage shock of a celluloid cock.

I watched the GTO's taillights. "That *is* a cool car."

"Yeah." Cryptic laugh.

"What?"

"Oh, something happened with that car once. A long time ago, when I was going with Glenn."

"What was that?"

"Oh, one night—this was in '80, I guess"—Pete's non-chalance seemed forced—"I was waiting for Glenn outside his studio on Wave Crest. And he pulls up in the GTO—I think he'd just got it—and says, 'Sorry I'm late.' And he's smiling, all boyish and innocent and all that. But there's all this jiz on the side of the car."

I quaked. "Jiz?"

"Yeah. Like he'd stopped somewhere and blown someone and they'd come all over the car. Very L.A. Drive-through sex. He'd probably been down at the beach parking lot. I wasn't naive, I knew he went down there sometimes. It wasn't like we were monogamous or anything. And at that time I wasn't worried about AIDS. But it still blew me out—that he was so sexually crazed he'd do something like that *a few minutes* before we were going to be together."

"I can understand that."

"So I flipped and we had a big fight. And that was it for us, in terms of being boyfriends."

I was shaken, even though I was pretty sure the similarities were just coincidental. Glenn had undoubtedly had that sort of encounter with any number of men in those days. Still, it might *as well* have been me.

"Were you in love with Glenn?" I said.

Pete hesitated. "No. I wasn't that stupid. But I could have been."

I didn't like to censor myself with Pete or revise my past and had seldom done either. But this was one time I was glad I'd kept my mouth shut.

*   *   *

We followed the GTO into the San Fernando Valley.

"Maybe they're going to score some more speed," I said.

"I think they just did that."

"In Valencia?"

"Yeah, I think some dance student sells it."

"Mark Morris by day. Crank queen by night."

"Something like that."

"Maybe they're hungry."

"I doubt that."

"Hey, I've got it," I said. "They're going to paste up more posters of Joey's assassination pictures. It's an art-squad escapade."

"I think they've already done that. They may have grown tired of waiting for someone else to take the hint."

"More than a hint, I'd say."

"The weapons do worry me," Pete said.

"The Sem-Tex worries *me*. I think that stuff's pretty hard to get this side of Beirut or Belfast. It comes from Czechoslovakia. Or used to anyway. It's not something you pick up at Builder's Emporium."

"It *is* disturbing," Pete said. "The last I heard, Glenn had bought *one* submachine gun from some black guy in Compton for six hundred dollars. I had no idea he was building up an arsenal."

"It all seems so Neanderthal. I mean, *imagining* something violent as a kind of cinematic fantasy is one thing. But to actually start fooling around with weapons—it's so dim-witted and heterosexual. There's no getting past the moronic Chuck Norris/Rambo connotations."

"Well, Glenn would say that if Rambo's coming through your door with a flamethrower, you'd better do something besides hold up a volume of Proust."

"And, of course, you agree."

"Well, what would *you* do?"

"It's a comic book situation," I said.

"So?"

"So, I *would* hold up Proust. The flameproof volumes.

195

Then, once Rambo had used up his fire, I'd rip out an extralong sentence and hog-tie him with it. Then I'd fuck him."

"He'd probably like that." Pete did a grunting Rambo impression: "*Yeah!* Fuck my greased ass! Slam that cock right up there! Don't worry about hurtin' me! You can't hurt Rambo."

"Why is it so easy to picture that?"

"Because he's right on the verge of that anyway," Pete said. "You know who should really be hog-tied and butt-fucked? *Arnold.*"

"Right," I said. "But look—*hoarding* weapons is one thing. A lot of paranoid speed freaks do that. That's not the same as *using* them."

"It wouldn't be the first time."

I looked at him. "Do I want to know about this?"

"Probably not. I wish *I* didn't know about it."

"So what is it?"

"Well—I think Glenn may have killed three people in New Mexico."

"Are you serious?"

"Yes. I can't vouch for all the details. This is all second-hand, through Joey. But supposedly Glenn went, alone, to visit an old friend in Santa Fe last winter. Another artist, who was dying of AIDS, and being forced to sell his house. Like he'd lost his health insurance and spent all his savings, so this house he lived in was up for sale. And while Glenn was there visiting, this Realtor came by to show the place to a yuppie couple."

"God, how heartless," I said. "I've heard of that happening in San Francisco. All these straight couples moving back into the Castro, into dead guys' houses."

"Yeah, it was like that, except Glenn's friend wasn't quite dead yet. So Glenn was in the bedroom with his friend, and after the Realtor showed the couple through the house, the three of them were standing out on the back patio, talking. And they didn't realize they could be overheard, but apparently the stuff they were saying was really callous and evil. Like: 'How much longer do you think he's going to live? 'Cause we'd like to be in by Christmas.' And the wife, this blond yuppie bitch, was supposedly especially awful. Like: 'Well, is he actually going to *die* in that *room?* Because we'd like that to be the *baby's* room.' "

"She was pregnant?"

"I'm afraid so."

"Oh, Jesus."

"So they kept talking like this out on the patio, and meanwhile Glenn's in there with his friend, who can also hear them, and this guy is like, you know, only a few weeks from death. And Glenn's finally had it. He flips and he's got a gun with him, that he's been using for target practice. This house is way out on the edge of Santa Fe, very isolated. So Glenn picks up the gun and walks out to the patio and says to the yuppie bitch: 'Do you know what it's like to lose someone you love?' And she shakes her head with this terrified 'No.' And he shoots her husband point-blank in the forehead and says, 'You do now.' "

"Good God. Are you making this up?"

"No. Then he shoots the yuppie bitch. In the mouth. Then he shoots the real estate lady, who's trying to get away."

"Jesus. What about the baby?"

"Well, Glenn found out later that they saved the baby. And he told Joey that was good, since the baby was the only innocent one there. That was the most disturbing aspect of the whole thing. Glenn felt absolutely no remorse. He said they were all three hateful pigs who deserved to die. And he told Joey he felt this incredible cathartic release when he killed them. That it was better than shooting speed and almost as good as the very best sex."

"Jesus."

"Yeah, Joey was very freaked out when he heard about it. That's the main reason he left Glenn two months ago. He felt that Glenn had really crossed a line—"

"I guess you could *say* so."

"And having done it once . . ."

197

I watched the GTO's taillights and wished we'd have car trouble again. "If you'd told me about this earlier, I would never have allowed you to go to Valencia."

"I know. That's why I didn't. I knew it would upset you."

I laughed. "I know this is going to mark me as a knee-jerk humanist, but I just can't see shooting a pregnant woman, no matter what a hateful bitch she was. I can understand why Glenn would be *angry* at people like that—"

"I can, too."

"But to actually *kill* them . . ."

"I probably wouldn't have myself," Pete said. "But I don't know. If someone I loved were dying and something like that happened . . . It's possible to do things in a moment of anger. . . . That's probably why I don't own a gun."

I finally said what I'd been thinking since I'd seen the artwork in Valencia. "I take it you shared a lot of our terrorist jokes with Glenn and Joey."

Pete sighed irritably. "I don't know that they were *our jokes,* Tim, in the sense that I was violating some sacred trust by repeating them."

"I'm not accusing you of anything."

"Yes, you are. Look—I probably *did* need to know I could still laugh about that stuff with someone. At that point I thought I was never going to see you again."

"I understand. I tried to do the same thing, I guess. Except Todd doesn't laugh at anything anymore. And Gregory . . . you know how he is about anything violent."

"Yeah, I know," Pete said. "He'd mince right into the cattle car—as long as they told him he could shriek at Bette Midler comedies once he got to Auschwitz."

"That's a bit harsh. I hope you'll try and get along with Gregory this time."

Pete sneered.

"Glenn and Joey must be crazy about your Baader-Meinhof song."

"*All right,*" Pete said. "Before you get carried away with this simpleminded guilt trip, I think you should know that far from *me* inspiring *them,* if anything, it was the other way around. I wrote that song *about* Glenn. *He's* been a terrorist buff for years—albeit on a kind of camp, ironic level. *Glenn's* the one who used to go on to *me* about the Baader-Meinhof gang. How there should be a sitcom about them, with a retro-seventies look. Remember?" We'd joked about this. To the "Brady Bunch" theme, Pete sang, " 'There was once a German leftist known as Ulrike / Who got so sick and tired of only talk. She met a wild young rebel named Andreas / And at his violent plans she did not balk.' That came from *Glenn!* He thought *Patty Hearst* was funny, too."

Pete and I had considered *Patty Hearst* an unintentional comedy, due mainly to its cardboard depiction of the SLA. Pete liked to parody the William Harris character's incessant politicizing, spitting, "Put the pig milk back in the fascist insect refrigerator, Tania!"

"So Glenn was still operating on a camp, ironic level last year?" I said.

"For the most part. Sometimes he'd get more serious. You know, talking about how easy it would be to kill certain right-wing people now. How no one's expecting anything like that now, in America. It's not like twenty years ago when bombs were going off everywhere. They feel safe now. They're smug and complacent." Pete smiled. "It's odd. We even talked about Bryer at one point. This was way before my mom went to work for him. We decided he probably didn't even have a bodyguard. We imagined him flashing through John Wayne Airport, with just his briefcase and his garment bag. We imagined blowing his fucking head off with an AK-47 in the parking structure."

"Yes, it's easy to picture that all right. Could you take me home now, please?"

"*No.* I'm concerned about Joey—"

"*Why?* Were you and Joey fooling around? I mean, I know you have a rule against that with newcomers in general, but—"

"I told you," Pete said tightly. "I haven't been with anyone since we broke up."

"I know you said that. But sometimes things happen—"

"Goddamn it, Tim. This could really piss me off."

Understandably. "I'm sorry. I know I'm being neurotic and insecure, but—"

"Not everything is about sex, you know. It *is* possible to care for someone without wanting to fuck them, you know."

"No, I didn't know that. Thanks for telling me."

I wished like anything I'd kept my mouth shut. But the old fear-logic was so strong. If Pete had messed around with Joey (who almost certainly had the virus) within the last two months, it was possible that Pete, even though he'd tested negative last winter, might now in fact—

"Joey's got AIDS," Pete said grudgingly, as if saying it made it more true.

I felt a rush of guilt for having been so self-concerned. And a guilty sense of relief, certain Pete wouldn't have fooled around with Joey, knowing he was sick.

"How long has he known that?" I said.

"Well, he knew he was positive, but they just stuck the AIDS tag on him a couple months ago. I took him to the doctor right after he left Glenn. He had a bad case of thrush. His T-cell count was eighty-seven or something."

"That's low."

"Yeah. He can't take AZT. He had a bad reaction. It doesn't look good."

We were starting up the steep grade of the Sepulveda Pass.

"The speed can't be helping," I said.

"No."

"Why didn't you mention this earlier?"

He shrugged. "I don't know. I guess I thought you might think it was pointless, trying to save someone who's going to die anyway."

FOURTEEN

AS SOON as we saw that they were getting off at Mulholland Drive, Pete said, "Look, I may as well tell you what I think they could be up to."

"Is it unpleasant?"

"Kind of. You know our decapitation jokes?"

"Oh, no."

Our decapitation scenarios for the most part involved gay-bashing entertainment figures such as Andrew "Dice" Clay, Axl Rose, and the late Sam Kinison.

"Yeah, Glenn got quite a kick out of those," Pete said. "Especially the Axl idea."

"Oh, Christ."

I saw it: the screechy white-trash homophobe stripped bare and held down by three men, the fourth yanking back his honey-blond hair, hacking his neck with a machete, blood squirting.

"Yeah, Glenn got seriously off on that," Pete said. "Except he wanted to do it to Mel Gibson. After Mel made those homophobic remarks in that Spanish newspaper."

I saw it happening to Mel: the corny movie star stripped and held down, his tired shag hairdo, his butt wriggling, as the machete—the serrated edge this time—sawed into his neck flesh, blood squirting.

"Oh, Jesus, Pete. Mel Gibson could live up here. That movie-star row is just east of here."

"No, he lives in Malibu. In a heavily guarded area." Pete slowed down to keep plenty of space between us and the GTO as we followed them off the freeway. "I think Mel can rest easy tonight. But I can't say the same for Dondi Hule. *He's* the one they've been stalking."

Dondi Hule—just the name filled me with rage and revulsion. He was the vilest of the vile, worse even than Kinison or Clay. As part of his act Hule did lisping imitations of dying AIDS patients.

"They followed Dondi one night from some club on the Sunset Strip," Pete said.

"How do you know this?"

"Glenn told Joey about it a few weeks ago."

"So he's been talking to Joey before tonight?"

"Yeah, I'm afraid so."

"So they just followed him—is that all?"

"Yeah," Pete said. "Through some fluke. Dondi was in this Porsche convertible—"

"A cabriolet."

"Right. With the top down. Some Jessica Hahn–type bimbo woman beside him. And Glenn and Dexter and Mikey were in the GTO. And they had a chain saw."

"Come on, this is a joke, right?"

"No. And at one point, Dondi pulls up to this red light at Doheny. And they pull up right next to him. And they're all set to jump out and do it."

"Do what?"

"What do you think? Cut off his fucking head."

"Oh, my God."

"When guess what happens."

"A cop car pulls up."

"You got it."

Pete slowed down even more as we followed the GTO through the series of turns that bridged the freeway and led up to Mulholland Drive. "You think that really happened?" I said. "Maybe Glenn exaggerated for effect."

"I think it happened, Tim. Because Glenn had the idea of using Dondi's head in one of his assemblages."

"Oh, come on."

"No, it's plausible. Aesthetically, I mean. Glenn's already done that with some of his stuff, using materials that will rot or decay. Dead snakes. Rats. A little Chihuahua somebody ran over."

"Are you serious?"

"Yeah, none of his stuff is supposed to last. It's all built to either decompose or fall apart or explode. Supposedly, he was going to have Dondi's severed head attached to a mechanical device that would make his jaws move up and down while a Walkman played a loop of one of Dondi's crueler AIDS jokes. Glenn planned to document it on videotape for posterity and art-history purposes, and also send copies of the tape to the TV sations. He wondered if they'd actually show something that grisly on the news. Or if they'd use that digital-square effect to obscure it."

"I'll bet they'd show it," I said, so appalled I didn't know what else to do except joke. "They show everything now. I'd like to see Mary Hart introduce that on 'Entertainment Tonight.' "

"Yeah, me, too."

We were some distance behind the GTO, but I was still getting worried. There was nothing out there except empty brush hills and orange-lit asphalt—no other cars. It seemed absurdly obvious that we were following them. Up ahead of us they reached Mulholland Drive.

"The thing is," Pete said, "I think Dondi Hule may live in the Hollywood Hills."

"Yes, it's easy to picture him in a leased house in Laurel Canyon." I imagined a *Clockwork Orange*–like sequence: doorbell ringing, the corpulent, ponytailed comedian coming from the bedroom, tying his silk robe. As he opens the door, four shirtless men burst in, faces hidden by glans penis masks. They yank Dondi down by his ponytail, exposing his fat neck. The raucous grind of the chain saw, Dondi's howls and splintering spinal cord, blood spattering the plate glass windows, the bimbo's piercing scream.

But instead of turning east on Mulholland toward the Hollywood Hills, the GTO turned west.

"They're heading into Bel-Air," I said. "Who would they be planning to decapitate over there?"

"Well, one name springs to mind."

"Yeah, but he's still got Secret Service up the bunghole. Anyway, I've driven by that place. It's got cameras, a guard booth by the gate. You'd need a fucking commando squad to get in there."

I couldn't believe I was talking about this stuff as seriously as I was.

The GTO's taillights were already out of view around the curves of the road as we turned onto Mulholland.

"I wasn't thinking of his *house*," Pete said.

"Oh, my God. Of course."

I knew what Pete had in mind because we'd driven out along this stretch of Mulholland before—the afternoon we'd parked to watch the sunset and had the problem with the dirt bikers. Before that incident, we'd come to the complex we now saw off the right in the moonlight. Built into a bluff overlooking the lights of the Valley, surrounded by picturesque pine trees, stood Bel-Air Presbyterian Church.

In the orange sunset light of the previous year, Pete had swung up through the church parking lot so he could point out what he considered a "wry juxtaposition." The lounge where he'd gone to a straight AA meeting a few times, and at the other end of the complex, the sanctuary, a pale, boxy, fifties-modern structure with a large cross in front of it, where Ronald and Nancy Reagan attended Sunday services. This troubling proximity had inspired us to wonder if there'd been AA meetings in Nazi Germany, and Pete had come up with joke meeting names: Berchtesgaden Discussion Group, Hitler Mädchen Step Study, SS Speaker/Participation. As much as Pete liked AA, he wasn't pious about it.

We'd also imagined a chance encounter at the church between Pete and Nancy Reagan. He might be arriving late for his AA meeting, walking along one of the breezeways, and suddenly there she'd be, small and birdlike and smiling in her red Adolfo dress, on her way back from the ladies' room, momentarily unattended by her Secret Service detail.

"What would you do?" I'd asked Pete.

He'd thought for a moment, then said, "Well, at the very least, I know I'd lose it. I'd start yelling at her, 'You murderous bitch, you vile genocidal cunt!' But just keeping it verbal seems somehow too impotent, as if all you can do in the face of evil is shout obscenities. So probably, I'd strangle her. That would be the most satisfying. To just choke the fuck out of her till her face turned red and her tongue lopped out. Then tear off her head, just twist it right off, and throw it through the stained-glass window like a stinking sack of shit. Or else set it on a stake in front of the sanctuary."

"No, no," I'd said, laughing. "You know what would wreck her even more? If you got the Gipper alone and cut off *his* head with a chain saw and tossed it in the tub while she was taking her bath. Can you imagine that scream?"

Pete slowed down as we approached the church. "Did you ever talk to Glenn about this place?" I said.

"Yeah. In fact—we came to the AA meeting here once. Glenn and Joey and I. Walked around afterward. Checked out the sanctuary. Imagined how we might do it."

"Do what? Decapitate them?"

"No. It was more like how you'd shoot them. Where you'd plant a bomb, that sort of thing."

"Oh, Jesus, Pete."

"It was still a joke though, at the time. I mean, we were laughing. Some janitor gave us a funny look."

Pete pulled over and parked.

"What are you doing?"

"There they are."

The GTO was parked off the road about fifty feet ahead of us, just past the exit driveway. With the moonlight shining through its windows we could see that the car was empty.

Pete shut off the engine. "I'm going to talk to them."

"Are you out of your mind?"

Pete was already getting out of the car. I got out as well and caught up with him as he climbed the steep driveway. As the church came into view, illuminated by white security lights, so did the four men. They were going up the steps to the sanctuary, under the long shadow of the large cross—

a case of found religious kitsch. Dexter was carrying a white package about the size of a bed pillow.

There was a moment before they saw us when we could've turned and gone, and that's what I wanted to do. But Pete said to me, "This is too insane," and called out, "Hey, Glenn!"

They all jumped and whirled around as Pete kept walking toward them. Only Mikey appeared to have a weapon— one of the machine pistols we'd seen at the house. I don't really know how close he came to firing in panic, but I'm glad Joey said to him, "No, Jesus. It's Pete."

Glenn stepped up to Pete. "What are *you* doing here?" He spoke with a snakily sardonic voice that reminded me of William F. Buckley's. "Someone must've mixed up the call sheets, Pete. *This* isn't your scene, dreamboat."

"Don't do this," Pete said. "You don't have to do this."

Mikey was moving back behind us, covering us with his machine pistol. Dexter's package, I saw now, was plastique, a fairly horrendous amount of plastique, with a timer and detonator attached.

"We don't *have to?*" Glenn slid his hand across Pete's shoulder. "What do you mean, why not? Because he died last night? He had a heart attack or a stroke or fell off his horse?"

"Glenn, you can't kill all these people just to get him."

"Who says?"

Joey looked considerably worse here than he had at the house, jacked up and crazy eyed, waxy with dried sweat. "What the fuck are you doing here?" he said to Pete, his teeth clenched in what you *wished* were only a parody of rage. "Are you fucking crazy?"

"No, I'm the sane one, Joey."

"You must want to *die,*" Joey said. "Who *the fuck* do you think you are? *Our conscience?*"

"Let's hope not," Glenn said with an airy laugh. "At *our* house, Jiminy Cricket gets stepped on and squashed."

"Yeah, I know," Pete said.

"You know quite a lot, don't you?" Glenn brushed Pete's hair back with his fingers. "Peter Cottontail, hopping down the bunny trail. I think you've just come down on a land mine, love boy."

Suddenly there were headlights, a car turning up the church driveway.

"Shit, it's the fucking patrol!" Mikey said.

Glenn grabbed Pete's arm. "Back in the bushes. You've been *there* before, I know."

Mikey pressed the muzzle of his pistol to the back of my neck. "If you make one sound, I'll blow your fucking head off."

"Frightfully cardboard butch, I know," Glenn said to me. "But he means it."

We were all back in the bushes by the time the headlights reached the top of the driveway. It wasn't a security patrol car though. It was an old panel truck, EDUARDOS CLEANING on the side, a sticky Julio Iglesias love song spilling out. It pulled up to the sanctuary steps and stopped. Three stocky Latino men got out, talking in Spanish as they opened the back of the truck and took out a vacuum cleaner and a waxer.

"What the fuck is this shit?" Dexter whispered.

"It *is* a bit odd," Glenn said. "What time is it?"

Joey looked at his wristwatch. "Three-forty."

The Latino guys went up to the sanctuary and unlocked the glass doors. One took the waxer inside, the other two came back to the truck for more supplies.

"This is fucked up," Dexter said. "They're right where we need to go."

"I'm afraid so," Glenn said.

Mikey had his arm around my neck, the muzzle of his weapon against my lower back. "They look like Salvadorans to me," he said. "They've probably lost people to the fucking death squads *he paid for*. They'd probably *help* us."

"This is fucked," Dexter said. "I knew something would go wrong."

"I'll bet anything they'd help us," Mikey said. "We could stick it in the fucking pulpit. Or right under his pew."

"I think the Secret Service glances under his pew," Glenn said.

The Latino guys had stopped to prepare their equipment

at the sanctuary door. A balcony extended back along the side of the building. I guessed that it was somewhere along there that they hoped to place the bomb. I considered how a relatively small amount of plastique, hidden in a cassette player, had taken down that Pan Am jet over Scotland, and there was many more times that amount here. I pictured the sanctuary in ruins, as gutted as a South Central market, virtually everyone inside it killed.

"How long can they *be* here?" Dexter said.

"It looks like they're going to wax the floors," Glenn said. "This is starting to feel like an abort situation."

"This is too fucked," Mikey said. "Come *on*, we gotta do it. This has to be the first thing."

"We could do it the other way," Joey said to Glenn.

I didn't know what he meant at first. But from the way Glenn looked at him I figured it out.

"We'll discuss it," Glenn said. "Let's go to the camp."

"Glenn, let me talk to them," Mikey said. "They probably hate his fucking guts. They *know* he financed the right-wing death squads."

"*No*," Glenn said definitively.

"Then we should wait," Mikey said.

"*No!* The patrol will be along here eventually." Glenn looked at Pete and me. "All right, we're all going to the car."

"Glenn, I don't think we really need to be a part of this," Pete said.

"*Need?*" Glenn said. "What is all this about *need* tonight? What *do* you need, Pete? Besides a fat greased cock up your ass." He looked at me. "Or maybe you're getting that already." He mussed my hair. "You be good. No girlish screaming."

We climbed down through the bushes to the road. As soon as Glenn saw the Mercedes, he said, "Oh, now I get it. Of course. That's *Pablo's* car. I thought it looked familiar when we saw it by the house. Well, you've been quite the little spy tonight, haven't you, Pete?"

"I was worried about Joey," Pete said.

"I'm *fine*," Joey said. His eyes looked completely psychotic in the moonlight.

"Yeah, I can tell," Pete said.

"Why don't you fuck yourself, you condescending puke," Joey said through his teeth. "Fucking assfuck choirboy."

"Give Joey the keys to the car," Glenn said to Pete. "He'll follow us."

Joey took the keys and went back to the Mercedes.

Pete and I got into the backseat of the GTO along with Mikey, who kept the machine pistol trained on us. Once Glenn and Dexter had put the bomb in the trunk, Dexter got in behind the wheel and Glenn took the shotgun seat. We pulled out, heading west on Mulholland, Joey behind us in the Mercedes.

"This is a pisser," Dexter said.

"I know." Glenn seemed preoccupied.

"If these fucking pussies hadn't come along," Mikey said of Pete and me, "there wouldn't have been a problem."

"Yes, but these fucking pussies did come along," Glenn said, and looked at Pete. "And if you try and tell me it's God's way of saying *don't do it*, I'm going to take a sentimental journey down your throat with my braunschweiger-thick cock."

"I wouldn't presume to speak for God," Pete said.

"Fuck God in the ass," Mikey said. "And fuck you, too, Pete."

It was only then, from Mikey's tone, that I realized they had more of a history than Pete had indicated.

"Now, now," Glenn said. "Pete can't help being Pete. Can you, Pete?"

"I don't know if you realize how truly insane this is," Pete said.

"Oh, I think we do." Glenn smiled, checking me out. I was all but certain he didn't remember me.

"I don't blame you for wanting to nail Reagan," Pete said.

"Didn't think you would."

"But a church full of people, Glenn—"

"It's an aesthetic decision as much as anything," Glenn

said. "I *like* messiness—you know that, Pete. I abhor preciousness. I like paint and jiz and blood and crap smeared all over everything. I like to watch anal retentives *crack.*"

"Yeah, but Glenn—"

"Yeah, but *what*, Pete? Don't tell me you're not getting off on this. I know you too well. Your adrenaline's going crazy right now. You're jacked up right out of your mind and you love it. Don't tell me you're not elated that someone's finally *doing it.*"

"He's a fake," Mikey said, looking at Pete. "He's a fucking poseur. He sings all these fucking anarchic songs, but when it comes down to it, he's a fucking bourgeois humanist pussy. Look at the kind of guy he's attracted to."

"I'm not as conventional as I seem," I said.

"Oh, yes, you are," Mikey said. "You know what I'd like to do to you? I'd like to tie you up and take a giant shit right in your face."

"Now, Mikey." Glenn reached back and squeezed Mikey's knee and said to me, "He's being figurative. Mikey's really quite tender. Pete can vouch for that."

"That was a long time ago," Pete said.

"He fucked me in the ass in a Laundromat in Venice," Mikey said bitterly. "I wouldn't call that tender."

"*I'd* call it terribly exciting," Glenn said. "Any witnesses?"

"No, it was late at night," Pete said. "It was his idea."

"He stopped at one point to put another quarter in the drier," Mikey said angrily.

"Come *on*," Pete said. "You're acting like you didn't want it. I was trying to read *Crime and Punishment* and you were practically sticking your butt in my face." Pete looked at me. "This was eleven years ago."

"We've all got a past," I said.

We soon reached the end of the asphalt. From that point Mulholland continued out along the crest of the Santa Monica Mountains as a rough dirt road. Dexter kept going, the Mercedes behind us in the dust.

"If you're going to do it," Pete said to Glenn, "can't you get him when he's alone?"

"Oh, you mean like our Aldo Moro scenario?" Glenn said with a grin. "Grabbing him in a men's room in the *Die Hard* building? Chloroformed at the urinal, spirited away. His body found two weeks later in an Audi trunk in Palmdale. Nancy asked to identify the *badly* decomposed remains. 'Yes, that's him.' Vomit, upchuck down the front of her smart Adolfo dress. Like that?"

"There has to be some way to get him without killing all those other people," Pete said.

"Well—if you think of something between now and nine A.M., speak up."

"Then we're going to go the other way?" Mikey said guardedly.

"I don't see how we have much choice, if we want it done," Glenn said. "I don't know about you, but I'm all sexed up with someplace to go. My fat balls feel like a rumbling volcano—so you *know* it's too late to stop now."

"*I* should do it," Mikey said.

"We'll talk about it."

We passed the spot where Pete and I had parked and had the trouble with the dirt bikers. The road looked much cruddier at night, the headlights jerking over piles of trash, beer cans, dumped sofas.

"This'd be a good place to kill somebody," Mikey said. "Shoot 'em in the back of the head, executioner style."

"Yes," Glenn said. "Except see those lights down there? That's Encino. Do you know how lightly Valley girls sleep? 'Like, Dad, I heard some shots,' "

"So, you could strangle them," Mikey said. "Put plastic bags over their heads."

"That's true," Glenn said. "It would've been a good place to bring Dondi Hule. Except for that Valley girl again. 'Like, Dad, I just heard this totally gross chain saw.' " Foppish laugh.

I felt like pointing out how tired that Valley-girl bit was, but I kept my mouth shut.

"We should've done the club," Mikey said. "We could've wasted a bunch of those fucking veterans, too. Those guys make me sick. Fucking wheelchair baby killers, always whining about their fucking nightmares. That's what you *get* when you shove a flare up a Vietnamese woman's pussy, *moron*. Didn't John Wayne do that in *The Green Berets?*"

Glenn smiled pleasantly at Pete and me. "It was a comedy benefit for a veterans' group—Mr. Hule was performing. We had quite a fun skit worked out, all of us armed and attired in our deliciously ribald latex glans penis headgear. We planned to grab Mr. Hule on the stage, where, after I, with a full bladder, urinated splashily in his face, Mikey, who's quite clever with a samurai sword, would do his Japanese executioner shtick. For an encore, we would've opened fire on the audience, all of whom—let's not forget, Mr. Moral Quibbler—would have been only moments before weak with laughter over Mr. Hule's dizzyingly hilarious impression of a dying fag."

"We should've *done it*," Mikey said.

"Too much could've gone wrong." Glenn shrugged. "And in the final analysis, why run the risk of martyring a turd when you can stroll right into the Bel-Air shit factory and give America the heavy-duty high colonic she so desperately needs."

Dexter swerved to avoid hitting a dumped refrigerator.

"This'd be a good place to fuck two guys in the ass while you strangle them," Mikey said.

Glenn frowned. "That's not very loving, Mikey."

"I don't *feel* very loving."

"What *do* you feel, Mikey?"

"I feel like we should go back and nail Pete Schindler to that fucking cross in front of the church. And see if he gets a hard-on."

"A wry image," Glenn said. "But I'm afraid it might alert the Secret Service that something off-beat is afoot." Glenn squeezed Pete's knee. "All joshing aside, there's no way we could nail sweet little Pete's hands to a Protestant church cross—it's unthinkable. Why, he's written our anthem."

"I never meant that song to be a blueprint," Pete said.

"Oh, bullshit, you did, too," Glenn said. "Save the dis-claimers for the MTV news, assuming you get out of this alive. We've talked about all this far too much off the record, Pete. You've been hungry for something like this to happen. For someone to go 'much too far.' Someone, naturally, with nothing to lose. Well—here we are."

"I didn't mean killing innocent people."

"*Innocent.* Well, it's like this, Pete. If Hitler were in chapel at Berchtesgaden—"

"It's not the same thing."

"No, you're right, it isn't," Glenn said. "The damage is already done. This is payback. An object lesson. That not all queers are going to mince off to the hospice or be content to carry signs and blow whistles. That passive genocide earns aggressive retribution. Six hours from now, Ronald Reagan's head is going to look like a deflated football. His brains are going to be stuck to his grinning bitch's face— which itself will be stuck to a moldy hymnal." Glenn looked at me. "You're cute. Has anyone ever told you that? I mean cute in a butch way, not an icky way. God, you're trembling like a leaf. How exciting. Pete, what's your frightened friend's name?"

"Leave him alone," Pete said.

"Ooohhh, we're so protective." Oily sarcasm. "This must be serious then. With an *emotional* component. Not a sleazy tearoom tryst that's somehow escaped its proper bounds. But then you don't frequent that sort of place, do you, Pete? You're a good girl. The Amy Grant of the alternative music scene."

"You've really gone over the edge," Pete said.

"Oh, boy, have I ever," Glenn said. "And it feels so goddamn fucking good. I learned that in Santa Fe. Guess Joey filled you in on that stark little piece of high-desert minimalism. Well, how to describe it, Pete. When I blew those smug heartless fucks away, they were everyone who's ever called me a fag or a queer, every shitty hateful and/ or condescending straight fuck. . . . And it felt so exquis-itely fine. I'm here to tell you it beat aesthetic bliss by a long country mile. It made me want to spread the word to every queer and dyke in the land. The next time a hetero pig gives you some shit, talk back in *their* language: blow their fucking brains out. They understand that."

I knew I should keep my mouth shut, but I said, "Is that the kind of world you want to live in?"

"No," Glenn said. "Not at all. But it's the kind of world they've made."

Mikey looked at me. "He's a Gandhi queen, I knew it. He *wants* to be a victim."

"I'm not a Gandhi queen," I said.

"I don't know what you think you're going to do now," Pete said to Glenn.

"Well, then, let me spell it out for you—since it's all your fault, Mr. Good Intentions, that one of us must now hand-deliver the Gipper his gift."

"Who's going to do that?" Pete said.

Glenn looked at me. "I was hoping your chum might volunteer. In a proper suit, I'd say he'd pass quite nicely as a fresh-faced, white-bread Republican. 'Mr. President, sir, I'd just like to shake your hand and tell you how much I—' *Boom*." Glenn smiled. "But all whimsy aside, Pete, I wish I could say we're going to draw straws. But it's got more to do with T-cell counts, I'm afraid."

"You're deranged," Pete said. "You'll never get near him."

"It's a big bomb, *Liebchen*. We don't have to get that close."

"It's a fantasy."

"We've lived out all the others. Why not this one, too?"

"You won't get past the parking lot."

Glenn sighed heavily and went into a grating nasal psychobabble parody: "Do you *always* have to be so *negative*? I *really* think you *may* be a toxic person for me, Pete. We're *trying* to keep a positive attitude about this. It's Sunday morning and I just know *a lot* of those Secret Service men believe in Jesus Christ, too. I'll bet their guard's just about as low as it ever gets. And if *you* don't think so, *you* just keep it to yourself, Pete Schindler. If you can't be supportive and nurturing about this, we just may have to release you with love."

FIFTEEN

IN A FEW minutes we turned up a narrow rutted side road that led back through a grove of windblown eucalyptus trees to a fenced compound of run-down white wooden buildings. The faded sign above the gate read:

> *Camp Theodore Roosevelt*
> *Boy Scouts of America*

Glenn got out and unlocked the gate. Then we drove in, parking in front of the old meeting hall. Joey pulled up beside us in the Mercedes and cut the engine. Crickets. Out in the black night a coyote howled, followed by crazed dog barks. Mikey covered Pete and me as Glenn led us up to the meeting hall, Joey going in ahead of us to switch on an amber lamp.

The place was gutted and pretty much the way the Scouts had left it some years before, which didn't stop Glenn from giving us a mock designer tour. "I love the flags, don't you? American and California State, completely authentic, circa let's-fry-the-Rosenbergs. It's so good that patriotism's back—you can't disagree. And the portrait of Teddy R. Just look at that bully hog's head. No rough rider's spunk, nor suffragette's twat nectar, ever glazed *that* bristly facial brush. And over here, on this knotty-pine wall, the tree-trunk plaque with the Boy Scout pledge. I made this myself with my wood-burning kit. Actually, I used my penis and it hurt like hell. My own fault though. The Scout manual's clear as a bell about the right way to fuck wood. And over here, we have a 1940s pine-frame sofa with faded red cushions. A reproduction actually, based on a still from the colorized version of *High Sierra*. The matching chairs. In this one"—Joey was plopped in the chair—"we have a Ralph Lauren homosexual anarchist. There should be a little tag attached to him somewhere, explaining that the scuffed, used look, the imperfections, are part of what make him charming and unique."

Joey got up, giving Glenn a weary look, as if he were as tired of Glenn's pathological facetiousness as I was. "I'm gonna take a shower."

"Good idea, Joe." Glenn gave Joey's butt a jock pat. "Don't bend over for that bar of soap till I get there, *ha ha ha*."

Joey went into the green locker room in the back of the building and peeled off his shorts. Dexter came in and headed back there, too.

"And here's our TV." Glenn switched on the old 1960s cabinet set. After a long warm-up, a Madonna video popped onto the screen, her face a livid scarlet. "The bad color's deliberate," Glenn said. "Coordinated with the stripes in Old Glory and, of course, this." He flicked dried squirted syringe-blood from the tree-trunk plaque.

"And here we have our memorabilia." He pulled out a large cardboard box filled with an odd mixture of Boy Scout paraphernalia and sex toys—tent stakes and dildos, steel utensil kits and cock rings. "We're going to toss some of this stuff around eventually, casual reminders of a simpler time." He took out a foot-long, two-headed dildo. "From the Civil War. Lee surrendered this to Grant at Appomattox, I think."

"Come on, Glenn," Mikey said impatiently. "I wanna take a shower." He was leaning in the door, listlessly covering us.

"All right." Glenn dug two sets of handcuffs out of the box and came over to Pete and me. "We'll try to do this

216

as gently as possible. Why don't you cowboys park your butts on the love seat. But first, peel off your duds."

Pete sighed. "Is that necessary?"

"Of course not," Glenn said. "But it's sure gonna be fun. You're not seriously suggesting that I ignore the homoerotic potential of this situation, are you?" He ran his hand under the waistband of my trunks. "I'll bet my entire Colt pornography collection, *you've* fantasized being stripped and restrained by a gang of rowdy outlaws. Hands tied behind your back, a raunchy, sweaty-faced cowpoke sucking your veiny rod? Or maybe *two* drooling, unshaven hombres, fighting for it? Am I warm?" He pulled down my trunks. "Say, nice knob."

As I pulled my trunks back up, Pete said, "Don't mess with him, Glenn."

"Oh, please," Glenn said to Pete. "Is this your dagger-eyed Tyrone Power impression? You're nearly as bad an actor as he was. Don't pretend you haven't dreamt of a desperado dick up *your* bunghole, Pete, sans latex for those *extra sensations* of yesteryear." Glenn turned to me. "I'll bet you like to ride the horse cock, too." He pulled up my T-shirt. "Ooohhh, nice little body. Damn. I feel a jamboree coming on."

"Glenn, really," Pete said. "I think we may both be negative."

Mikey chuckled. "We'll leave a note to that effect with your bodies. So the morticians will know they don't have to wear rubbers."

"Really, Mikey." Glenn sneered. "What a repulsive notion. Not to say, an unfair slander against a largely above-board profession. Besides, I don't believe we've decided what we intend to do with our guests, other than make them as comfortable as possible. We'll steep some Earl Grey tea in a bit. And bring you something to read. Willa Cather perhaps. Or would you prefer Tom of Finland? I know, I have different moods, too. Do either of you gentlemen need to take a leak or a dump?"

Neither of us did. Despite another objection from Pete, Glenn insisted we take off our clothes. Once we'd done that, we sat down on the sofa and Glenn handcuffed Pete's left wrist to one of the pine arms, and my right wrist to the other, leaving each of us with one hand free.

"So you can smoke cigarettes and masturbate without our assistance," Glenn said. "And of course hold one another's hand, as I somehow know you do at motion pictures. I sense a passionate, fiercely volatile romance here. Oh, yes, I've noted your exchange of hot glances. But you . . ." He was looking at me. "Are you, by chance, a homo with a past? You look extremely familiar. Above the neck and below the T-shirt seam. I never forget a pretty cock. I'd swear that yours once grazed my lips in the misty parking-lot night of another time. Or do you merely *remind me* of a randy young man who once ejaculated upon my awed countenance and down the side of my black car?"

I was astonished, and somewhat horrified, that he remembered. I knew Pete was looking at me. "I don't think so," I said.

"Your nervousness betrays you," Glenn said. "I see it *was* as I remember." To Pete, he said, "Judge him not too harshly. The moon was very full that night. So were his fat, hairy balls. It was circa 1980. Who among us, after all, has not at least once found redemption in the kindness of a passing stranger's eager mouth without the sanctifying blessing of Pat Boone or Jehovah or Rome?"

"So you sucked him off at the beach twelve years ago," Pete said. "Who cares?"

"*I* care," Glenn said. "And I see no reason for bitterness. *Je ne regrette rien*, to quote the Little Sparrow. The times have grown mean, the city of Eros is now a necropolis, and all I have left are my memories. . . ."

I watched Mikey's smooth bare butt as he stepped into the shower and thought, with oblique envy, of Pete's encounter with him in the Laundromat.

"And memories"—Glenn slid into a jelly-voiced gay-auntie parody—"are *so dear!*" He pressed a prissy hand to his chin like Dirk Bogarde watching Tadzio. "Silly me, I remember every single fabulous *boy* I ever blew in Venice!" He sighed and rolled his eyes repulsively. "You drove a

Camaro. We compared engines. My gleaming 350, your throbbing 327. Your name was . . . *Tim*." He looked at Pete and mock-gasped. "Oh, my God." His own voice now, mock-serious. "Forgive me. Either this nutty little virus is doing somethin' to my brain, or else the crank's charred the old memory banks, or maybe it's just plain old self-obsession. But *Tim*—of course! *Your* Tim. *The* Tim. The very *same* Tim who broke your heart last year. How could I forget our *marathon* conversations after AA meetings at various neo-beatnik haunts about town as you rambled on *endlessly* into the neo-despair-ridden night, your eloquence marred only rarely with puerile drive-through psychology insights." In a Pakistani accent: "Welcome to Jock in thee Box! Cahn I take you odor, please!" In his own voice: "Yes, I'd like a codependent burger—withhold the onion—a large dysfunctional family, *with* emotional incest, a medium acting-out rageaholic love addict, and a large adult inner child *to go!*" A mock-smug grin for Pete. "Sorry, but I can't recall now whether Tim reminded *you* of *your* father, or if it was the other way around." Glenn drew tangled diagrams in the air: "Relationships are so dizzyingly Byzantine these days. But whatever happened"—Glenn looked at me— "you certainly raked poor Petey boy over the emotional coals. And yet—even then, as I stared into Pete's soulful blue passive-aggressive eyes, platonically squeezing his masculine hand on the marred tabletop, Morrissey keening peakedly through the sepia air behind us—*even then* the missing milk-carton schoolgirl inside my powerfully big-dicked man's body intuited the truth I see movingly demonstrated before me right now. That love—*if* it's love, to paraphrase Saint Thomas Aquinas and Sammy Hagar—cannot die and always *does* find a way. I told Pete then it wasn't over. I did a tarot reading. We got Death upside down. Which means that a sandy-haired prince will fuck you in the butt once again."

In the shower room, Dexter yowled, playfully grabbing Mikey. "Why don't you go take a shower?" I said to Glenn.

"What's wrong?" he said. "Are you finding my personality wearing?"

"How did you guess?"

"I'm sorry you feel that way. I find myself endlessly amusing."

"That's because you're on speed," I said. "You'd find a piece of dog shit endlessly amusing, you snide, demented queen."

Glenn let his jaw drop. Pete put a cautionary hand on my arm.

"Now *that* wasn't very nice," Glenn said. "*Snide* I don't mind. I simply *am* superior to nearly everyone in almost every way, and humility has always struck me as a wasted genteel flourish. *Queen* is plainly inappropriate. I'm far too naturally butch for that designation. *Demented,* however— now there you touch a nerve. Not that I am—demented, I mean—not yet anyway. But Rick was, towards the end, and it wasn't very amusing. He was like that on our last trip. Had to keep him doped up on the plane. Still, he babbled. 'Could you fasten your seat belt, sir?' His reply resembled nothing so much as gay Tourette's syndrome: 'Buttfuck cockhead asshole jiz Proust.' Are you finding this in poor taste? Would you rather not hear about it? Or perhaps you'd simply prefer a more subtle, exquisitely attenuated version. Speaking of which—Rick finished his novel before his mind went. And that was subtle enough. You know Rick. He spent seven years on that novel. There were, as they say, gay elements. But it was a highly refined work of literary art, nothing you couldn't excerpt in, say, *The New Yorker*. Know what happened to it? Did I ever tell you that story, Pete? Let me tell *you*, Tim. Rick and I flew to Spain and that's where he died. In a hospital in Barcelona. By the time I got back the breeders had been there. His brother Ted and Ted's pregnant wife, Sue. They'd come into the house, which was all right with me. I'd called them from Spain. Thought they were on our side. Found out differently. When I got back, Rick's novel was ashes in the fireplace, black pages. The only copy. Seven years of his life. Guess the gay elements, tasteful or otherwise, offended their breeder sensibilities. Guess what I wanted to do to them. But I was sane then. I held it in. For another whole year. Until Santa Fe."

"I don't blame you for being mad about something like that," Pete said.

"Didn't think you would."

"But I still think you've blown it. You could've had years, Glenn."

"To do what? Die slowly? Make art? Perhaps a little of both?"

Pete didn't answer.

"Oh." Glenn went snaky. "He's looking down. He doesn't want to say. How sensitive."

Pete looked at Glenn. "I believe art can affect things."

"Things?"

"*People*. How people perceive things."

"What people? Where? Jesse Helms? I know a better way to affect him."

"You've certainly shaken people up with your work, Glenn."

"So have you," Glenn said. "You've shaken us out of our catatonic grief with your inflammatory call to violence. I predict network sound bites of your Baader-Meinhof song over grisly visuals of our escapades."

"Glenn, I wrote that song so I wouldn't have to do it!"

"Oh, *I see*," Glenn said with stagy British gravity. "The depressingly chickenshit truth comes out. Art as catharsis. Art as therapy. Give the mental patient some clay. Let him make an ashtray. Well, I like your ashtray, Pete. I like it just fine. Let me pick it up and use it to batter in Ronald Reagan's skull and dig out his brains with my fingers and throw them in his wife's face, stuff them into her mouth and make her eat them. Chew, you grinning fascist bitch. Now swallow."

"It's one thing to throw out an image like that," Pete said. "It's another whole thing to try and make it real."

"Boy, you aren't kidding." Glenn did a technically perfect robust laugh. "It's damn hard work! Excuse me while I go wash off the sweat."

221

Glenn went into the locker room, where Joey and Mikey and Dexter were drying off. In the moment that we had alone, Pete said to me, "Just hold on." Whatever that meant.

Joey came out, drying his hair as he went to the TV, which he switched to CNN. A head shot of George Bush, his face as red as a monkey's penis. It was the same shot I'd seen the previous morning. He was talking about the need for family values in South Central. The ocean behind him was purple.

Mikey came out, pulled on his khaki shorts, and went out to the car.

Dexter came out naked, his uncut cock swinging like a pendulous turkey neck as he padded into the kitchen. In a moment he called, "Anybody want a sandwich?"

Nobody answered. Joey pulled on his gym shorts, lit a cigarette, and sat down in the chair facing the TV. Using the chunky 1960s brown-plastic remote control, he flipped through the channels, stopping at *Dr. Strangelove:* the scene where Sterling Hayden as the psychotic Air Force general explains to Peter Sellers his cracked theory of "preserving bodily fluids." In the harsh light of the black-and-white film Hayden's resemblance to Gerald Bryer was especially pointed, and it wasn't hard to imagine Bryer speaking of bodily fluids in a far more contemporary but equally paranoid context. (Bryer had once spoken of AIDS "spores" being released in the air "like tiny microscopic warheads.")

Joey flipped through the channels again, stopping on C-SPAN. Then he looked at Pete. "I'm sorry you had to get involved in this, but it's your own fucking fault. You shouldn't have come out to Valencia. You shouldn't have followed us."

"I don't believe you," Pete said. "You leave these fucking messages all night, practically begging me to come and rescue you—"

"I left *one message* like that at the club," Joey said blandly, and shrugged. "I had some ambivalence at a certain point, what can I say."

"Joey, why don't you fuck yourself?"

"*Look*—" With some effort Joey held in his anger. "I appreciate what you did for me, Pete. I had a couple of months that weren't that bad. I know it was awkward for you because you couldn't really make all the usual AA promises. About a long sober life and all that. You could've, but you didn't. All you could promise *implicitly* was that I'd be able to die sober. For some reason that just doesn't do it."

Joey stared at the TV: a strange, endless, seemingly candid shot of Barbara Bush sitting on a chartreuse lawn, playing fetch with Millie.

"You don't have to do this," Pete said.

"I *want* to do this."

"I don't believe you."

"I don't care," Joey said. "Look, I don't want to talk about it. I don't want you to fuck with my head."

"You've got a lot of talent, Joey—"

"So do a lot of dead people."

"You're not dead yet."

"I will be in a few hours. So just shut the fuck up, *okay?* Let me enjoy the time I've got left."

Joey switched to MTV: a black-and-white R.E.M. video, bleeding red, Michael Stipe and some women dancing bare chested, their nipples blocked out with black bars.

Glenn stepped into the room, drying off. "Are we talking out here? You're not trying to *influence* Joey, are you, Pete? You wouldn't do that, would you? Not when you're our guest."

Pete didn't respond. He looked profoundly depressed.

Mikey came in with the bomb, which he carefully placed on the red braided carpet. Then he emptied a canvas backpack out on the floor and began stuffing the bomb into the pack.

Glenn pulled on his baggy shorts and stepped to the white stucco wall with a felt-tip pen in his hand. "May as well leave the Mormon G-men something to ponder."

"Hey, what are you doing?" Dexter said from the kitchen door as Glenn began to draw on the wall.

223

"We shan't be coming back here again, Dexter. I don't see how it matters if we deface your sentimental shrine now."

Dexter said nothing more, but he didn't look pleased. He walked over to the artist's supplies piled in one corner of the room and picked up a dusty sketchbook, which he examined with an air of secretive reverence, his back to the rest of us, as Glenn continued to draw on the wall.

"Are you paying attention, Joseph?" Glenn said.

"Yeah." Joey had one leg up over the chair, exposing his genitals in his shorts leg.

"Very well then." Glenn explained as he went. "This . . . is the church. This . . . is the steeple. You can look through the glass doors . . . and see many of the key vile scum who are destroying this planet. *Ha ha ha.*"

I finally realized who Glenn's laugh reminded me of: Louis Hayward, the 1940s actor who'd specialized in the dual-persona costume pictures I'd watched on TV (and identified with) as a boy. Effete, powdered-wig court fop by day ("M'lords, M'ladies, *ha ha ha*"), dashing clipped-speech masked-rebel swordsman by night.

"*Here,*" Glenn continued, ". . . is the pulpit. This . . . over here . . . is our former president's pew. Up here . . . is the stained-glass window." He sighed. "Damn. If only we could've just got our hands on that Stinger miss-ile!" He did the choir singing: "Holy, holy, holy," followed by a whistling missile and an explosion sound. "Ah, well! To quote Vince Lombardi—or was it Guy Lombardo? Or was it Leonardo da Vinci?—it's not how you play the game that counts, it's whether or not you win it by obliterating the Gipper and as many of his fat-cat teammates as you can." He drew on the wall. "This . . . is the small glass door from the balcony. Now, recon tells us that a single Secret Service man will be standing just inside—"

"What if he steps out on the balcony?" Joey said. "He'll see me climbing up from the ravine. If I shoot him *then*—"

"Goddamn it, Glenn!" Mikey said. "You're going to let

this pussy botch one of the greatest moments of the twentieth century—"

"Don't you call my boyfriend a pussy, mister," Glenn said in a stiff Gary Cooper parody.

"This is bullshit," Mikey said. "I could come up through the lot and take that guy out without a sound."

"Yes, I know." Glenn slid his hand across Mikey's back. "You're our favorite little ninja. Which is precisely why we're going to need you in the weeks and months to come. We must be pragmatic. You've only recently sero-converted. You're far more likely to die in an FBI fusillade, Mikey, than by [with French pronunciation] *complication du HIV*. Or if, by a fluke, you're taken alive—why, there might even be a cure for you several years down the line in federal prison. You've got everything to live for, not the least of which is helping us kill as many powerful rightwing pigs as we can. And when Dexter and I begin to fade, as we no doubt shall before you do—why, the bomb with the burning fuse will be in *your* hand. So you see, you're the *last one* who should bear Ronald Reagan his gift. Whereas Joey"—Glenn took off his glasses and looked at Joey—"how I wish it weren't the case. But I think we all know that any way you slice it, *this* is Joey's last summer."

"Glenn, this is despicable!" Pete said. "You are morally insane!"

Everyone looked at Pete. For a moment I even imagined that Glenn was sobered.

Joey got up and came over to Pete. He was mad. "That's just a tad disingenuous, coming from you, Pete. Or does it make a big difference because you know me? Because I'm not some distant AIDS kamikaze you can cheer on the news, but someone you know and *really care about?* What do you want me to do, Pete? Die a miserable death? To pay for my sins? You want me to die in some fucking hospital after endless days of agony like everybody else? So that everybody can say he was a fighter who died with dignity? Is that what you want?"

"No."

"Because *fuck dying with dignity!* Too many people have died already, and there's nothing dignified about a corpse pile! I want to see *another* corpse pile—in that fucking church! I want to see Ronald Reagan's guts pulled out and thrown all over the room! I hope a bunch of stupid little cunt girls die, too! The more innocent victims the better! *We've* died and *we're* innocent! Let the slime who let it happen see what it's like!"

"I understand how you feel," Pete said.

"No, you don't," Joey said. "*You don't have it!* You used to say a lot of radical things, Pete. You used to say that if you ever got it, you'd take someone with you, some vile pig who deserves to die. Well, I guess you've kind of lost interest in that now that you know you're negative. You're into expressing your anger through art now. Well, *I don't have that luxury!* What do you think I should do? Paint one final big picture? Well, that's what I'm doing. I'm Mi- chelangelo. I'm going to dip my brush into Ronald Reagan's blood and paint the fucking ceiling!"

Glenn put his arm around Joey. For the first time ever, Glenn dropped his facetiousness as he said to Pete, "Do you think this is the way we want things to be?"

"I don't know," Pete said. "You're the terrorist buff. You tell me."

"I'll tell you this," Glenn said, "even though it's turning gold to shit to put it into words. But it's like this. I love Joey. We're both extremely fucked up and bad for each other, but I love him. I'd like nothing more than for us to go on being bad for each other, fighting and fucking and making art, for the next thirty years—but it's not happening. You know, last year when we got sober, that was a good time, Pete. We had a lot of fun then, no small thanks to you. I wish we could have long lives like that, but we can't. The fuck upstairs works in mysterious ways. But so do we. We're climbing the stairway to His office right now. He'll still be on the speakerphone, watching atrocity footage on one of His monitors, when we come through the door and blow His fucking brains all over heaven."

Glenn stepped to the wall and drew a crude pornographic

sketch. "This bullshit's over," he said. "Joey knows what to do. It's not really very complicated. What time is it?"

"Five-thirty," Joey said, looking at his watch.

"Dexter, recon the church," Glenn said. "Let's make absolutely sure the Gipper's sticking to his schedule. Mikey, how's that bomb look?"

"It's fine," Mikey said. "I just have to take off the timer."

"Good." Glenn captioned the sketch: *J. Edgar Hoover sucking John Dillinger's cock in his dreams*. "Then let's get moving."

Glenn looked at Joey. In a tone both ironic and genuinely tender, he said, "I think we should spend some quality time together now."

SIXTEEN

GLENN and Joey went into the bunkroom and closed the door. Dexter put on a pair of Nikes and a UCLA tank top and said to Mikey, "How do I look?"

"Fine. Except yuppie joggers don't usually have tracks on their arms."

Dexter pulled on a long-sleeved Loyola sweatshirt. "Back in thirty minutes."

Through the open door we watched Dexter drive off in a shiny new silver Range Rover. The sun was coming up, the sky in the east turning pink.

Then we were alone with Mikey, who sat on the floor, working on the bomb. The dawn light made his skin look especially smooth and glossy, a flattering photographic effect—Bruce Weber goes to Japan. I'd never slept with a Japanese-American man, but Mikey was just the sort I'd often found attractive. A *chunk*, as Ken, a gay Japanese guy I'd known in film school, would say. He'd meant *hunk*, but because of his accent it had come out *chunk*, which seemed much more expressive. I thought of a personal ad I'd once seen in the *Advocate*, reflecting an Asian man's bad experiences: "No 'rice queens,' no guys 'into Orientals,' no Vietnam veterans . . ."

On TV, Aretha Franklin was singing "Chain of Fools" in a smeary twenty-five-year-old videotape, and I was nervously tapping my foot to it, when the picture suddenly cut to snow and harsh white noise.

"What the fuck—?" Mikey turned down the volume and tried several other channels, but all of them were snow.

"Are you Century Cable up here?" I said.

"I don't know." He stared at the TV. "I think it's Mengele Cable."

"I think you *are* Century up here," I said. "It's been going out a lot lately."

Mikey came back to the bomb.

"I'll bet you get 'Nightline' on Monday," I said.

"I think we're going to have 'Nightline' for a long time to come." Mikey smiled. "That's Glenn's idea, that they'll have two experts to discuss it. From L.A. that Rand Corporation guy, Brian Jenkins, who always talks about terrorism. And from New York, Susan Sontag, author of *Notes on Camp,* the seminal study of homosexual humor."

"I don't think anyone's going to mistake this for camp," I said.

"You never know."

"Doesn't the idea of killing innocent people bother you?" I said.

"Who says they're innocent?"

"Well, you can't tell me everyone in that church deserves to die. What about the children—"

"*What* children?" Mikey said irritably. "What do you think the Sunday school is for? *That's* on the far side of the complex. If we really wanted to be nasty, we'd lob a grenade in there. I'd *do it.* You know why? Because I *like* senselessness now. I've changed that way. I used to be just for killing the politician or CEO or whoever, but sparing his family. Now I'd kill his family first and make him watch. So that *he* could know incomprehensible loss. If I were on my own, I'd go further. I'd kill people at random. I'd go down to Disneyland with a submachine gun and mow down as many breeders as I could. I'd turn the happiest place on earth into the saddest place on earth. But this is not that. These people aren't innocent. I've already killed an innocent person. I know what that's like. It didn't feel like this."

"That wasn't murder though," Pete said, "if you mean Mark."

Mikey stopped what he was doing and looked up at Pete. "Joey's got a big mouth."

"That must have been a difficult thing," Pete said.

Mikey went back to work on the bomb. "It wasn't something I wanted to do."

"Mark was a good poet."

"Yeah, he was," Mikey said blankly. "We had a good life together. For almost two years. Before he got sick. We tried different things. Drugs from Mexico. Chinese herbs. We went to a healer who said it was his anger. That if he'd let go of his anger, he'd get well. He did that, I think, but he didn't get better. I think the healer was wrong. He should've aimed his anger outward. Then he might be alive today. But finally he got the brain lesions, so he decided to end it. He told some people, if he thought they'd understand. So some friends came by that afternoon. It was very moving. Then he took the Seconals, but six hours later he was still breathing. So I held the pillow over his face. I loved him more than I've ever loved anyone."

Mikey got up and lit a cigarette.

"I almost killed myself after that," he said. "Some kitsch idea that I could join him in heaven. Glenn talked me out of that. He convinced me that I'd be killing the wrong person. He was right about that." Mikey looked at me. "You used to live in Venice."

"Yes. About six years ago."

"Yeah, I used to see you on the boardwalk." He said dryly, "We should fuck. To make the circle complete. Everybody else has. Me and Pete. Pete and Carlos. Me and Carlos. Maybe you and Carlos."

"Not to my knowledge."

"Not to your knowledge—that's funny."

"Who do you think killed Carlos?" Pete said.

"I *know* who killed him." Mikey paused deliberately. "Don't look at me that way. It wasn't me. Did you know Frank Childers?"

230

"Vaguely," Pete said. "You think Frank did it?"

Mikey nodded. "He told me about it a few weeks before he died. He knew I'd understand. Because Carlos did the same thing to me. To you, too, I guess. To a lot of guys."

"But Frank went with Carlos back in '86," Pete said. "He wasn't still angry after five years, was he?"

"Well, I think he blamed Carlos for his AIDS."

"But Carlos was *negative*," Pete said. "I don't think he lied about *that*."

"No, probably not," Mikey said. "But after Carlos fucked him over, Frank went sexually insane for a while. You know, trying to get lots of validation to compensate for what Carlos had done to him. Trying to fuck Carlos out of his system. He was sure that was when he got it. So one night last fall he went by Carlos's garage apartment."

"*That* place," Pete said. "The red bougainvillea spilling out across the stairs. No furniture, no place to sit, even though he'd been there for years. The single bed, to discourage people from staying over. I can still see Carlos coming to the screen door, shirtless. His warm brown skin. His wet greeting kiss. We'd always kiss deeply, since I knew he was negative. *God*—we used to make love for *hours*, hours on end, with the Jesus and Mary Chain playing, *Darklands*, over and over, while the bedroom got dark as the sun went down."

Mikey smiled, as if he had similar memories. "Frank said he wasn't even consciously angry at Carlos the night he went by. On the contrary, he said, it was almost a sentimental visit. He'd been in the hospital twice already. He knew his time was running out. He just wanted to say goodbye to Carlos, to tell him that in spite of how badly their affair had ended, he'd really loved him. But Frank said Carlos wasn't happy to see him at all. He was just stepping out of the shower when Frank came by, getting ready for a date. So Frank told Carlos he had AIDS and Carlos said something like, 'Gee, that's tough, I don't know what to say.' Then Carlos said he'd just taken the test again, for the third or fourth time, and come up negative again. They were standing in Carlos's kitchen. You know how his front

231

door opened onto the kitchen? Frank said he noticed a big knife in the dish rack."

"How bizarre," Pete said. "I *remember* that knife. I used to keep my *toothbrush* in the dish rack, 'cause there was just that one sink."

"Right. You had to brush your teeth in the kitchen."

"Yes, exactly," Pete said softly. "And once early on, even when everything was still idyllic with Carlos, I remember noticing that knife and wondering almost as a joke if I'd ever want to use it on him. Which is very strange, 'cause I don't usually think things like that about people. What was it *about* him?"

"He was a vampire," Mikey said. "He *liked* having ex-boyfriends angry at him. He could say they were 'obsessed' with him. His sick ego craved that the same way Dracula craves blood. That was my fantasy: to drive a stake through his heart. Or else burn his house down. Throw a Molotov cocktail through his bedroom window."

"Yeah, I thought of that, too," Pete said. "Like that X song, 'Burning House of Love.'"

"That was Carlos's favorite group."

"I know. I'm surprised though. Frank always seemed so shy and sweet-natured."

"He said the first thrust was to Carlos's heart. He drove the knife in right up under his rib cage. Then, he said, he went into a kind of blackout state of 'uncontrollable demonic ecstasy.' That was his term. And when it was over, when he was finally spent and he saw all the blood, and the body of the man he'd once loved so tenderly torn and destroyed with intestines spilling out, he threw up. But he didn't regret what he'd done. He felt that Carlos, in his soul, was genuinely evil."

"I can see why he'd think that, but—"

"I think Carlos may have given me the virus," Mikey said.

Pete looked stunned. "I don't understand. If Carlos was negative—"

"Well, *I* was negative then, too," Mikey said. "So we had very unsafe sex. And after Carlos, I was very careful again until Mark. Mark was also negative at first, and we were monogamous." Mike shrugged. "Who knows? I only went positive a few months ago. But now they're saying it can take as long as three years for the antibodies to show up in the test. It's *been* almost three years since I went with Carlos. So maybe he had it but it wasn't showing up yet. We'll never know now."

Pete looked shaken, and I didn't want to think about this. I'd heard the same news about the extended incubation period, but I'd pushed it aside when Pete told me he'd tested negative. I still wanted to believe it was only in rare cases where it would take as long as three years to show up. I still wanted to believe that Pete was really all right.

Glenn came out of the bunkroom, naked and smiling. He wiped his greasy cock off on the American flag and put on his glasses. "How's that bomb comin', Mikey?"

"It's ready."

"Then we're only waiting for the final word." Glenn opened his knapsack and dug out a syringe and a packet of speed. "Assuming we're on, I believe it's time for a light breakfast of bliss."

Glenn and Mikey went into the kitchen, as if, despite their lack of other inhibitions, they wanted to keep their speed-shooting ritual private. As Glenn prepared the drug, he sang bits of popular songs, changing the word *love* to *hate*, e.g.: "All You Need Is Hate," "Just an Old Fashioned Hate Song," "(Once I Had a) Secret Hate," "Hate Is a Many-Splendored Thing," and "I Honestly Hate You." The only exception to this pattern was a revised Beach Boys' lyric about having fun, fun, fun till Daddy takes the T-cells away.

In a moment, Joey came out of the bunkroom, naked and honey blond in the hard morning sunlight. He paused to wipe his greasy butt on the American flag and look at the striped cloth and scowl. "Shit—this fucking thing's *filthy*. I got *dust* all over my *butthole*." Giggling, he padded on into the kitchen.

While they were off, Pete whispered to me, "Just take it easy. This is what I've been waiting for."

I had no idea what he had in mind.

In a moment Glenn stepped into the kitchen door, looking breathless and ecstatic. "Ah, yes," he sighed. "And on the eighth day, the petrochemical Dad created crank. And He said, 'This will be for my sons who will die young.'"

"Glenn, I don't understand why you're not going to La Jolla," Pete said offhandedly. "That's a golden opportunity if there ever was one."

Glenn stared at Pete. When he spoke, he sounded oddly childlike and vulnerable. "What are you talking about?"

"That conference. What's it called? The American Family Foundation—"

"You mean, the American Values Foundation?" Glenn looked puzzled, as if he were struggling to concentrate and not space out.

"Yeah, *that's* it," Pete said. "They're having a four-day conference down there. I can't believe you don't know about that."

Joey stepped into the doorway, his arm bent. He looked seriously over-amped, as if he might be about to pass out. He was pouring sweat. "This sounds like bullshit," he said to Glenn. "He thinks if we're tweaked, he can fuck with our heads."

"I'm not trying to fuck with your head," Pete said calmly. "I'm trying to save your life."

"So who all is attending this reactionary powwow?" Glenn said wryly, as if the *idea* of it at least amused him. "Do you recall any names?"

"I've got the guest list," Pete said. "It's in my knapsack."

Oh, Christ, the mailing list. Even with his brains on fire, this was going to fool Glenn for about three seconds.

Glenn got Pete's knapsack, dug out the computer list, and opened it. Mikey and Joey gathered around, looking at different pages of it. They were impressed by the names, as well they should've been.

"Here's that antiabortion guy," Mikey said. "You know what he said, don't you? 'You fags are next.'"

Of a powerful Orange County defense contractor, Joey said, "Isn't this that Reagan kitchen-cabinet guy?"

"Yes," Glenn said. "And look here. *AIDS Cure*." The congressman in Joey's assassination painting. "And here is our East Coast neocon contingent, featuring not one but *two* key presidential hopefuls, their eyes fixed on '96."

"This would save us a lot of trouble in D.C.," Mikey said.

"It would at that," Glenn said.

I was still waiting for them to realize it was only a mailing list when Glenn looked at the last page and said, "Here's the schedule. Ah! Excuse me while I cream. *Luncheon*—noon Sunday. Guest speaker . . . everybody's favorite right-wing patriarch—the one *I'd* like to say 'Howdy' to, before it's too late and I'm dead." He was paraphrasing Pete's song. "I *would* like to see the look in his eyes, right before I blow off his head."

I was trembling with an adrenaline surge by then, realizing that it *was* a conference guest list. And a virtual who's who of the American right.

Glenn looked at Pete. "Where did you get this?"

"A friend of mine was doing some temp work at Gerald Bryer's district office. She lifted it."

I didn't blame Pete for not wanting to tell Glenn about his mother.

"Well, bless her heart." Glenn looked back through the list. "Yes, I see that Representative Bryer's right here among a number of other interesting *B* names. Something tells me he'll be sitting very close to the senator." Glenn looked over his glasses at Pete and slid into a Southern accent much like the senator's: "Why are you providing us with this option, sir? I thought you had serious reservations about violence."

"I have serious reservations about Joey throwing his life away on what's basically an incredibly sloppy vendetta," Pete said. "Especially when you can do something else that will affect the *future* in a very profound way. These are the people who *invented* Ronald Reagan, and now they're setting the agenda for what's to come. That's what this conference is all about. You'll never have another chance like this. And the thing is, if you all go in together, with automatic weapons, you can probably take most of those people out. *And* you can probably all get away."

"*Probably*. Hmm." Glenn continued his Southern accent. "It's just very difficult to know what to expect down here in the"—he looked at the conference schedule—"the Neptune Room of the La Jolla Coast Club."

Oh, God. I closed my eyes. And saw the Neptune Room, its pale blue and green nautical friezes. I'd been there innumerable times.

"With all these decent Americans gathered in one place," Glenn said, "they'd be fools if they didn't have security."

"I'm sure there's security of some sort," Pete said. "But it's like we used to talk about. Nobody's really expecting anything to happen, not in America, not in a place like La Jolla, not now. They're complacent."

Glenn kept looking over the list. "Oh my! *My, my, my!* It *is* a tempting scenario." He saw another name. "Excuse me while I convulse in a sudden ecstatic spasm of ejaculatory glee. Flying in from Manhattan we've got the right-wing cow herself. *Moo,* honey! Rump roast Sunday! Tears on Pinochet's pillow. Yes, in my mind's eye, it would be like shooting crypto-fascist fish in a barrel."

"That's probably what it will in fact be like," Pete said.

"There's that *probably* again." Glenn smiled glumly. "We could all die trying to act out that fantasy. Is that what you want, Pete?"

"On the contrary."

"There's something fucked-up about this," Joey said. "It sounds way too easy." He glared at Pete. "He's a closet humanist. He's a fucking pantywaist wimp sentimentalist. He's just worried that I'm going to maim some fresh-scrubbed Christian twat in the choir. He wants me to die a miserable death in a hospital like another fucking martyr."

Pete gave Joey an incredulous look. "Fuck you, Joey. Go ahead and do it. Fuck you in the ass."

"I wish you had," Joey said. "I know you wanted to."

"Right," Pete said. "You've got it. You really understand what everything's about."

We heard a car outside—Dexter coming back in the

Range Rover. Glenn and Joey went out to meet him. Mikey was still looking at the list, shaking his head regretfully. "I wish we'd known about this sooner."

"If you guys are gonna be terrorists," Pete said, "you should start reading the newspaper."

"Why?" Mikey said sarcastically. "Maybe we want to be *wacky* terrorists. Hapless cutups sending letter bombs, by mistake, to Mother Teresa." He chuckled.

I had to make a decision and I didn't have time to ponder all the moral nuances and ramifactions. I knew that if I could convince them to go to La Jolla, I'd have to bear some responsibility for what happened. But if I said nothing, they were going to do something just as horrendous—in fact, more horrendous; that's what I decided. That's what it came down to. If Joey went to the church, a lot of more or less innocent people were going to be obliterated along with the two—and their circle of wealthy benefactors—whose narratives blatantly urged violent closure. Whereas in La Jolla, in the Neptune Room, the ratio of innocent bystanders to guilty participants was inevitably going to be far lower.

That logic wouldn't win Sam Waterston's endorsement. "Good God, man! They shot off a busboy's hand!" But I had exhausted my appalled-humanist response. I thought of something Todd had once said, even though he opposed violence. "Assassination *does* change things profoundly. You can't say it doesn't." It was just that usually the wrong people got assassinated.

Pete was right. It was a rare opportunity to decimate the right wing and thereby affect the course of American politics, the state of humanity, in an incalculably ecstatic way. There's no point in pretending that I didn't find the prospect exhilarating, that I didn't also long to see the right people die for a change.

But I hesitated as Glenn and Joey and Dexter came in the room. Dexter was limping, as if he'd injured his leg while he was jogging. Glenn looked extremely disturbed. I wondered if Dexter might have discovered that the Reagans weren't going to church this morning after all. If that was the case, I wouldn't need to say anything, of course. But the possibility that *nothing* might happen, nothing at all, suddenly seemed unacceptable, an intolerable visceral disappointment, as if a momentum had been building, a drive toward catharsis, and I had become caught up in it as much as anyone. So I felt an awful sense of relief when Glenn said to Mikey, "He's coming to church all right."

"Look, I know the La Jolla Coast Club," I said to Glenn. "I used to go there. I grew up in La Jolla. We were members."

Glenn stared at me. "Yes, I can believe that. I can tell just by looking at you that your little WASP bunghole's as tight as a Chinese handcuff."

Dexter sat down and rubbed his leg, wincing.

"The Neptune Room is right on the beach," I told Glenn, and flashed back to a claustrophobic night in 1970: dancing stiffly with Tricia Nixon look-alike Bonni Hunnicutt, who was married to a Bechtel executive now. Her cold, wet palms, her soft white neck and insipid perfume, the slippery strains of "More"—I'd needed air.

"There's a veranda," I told Glenn. "A long row of French doors. The beach is public. There's really nothing to stop you. . . . I can draw you a map."

"Okay." Glenn looked at the other guys. Something funny was going on. "Joey, unlock Tim's cuff, would you?"

Once I was free, I picked up the felt-tip pen and stepped to the wall, feeling a bit self-conscious about being on naked display. For a moment I imagined I had Gregory Peck's role in a gay porno remake of *Twelve O'Clock High:* This briefing would give way to an orgy in a B-17 cockpit, somebody creaming on the Plexiglas of the machine-gun ball-turret.

I drew on the wall. "Here's the club. This . . . is the Neptune Room here. This street, alongside the club, is Corral Avenue. It dead-ends at the beach right here. It'll probably be crowded down there today. But you can park in the red zone here, if you don't mind getting a ticket."

"Please." Glenn lowered his eyes.

238

Mikey playfully grabbed at my cock, chuckling when I jumped back. Dexter was still rubbing his leg in pain.

"So that's it," I said. "I'm sure on a warm summer day the veranda doors will be open to let in the sea breeze."

Glenn and Joey asked me questions, and I showed them where the interior doors were, the kitchen, where the dais would be, the "most important" tables. They began to plan how they might do it, who would go where.

"We could go in with the MP5s," Joey said. "Extra clips. Once we start shooting, there'll be total hysteria. While they're shitting, we reload—"

"And as we're leaving, toss a few grenades back into the room as party favors." Glenn smiled.

Mikey warmed to the notion as well. "This could actually be quite a blast, Glenn. People are gonna shit. Especially when they find out a bunch of queers did it!" He grinned.

In the back of my mind I heard Gregory saying, "My God, what about the *backlash?* This will set us back thirty years! They'll create a police state!" But I knew how Todd would react. He'd "empathize with the rage" of the attackers, while abhorring the actual violence. While visibly trembling with elation that someone (else) had finally *done it*.

"I think it's worth considering," Dexter said. " 'Cause I really don't think anybody's getting near that church this morning."

"What are you talking about?" Mikey said.

"The Gipper's got company," Glenn said. "It seems that our current president and Mrs. Bush are attending services with Ron and Nancy this morning."

Oh, Jesus, I thought. Of course. George Bush was in southern California. The shot on CNN with the ocean behind him—he'd been addressing the conference in La Jolla on Friday.

"You're kidding," Mikey said. "Then we *gotta* do it!"

Dexter shook his head. "They've got the road closed off. It's a whole other ball game now, Mikey."

"It's too good," Mikey said. "It's like a double fucking jackpot! We gotta go for it!"

"But you'd be making Quayle president," I said.

"Not an entirely unwitty prospect," Glenn said. "A wry postmodern, retro-dementia, crypto-kitsch, neo-Dada prank—like giving a Nobel Peace Prize to Henry Kissinger. Of course, once the tittering tapered off, you'd be left with a horse-faced Christian cooze in charge of everything, which wouldn't be very funny. It's a moot point anyway. Dexter's right. An ex-president's one thing, George Bush is another. Don't think we'd get past the parking lot, even if we all went in *Wild Bunch* style. But contrary to what Pete may think, we're not gratuitously suicidal."

"A plane!" Mikey said. "I could steal a plane!"

"Mikey, you don't know how to fly a plane," Joey said.

"I can grab a pilot at gunpoint!" Mikey said. "Some fucking Sunday pilot! Make him crash his Cessna into the church!"

"It's a fantasy, Mikey," Joey said.

"*So what?*" Mikey said. "Everything *starts* as a fantasy! You're just chickenshit, that's all. You're just glad you've got some more time."

"You're fucking right I am!" Joey said. "I don't *want* to die, Mikey." Joey wiped dripping sweat from his eyes. "This makes a lot more sense."

"It does at that," Glenn said. "Yes, I'm beginning to have a very warm, glowing feeling about this La Jolla adventure. I see a rare, open window of opportunity. If Bush was there on Friday, that was surely their moment of keenest alert. They'll be relaxed now, in the wind-down stage, the afterglow. There still may be the remnants of protest—so much the better. While the ACT UP and Queer Nation kids are out front whining, 'Shame, shame, shame,' we'll be slipping in the back way to cut the shit and take care of business. Yes, this is starting to look like a seriously fun way to kick off the bitchin'est summer ever. It's also smacking loudly of karmic inevitability. I know that sounds a bit mystical, but what can I say? I've learned the hard way to trust my feelings, to listen to that little voice inside—which in this case is saying: *Do it. Grease those right-wing pigs.* We should dress for the beach. It will be a hot day. A sparkling sun-drenched setting for death in the afternoon. What sort of architecture is the club?"

"It's art deco," I said.

"Perfect." Glenn looked out the window into the harsh sunrise glow. "Yes, I see it all now. The blood on the walls, on the white tablecloths. Is that the shrimp Louie or the senator's brains? I believe in the power of visualization."

Glenn led me back to the sofa, thinking out loud as if he were in a trance. "We'll have to get beach towels to cover the weapons. We'll have to swing by the house in Valencia. We should get going. How long does it take to get to La Jolla?"

"It's about two hours from L.A.," I said, as Glenn massaged the back of my neck.

"Good," he said. "A pleasant Sunday drive down the coast. Yes, La Jolla. Perhaps if we have a few minutes to kill, we can swing by the Salk Institute and see how that AIDS vaccine's coming. 'Tell me, Jonas, is it true what they say? That this whole thing began with a green monkey's kidney used to make a bad batch of polio vaccine? A *very* bad batch. But never mind that. It's the *new* vaccine *we* want to know about. The one that stops HIV dead in its tracks. That stops the right-wing virus feeding off love's body.' Yes, I see an elaborate analogy emerging, a fearful Blakean symmetry—if only we had time for true literary density. For the Salk approach, in layman's terms, uses *dead* HIV to 'stimulate' *killer cells!* Which flood the body's Neptune Rooms, cleansing them of the living virus of hate! Washing it all away in the rivers of blood flowing down to the shimmering La Jolla sea! In the trials so far, men have gone from testing positive to negative! *A miracle!* Ah, La Jolla! Are you the alpha and omega of the pandemic? Or are you just salt air and old money and surfer's spunk and fat rats in the palm trees? *La Jolla!* I say your name as a word of magic, as an incantation. *La* Joll-*ya!* I wonder what you mean in English."

"Carlos would know," Mikey said. "He was bilingual."

"Raymond Chandler lived there in the fifties," I said. "Just across the alley from us. Our cat used to fight with his cat. At least I think they were fighting. But once, I remember—"

"I'll read your memoirs, I promise," Glenn interrupted. "Right now I'm going to recuff you, Tim, but don't worry. As you've no doubt suspected, we've always intended to set you and Pete free—physically as well as metaphysically, as well as every other way."

SEVENTEEN

THEY ALL got ready to go, except for Dexter. He'd injured his leg badly enough that his knee was swelling. He took a couple of codeine tablets and lay back in the pine-frame chair with his leg stretched out on a plastic milk crate. He was going to stay behind and eventually release us before he took off to rendezvous with the other guys (in Mexico, I guessed) that evening. Glenn felt that he was doing us a favor by keeping us restrained awhile longer. "Should the FBI learn of your presence, you can say with all honesty that you *couldn't* warn anyone."

Mikey "borrowed" my tropical swim trunks. He looked good in them, too. (Bruce Weber, still in Japan.) Mikey was in a bright, cheerful mood now, as were Glenn and Joey. The speed, no doubt, was a major factor in that, but their mood was almost one of joyful anticipation. They might have been good-natured jocks getting ready for a game.

"That Laundromat," Mikey said to Pete. "It was called the Sand and Suds?"

"Suds and Surf, I think," Pete said.

"That's right. Suds and Surf." Mikey grinned. "I still think about that whenever I smell Tide detergent." He chuckled and picked up his knapsack and his machine pistol and went out the door.

Joey came over and crouched down in front of Pete. With

his round wire-frame glasses on, Joey looked like a cracked blond 1920s anarchist. He took Pete's hand. "I don't know what to say. I don't want this to get sticky. But I don't see any point in doing some sort of tight-lipped macho number either."

"Just be careful," Pete said. "Try not to get shot by some moonlighting cop with a .38 under his blazer."

"I'm alert, I'm leveled out now, don't worry," Joey said. And in fact he'd stopped sweating and seemed much steadier. "I know you used to say you'd do this sober, Pete. Like that AA bumper sticker: 'Do it sober.' " Joey smiled. "So your aim would be better."

"I know I said that, but—"

"Well, who knows, maybe you'll still get a chance to see if you really meant it." Joey seemed to instantly regret the caustic tone of the remark. "I hope not," he said. "I hope you guys are really okay. That you stay together and all that. Play house, fuck a lot, don't cheat on each other. Don't bring home that HIV. I hope someone lives into the next century. I really did love you, Pete. I don't mean in a sexual sense, but—"

"I know."

They hugged awkwardly, Pete only able to use one arm. Then Joey went out.

Glenn came over to us, looking first at Pete. "Well, I suppose the time has come to say my kitsch good-byes, Mr. Chips. Good night, sweet prince, with your little gray Citroën, and your pocket full of Trojans, some of them used. *Arrivederci*, my Venetian sodomy chum. *Ciao* to those sun-drenched butthole afternoons on Wave Crest—how we took them so for granted. *Auf Wiedersehen*, pale blue eyes. *Vaya con Dios*, young lovers, wherever you are. *Au revoir, amour fou.*" Glenn looked at me. "Happy trails, Tim, with your throbbing 327. You've got a good man riding shotgun now. Don't fight on the freeway. Don't pick each other apart. Don't wish us luck. Tell us to break a leg and drop a rod on the 405 and lose our erections, if not our religion."

"I still think you're insane," Pete said.

Glenn smiled. "And I'd still like to eat you with a white

plastic spoon. We'll save a seat for you at that big AA meeting in the sky. Who knows, by the time you get there, I could have thirty or forty years. I might be the main speaker."

"I'd leave," Pete said.

"All right"—Glenn slid into his quavering gay-auntie voice—"I'm going to go now. Before one of us starts to cry." He picked up his knapsack and went out the door.

Dexter followed Glenn out to the porch, where the two of them talked for a few minutes. Then Glenn got into the Range Rover where Mikey and Joey were waiting. Glenn started the engine. The tape deck was blasting "Date Night at Dachau" as they drove out through the gate in a brown cloud of dust.

Dexter limped back inside, wincing painfully. The TV picture was still snow. Dexter picked up the VCR remote control and used it to roll a tape as he dropped down into the chair.

"My boyfriend's stuff," he said with casual pride as Rose Parade footage appeared on the screen: innocuous floats, a bland narration.

"This is why I went to prison," Dexter said, which I didn't understand—until, with the audio narration continuing, the picture cut to a glossy close-up from a gay porno film of one man eating another man's butt.

"Oh, right, I heard about this," I said. An infamous video art prank in the Bay Area, the Rose Parade signal overridden for a few minutes in several hundred thousand homes. "What year was that? 'Eighty-three?"

" 'Eighty-two," Dexter said. "But by the time the case came to trial the next year, homo stuff had got a really bad name, people freaked out about AIDS and all that. So they threw the book at us."

The big wet pink tongue licked the hairy butthole.

"Bad timing," I said.

"Yeah. People were incensed."

I looked at Pete and he did a little girl's voice: "Mommy, what are those two men doing?" followed by a flabbergasted mom's reaction, "Oh, *my God!*"

I laughed but I wasn't really sure how I felt about kids seeing something like this.

The TV picture cut to a black-and-white scene from *Sitting Pretty*, the first Mr. Belvedere film, starring Clifton Webb.

"This is some other stuff Randy did," Dexter told us. "He liked to have fun with everything."

Clifton Webb was talking with Robert Young and Maureen O'Hara, who played the couple he worked for, in their postwar suburban living room. But all the dialogue had been skillfully redubbed. You weren't really fooled, but the voices were fairly accurate impressions, the new dialogue written to fit. It becomes apparent that Mr. Belvedere has recently been arrested by the vice squad in a department store men's room. "But we thought you were a eunuch," Maureen says pleasantly. "As far as you're concerned, I am," Clifton replies in haughty clipped tones. "If I choose to suck cock on my day off, I don't really see how it concerns you. Would you prefer that I bring stray tricks back to my room?" "Now, that will do!" harrumphs Robert Young.

Dexter was falling asleep in his chair. He perked up for a moment when the next segment came on, a redubbed sequence from *The Searchers*, John Wayne talking to Jeffrey Hunter about pussy. Dexter smiled, then closed his eyes again. It becomes apparent that John Wayne is just trying to get Jeffrey Hunter hot so they can jack off together.

Dexter started snoring. And Pete whispered to me, "Get the watch."

I saw that he meant Dexter's wristwatch, which was lying on his T-shirt on the floor beside his chair. Using my toe, I was just able to reach the shirt and pull it over. I gave Pete the watch. It was a little before ten. Pete reset the time to one forty-five.

"What's going on?" I said.

Pete shushed me. He was obviously planning to fool Dexter so he'd let us go early—in time to do what? Warn the crowd in La Jolla? That seemed unthinkable. But it was hard to reach any other conclusion.

Pete tossed the watch and T-shirt back by Dexter's chair.

Then he considered the TV, which was now showing a redubbed Last Supper sequence from Nicholas Ray's *King of Kings*, in which Jesus (Jeffrey Hunter again) and the disciples are sharing stories about their raunchiest homosexual adventures. "I tell you, I've never *seen* so much smegma!" Judas exclaims. "Why don't we all pull our cocks out under the table?" Christ suggests, lowering his eyes. "Wow, mine's so hard it hurts!"

"Can you get the remote?" Pete whispered.

Again using my toe, I was able to knock the VCR remote control off the arm of Dexter's chair. He stirred when it hit the floor, but continued snoring. I used my toe to pull the remote over to where I could pick it up and hand it to Pete.

Pete pressed fast-forward and Dexter almost woke up as the sound turned to gibberish. Pete hit the mute button just in time. The tape moved rapidly through scenes from other films, shots of two men talking, often exchanging ambiguous looks: Robert Redford and Paul Newman, Clint Eastwood and Jeff Bridges, Mel Gibson and Danny Glover. Straight guys in love. Finally the tape clicked off and Dexter stirred again.

Pete tossed the remote back across the floor and said, "Hey, Dexter? *Dexter*."

Dexter opened his eyes. "What?"

"You think maybe we could take off now? I'm sure it's over by now."

Dexter sat up and reached for his watch. When he saw the time, he said, "Shit. I can't believe it. It seems like I just fell asleep."

"Yeah, we took a nap, too," Pete said. "So how about it? It's gotta be over by now, right?"

"Yeah, I guess so." Dexter stared at the snow on the TV screen. "Shit, I wish we could get the news. I'll bet there's already something about it."

Dexter winced in pain as he got up and limped over to us with the handcuff keys. "Hey, do me a favor though, will you?" he said. "Help me load some stuff into the car."

"Sure," Pete said.

Dexter unlocked our cuffs.

Pete pulled his jeans on and put on his shoes. I pulled on Mikey's fatigues, which were much too tight, squashing my dick down my pants leg so that I felt like a lewd 1970s clone.

Dexter hobbled over to the art supplies and pulled back a sheet to reveal a dozen or so canvases resting in two stacks against the wall. "I gotta take these with me," he said.

Pete and I took the paintings out to the GTO in several trips while Dexter rested in a rocking chair on the meeting hall porch, rubbing his knee. They were all paintings by his dead boyfriend Randy, dated '83 through '86, in a strange kind of glazed, hyperrealist style. They all featured the same two clean-cut young guys, one blond, the other dark haired, in ostensibly wholesome Americana settings. In one, for example, they were in a country kitchen, like the kitchen in the old "Lassie" series, Mom smiling in the background, making flapjacks at the griddle. But on the checkered tablecloth in the foreground, one of the clean-cut grinning young guys was getting ready to suck the other's cock, which was so pink and juicy it looked like a glistening 1950s *Good Housekeeping* dessert illustration.

The other paintings employed similar strategies, but my favorite was probably the least overtly sexual. The two guys were sitting naked by a skinny-dip pool, their arms around each other, the dark-haired guy with his other arm around a beautiful collie. The blond-haired guy did have a hard-on, but the image had a strange kind of defiantly genuine innocence. That was the last painting we stuck in the trunk of the GTO, on top of the deactivated Sem-Tex bomb.

"You guys might as well go on now," Dexter said to us from the porch. "I wanna spend a little more time here by myself." He looked across the weed-infested quad at the other decrepit white buildings. "This was gonna be our place. We were gonna renovate it and live in the meeting hall and rent out the other places to our friends. Like an art colony place. Now the Scouts wanna buy it back. Guess scouting's picked up again in recent years."

"It wouldn't surprise me," Pete said. "Are you okay?"

"Yeah. I'm fine," Dexter said. But he had a funny forced smile. "You guys better get going."

Pete and I got into Pablo's Mercedes. Dexter was still sitting in the rocking chair on the meeting hall porch as we drove out through the gate. I looked back and almost waved, but Dexter wouldn't have noticed. He was staring out across the hills, still smiling.

As we bumped down the rutted dirt road I said to Pete, "So what the fuck is going on? You're not going to warn those people in La Jolla, are you?"

"No, no. I don't see how I could do that. But there *is* one aspect of it that might be very bad. I've got to check on something."

"What?"

"Well, I wasn't completely honest with you about my mother and Bryer."

"What do you mean?"

"Well, I think she's been seeing him."

"Seeing him?"

"Yeah. Like it's serious."

"But isn't he married?"

"Not now. His wife died of cancer a few years ago."

"What are you saying? That he really didn't fire her?"

"No, I don't think so. I think they *did* have a fight though."

"Then why did you say he fired her?"

"I don't know! Wishful thinking, I guess. How do you think I feel, knowing my mom is in love with Heinrich Himmler!"

"So what are you saying? That you think she'll be with him at the luncheon?"

"*I don't know!* That's what I want to find out. She was very upset when I talked to her last night. She was crying. They'd had a very bad row at his office after we left. He was going to have me arrested for attempted murder, and she was trying to talk him out of it . . . so I don't *know* what's going on at this point. But it's not inconceivable that they could've kissed and made up."

249

"If she's there with him, what are you going to do?"

"I don't know. What would *you* do?"

"She's not my mother, Pete. I can't say."

"Come *on!* For God's sake! You gotta give me more than that! This is a major fucking moral dilemma! We gotta come up with something fast!"

In a few minutes we came to a narrow paved road that led down through the brush to Mandeville Canyon. As we drove past the ranch houses lining the canyon road, we heard sirens coming toward us. Pete pulled over as two fire trucks roared past us. Looking back, we saw a cloud of black smoke above the rust-colored hills. Dexter, it seemed, had opted to torch the camp rather than let the Boy Scouts of America reclaim it.

EIGHTEEN

IT WAS almost eleven-thirty when we pulled up to my house in Santa Monica Canyon. Pete parked by the fireplug since all the other spaces were taken by beachgoers' cars. I knew someone had come by to see me that morning because the Sunday *L.A. Times* was up on the porch doormat instead of in the driveway where they always tossed it. I pictured Jay Sutter knocking on my door, out of breath in running shorts, his smooth body slick with sweat.

As I unlocked the door, Jefty came up from the neighbor's yard, rubbing against me, yowling hungrily. He had a scratch on his nose, as if he'd either been fighting or playing *Body Heat* again with the neighbor's cream-colored Persian. I went into the kitchen and poured out some Science Diet.

Pete was already holding the phone. "Tim, come *on.*"

We went over our plan one more time. I psyched myself up as Pete got the number of the La Jolla Coast Club from information. If it turned out Pete's mother was in fact there with Bryer, we'd considered several possible ways to draw her away from the luncheon. The first idea was to make her think that something terrible had happened to Pete's niece, the little girl whose photo she kept next to Pete's on her desk in Bryer's office. I could say that Debbie had been in a car accident somewhere far away, like the Simi Valley. By the time Pete's mother got there and realized it was a ruse, they'd be mopping up the blood in the Neptune Room. But Pete had been afraid that if we used that story, Bryer might accompany his mother. Even though the luncheon was an important political event, the congressman might feel compelled to forgo it if a little girl's life were involved.

Then we'd considered saying that something had happened to Pete's aunt's dog. His aunt lived in Lancaster, on the distant outskirts of L.A., and she had a chow. I could pretend to be a veterinarian and say the chow had been killed by a pit bull and Pete's aunt was so distraught she was unable either to come to the phone or to drive. But Pete was afraid that wouldn't work. His mother, while sympathetic, would almost certainly suggest that I call a friend of his aunt's in the Lancaster area. Finally, I'd hit on the idea that we used.

Once Pete had dialed the La Jolla Coast Club, he handed me the phone. When a woman answered, I identified myself as a doctor and asked her to page Doris Schindler. "It's a medical emergency."

She put me on hold. We waited. I could see that Pete was hoping his mother wouldn't be there. I was trying not to replay the sex scene in Bryer's office, trying not to recall the quick shot of Mrs. Schindler's sloppy wet vagina, when she suddenly came on the line. "Hello?"

"Is this Doris Schindler?"

Fearfully: "Yes, it is. What's wrong?"

"This is Dr. Genet at Sylmar Presbyterian Hospital."

Jefty yowled. I covered the mouthpiece and motioned to Pete to get the cat out of the room, which he did, putting Jefty out on the deck, shutting the door.

"You have a son, Peter Schindler?"

"Yes, I do. What is it? *Does he have AIDS?*"

"No, ma'am. But he has been severely injured. He's in intensive care. He's lost quite a lot of blood—"

"*Blood?* Well, you'd better be careful. He's got that AIDS virus, you know."

"He's in critical condition, ma'am. I'm not sure he's going to live."

"What happened? Was it a car wreck?"

"No, ma'am. It looks like he was crucified."

"*What?*"

I heard Bryer's deep voice in the background: "What's wrong?"

"Something's happened to Pete," she told him. "They're saying he was crucified."

"*Crucified?*"

I covered the mouthpiece and told Pete, "Bryer's there."

"*He can't come with her,*" Pete whispered vehemently.

"*Hello!*" Bryer barked into the phone. "Who is this? Who am I speaking to?"

"This is Dr. Genet in Sylmar Presbyterian—"

"Doctor who? Speak up!"

"Dr. Genet."

"Genet? What's the problem?"

"I was trying to inform Mrs. Schindler that her son's dying."

A beat, then: "*Good!* Serves him right! One less queer givin' AIDS to decent people!"

"*Gerry!*" Pete's mother whimpered in the background.

"What happened?"Bryer said.

"Well, according to the police," I said, "he tried to stop some Latino youths who were torturing a dog. Gang members, it seems. And there was some sort of altercation. And they nailed him to the side of a doughnut shop and left him there."

"A doughnut shop? Where was this?"

"Here in Sylmar."

"*Sylmar?*"

"That's right."

Bryer said nothing for a moment, and I wished like anything we'd come up with something more "realistic."

Then Bryer said, "*Good!* Why didn't you *leave him there* till all the goddamn AIDS blood ran out of his body!"

"I wonder if I could speak to Mrs. Schindler again," I said sharply, as I imagined a doctor would.

She came on the line: "Yes?"

"He's been asking to see you, ma'am. I'm really not sure if he's going to last the afternoon."

To Bryer, she said, "I've got to go up there."

"*No!*" Bryer said. "You're too upset. You'll crash the car."

"Then you drive me, honey. *Please*. I know how you feel. But he's still my son." She started to cry.

"Doris, I can't miss this lunch," Bryer said. "Why don't you have Grace go with you?"

Mrs. Schindler struggled to stop crying. "All right." To me she said, "*Where* are you?"

I gave her a fake Sylmar address.

After I hung up, I said to Pete, "It worked. She's going with Grace, whoever that is."

"Some sour right-wing bitch, no doubt, who thanks God every night for killing the queers."

Pete and I put our arms around each other for a moment in the bright, hot living room. I felt safe at last, but drained.

While Pete took a shower, I let Jefty back in and examined him for other injuries. I didn't find any. I told him, "Man, you are playing Russian roulette." He yowled.

I played back my messages. The first was from Gregory. "Hi, Tim. It's Sunday morning. Just thought I'd see how your dream date went. I know why you're not answering. You're in the bedroom, making passionate love with Victor. *Just kidding*." Shifting gears: "I'm so depressed. This thing with Sean is driving me crazy. I'm completely obsessed with him, but I can't do a thing. I don't know *why* I keep doing this. Call me when you can."

The next message came on: "Tim, this is Jay. I guess you're still not home yet. I came by around eight. Was really hoping you'd be there, that you'd come to the door with a big fucking hard-on. I've got one right now. Don't know how much longer I can last. I'm at 1943 Amalfi, just up around the next bend. I wish you were walking in the door right now, peeling off your trunks. I'd have you stick your dick right in my face. I wish I had your cock in my mouth right now, just sucking the fuck out of it. I wish you were sucking mine. I could look down, see your hot butch face . . . Oh, Jesus, I'm gonna shoot, Tim. Oh, yeah, here it comes. Oh fuck, yeah!" He groaned repeatedly, then sighed, relieved. "All right. Hey, that was great. Thanks. Look, I'll call you, okay?"

The last message: "Tim, it's Kevin. Just found your number. I hope you're okay. I think someone was putting mescaline in the drinks last night. I had *quite* an adventure after you left. I'll be at 213-229-8401 until tomorrow. Hope nothing I said freaked you out. I love you."

I went back to the bedroom and switched on the TV. The picture was snow here, too. Pete stepped out of the bathroom, drying off.

"Are you hungry?" I asked him.

"Not really. I think I'd like to take a nap."

"Yeah, me, too."

I took a shower. When I came back into the bedroom, Pete was lying naked on the sheets, Jefty curled up against his leg. I lay down on the bed next to Pete. The windows were open, the ocean breeze puffing the white window shades, bright sunlight leaking in across the white walls. Pete and I held each other. He smelled of Ivory soap. We kissed lightly. We both got hard-ons, but I knew we weren't going to make love now, we were too exhausted. He rolled over and I held him from behind.

Within a few minutes he was sleeping. I listened to the waves crash in the distance, children squealing in the surf. I looked at the clock. It was 12:07. I imagined the gunfire and screams in La Jolla, Gerald Bryer with a bullet hole in his forehead, pitching hard across the tabletop like Sterling Hayden after Al Pacino shot him in *The Godfather*. I pictured other grim conservative faces I'd seen on TV, the tops of their heads exploding in misty pink Zapruder sprays, blood and brain tissue spattering the delicate art deco nautical friezes that lined the Neptune Room's walls. I kissed Pete's pale, warm shoulder.

I looked at the colorful 1950s Mexican travel poster on the white wall, the poster Jeff had given me. Saw Jeff sleeping naked on his bed in Mexico. Thought of Joey's painting of his boyfriend asleep the same way. Thought of Joey's painting of the two men asleep together.

I imagined I was looking at a painting of Pete and me, as we were right now, the way Joey would have painted it.